ONE HOOF IN THE GRAVE

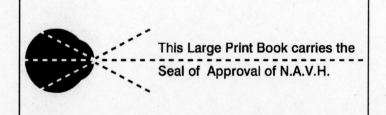

ONE HOOF IN THE GRAVE

CAROLYN MCSPARREN

THORNDIKE PRESS
A part of Gale, Cengage Learning

GALE
CENGAGE Learning·

Detroit • New York • San Francisco • New Haven, Conn • Waterville, Maine • London

GALE
CENGAGE Learning

LIBRARY OF CONGRESS CATALOGING-IN-PUBLICATION DATA

McSparren, Carolyn.
    One hoof in the grave / by Carolyn McSparren. — Large print ed.
      p. cm. — (Thorndike Press large print clean reads) (The Merry Abbott carriage-driving mysteries; bk #2)
    ISBN 978-1-4104-4974-0 (hardcover) — ISBN 1-4104-4974-2 (hardcover)
    1. Large type books. I. Title.
    P*
    813'.6—dc23   2012014639

Published in 2012 by arrangement with BellBooks, Inc.

DEDICATION AND ACKNOWLEDGEMENTS

Thanks to Meredith Giere, who took the time to write me after she saw a picture of me and my driving horse, Zoe, in the national driving magazine. She gave me Hail Columbia for all my harnessing mistakes and has become my friend and go-to person on all things technical.

Thanks to Beverly Hollingsworth, my co-driver and trainer, who cajoled and threatened me into driving in my first actual driving show, The Nashoba Carriage Classic. I didn't fall out of the carriage and Zoe was an angel.

Thanks to Sam Garner, who trained Zoe and me to drive in the first place and fixes my carriage when it breaks down. And to Patsy, his wife, who puts up with all of us.

Thanks to the folks at Nashoba Carriage

Association, and to Pam Gamble, who drives draft horses to carriages for hire in Memphis.

Thanks as always to my critique partners, Phyllis Appleby, Patricia Potter, and Barbara Christopher, who shepherded me through my first draft, and to Debra Dixon and Patricia Van Wie, both wonderful editors.

Finally, thanks to Zoe, who is usually a saint, but can be a demon. I learned a long time ago that when things get really bad, go hug a horse. It helps.

I hope you like this second driving mystery. I'm working on the third Meredith and Peggy mystery right now.

CHAPTER 1

Saturday morning
Merry

Marathon day is always tense at a carriage driving show. There was enough adrenaline floating around to win every gold medal at the Olympics. I breathed deeply of the scent of pines that crowded both sides of the starting track and tried to relax.

It was barely dawn on a chill north Georgia morning in early May. Around me horses put to carriages paced the staging area atop the Tollivers' hill as they waited for their signal to start down to the first obstacle.

Harness jingled, drivers and grooms cajoled their teams to settle them. Eager to start, the horses whinnied, stomped, and snorted. Peggy Caldwell, my landlady and first friend in Mossy Creek, Georgia, was driving our pair of Halflinger horses, Golden Boy and Ned, over her first marathon course. She's a natural reinsman, but I'd been training her less than a year. Now, she needed the experience of driving a pair in an actual show.

I was more nervous than she was. At least I would be with her, standing behind her seat on the steel marathon carriage as her gator — short for Navigator. My friend Pete Hull swears that some anonymous driver shortened the term because "gators" are mean suckers with big mouths, the better to snarl at their slow or downright dangerous drivers.

As gator, I was supposed to keep us on course, on time, and use my not inconsiderable weight to counterbalance the carriage around turns.

Until we got the signal to start, I was standing in front of our Halflingers and slipping them sugar cubes to keep them calm, so Peggy wouldn't tense up even more. I was tense enough for both of us.

"Where the hell is Raleigh?" I heard Pete Hull shout. "Wasn't he supposed to start first?"

Peggy and I were due to go second, after Giles Raleigh's four-in-hand team of Dutch warmbloods. I saw the judge in charge of starting speaking on his cell phone, and a moment later he came over to us. "Peggy,

Merry, that was Raleigh on the phone. He's got to replace a broken pole chain on his lead horses. He'll be here in a couple of minutes, but we can make up the time if y'all go first. How about it?"

"Oh, Lord," Peggy whispered. "Do we have to?"

I gave her a thumbs-up. "Our boys are getting more antsy by the minute."

"Why don't you take over the reins?" she asked me.

I shook my head. "You've trained with both Ned and Golden. You know the course. I'll be on the step right behind you coaching you. You'll do fine. Have at it."

She sucked in a deep breath and squared her shoulders. "Then let's do this thing."

I gave Ned and Golden a final pat, walked around behind the cart, climbed on the gator's step, and patted her shoulder. "Okay, kiddo, let's have some fun."

"Oh, Lord," Peggy whispered and clicked to the pair of Halflingers. "Trot on."

They trotted smoothly down the path toward our first obstacle. We were off.

Peggy and I had agreed on one goal. No disasters. Like all the competitors, we wore hard hats and body protectors, even though we had no intention of driving our horses at a dead gallop the way the more experienced drivers did.

"We might as well be driving through the clouds in the Alps," Peggy said. She had a point. Heavy mist nearly obscured our path. It rose in thick clouds from the surface of the little lake in the valley. "We're driving into a witch's cauldron," Peggy whispered. "I'll never be able to see where to turn onto the bridge."

I could feel the tension in her shoulder when she leaned back against the seat in front of me, but her hands seemed steady on the reins.

At the bottom of the hill we had to make a sharp right turn beside the lake onto a causeway that led to a wooden bridge. The bridge wasn't steeply arched or narrow, but some horses hated the sound of their hooves on the wood so much they took one step, stopped dead and refused to cross. Peggy and I had practiced driving across boards with the Halflingers for the last couple of months. We figured they were cool, even if we weren't.

On Friday evening, all the drivers and navigators had ridden over the marathon course on the back of pickup trucks, so we knew what obstacles we'd encounter and where. The bed of a truck, however, gives a different perspective from when you're handling the reins of sensitive horses who'll pick up on every emotion transmitted through your hands.

"Good boys," Peggy called. Their fat little yellow butts jiggled from side to side as they sped up. Halflingers are the size of large ponies, but they are classed as draft horses. That means they can be a handful to drive.

She'd driven in a couple of short non-rated marathons, but always in single harness with my Halflinger, Golden Boy. What he didn't know about driving hadn't been figured out yet. But Peggy'd never before driven a pair in a recognized event.

The mist lifted some as we neared the bottom of the hollow. Drivers not scheduled to go until later, grooms, spectators, and hangers-on straddled their ATVs or stood out of the track of the carriages where the teams made the turn, so they could watch the first carriages cross the bridge and plan their own runs.

I caught the odor of coffee from the big cups most of them held and wished I could swap places with them.

The sun now glittered off the lake so brightly that I wished I could fit Golden Boy and Ned with their own Polarized sunglasses, like Peggy's and mine. Their golden coats and flowing white manes blazed nearly as bright as the sunlight.

"Easy," she called.

"Half halt right," I said. She gave a short tug on her reins and tapped her brakes to slow down the horses and set them up for the last part of the trot downhill.

In yesterday afternoon's hazards class, where we threaded the carriage through the various hazards set barely wider than our tires, our boys — Golden Boy and his new teammate Ned — had performed as though they'd been working together all their lives. Golden Boy, actually *my* Halflinger, inherited from my father, was an old pro. As right hand horse, he kept the younger and less experienced Ned in line admirably. Ned was Peggy's new acquisition — willing, but green. Green horses always worried me.

Peggy slowed and swung the team right onto the causeway. Perfect. Right down the center. Even though it was narrow, there was plenty of room between the banks.

"Horses are slaves. Free them now or die in their place!" The voice was so loud it sounded as though God himself were issuing a new commandment. A second later, a garish banner flapped open across the bridge dead ahead of us and popped noisily in the morning breeze.

I yelped, levitated two feet straight up in

the air, and almost fell off the carriage. Peggy hauled back hard on the reins and stomped the brakes. Even Golden Boy was startled. Of all the crazy . . .

Terrified, Ned reared and pulled hard to his left. His left hind hoof slipped in the mud at the edge of the causeway and slid down the bank toward the water, canting the carriage to the left. Peggy hauled right on the reins as I threw my weight to counterbalance the listing cart.

Too late.

We drove straight into the lake. The team's momentum dragged us a dozen feet into the water. Both horses and carriage sank instantly. The horses thrashed, trying desperately to free themselves from their harness and keep their heads above the water.

Even in May the water hung on to its chill. All I could do was suck in a breath and pray. Choking and spitting, weighed down by clothes, boots and body protector that felt as heavy as chain mail, I fought my way to the surface. My eyes stung and then my hard hat spilled an icy waterfall down my face.

I dashed the water out of my eyes with one hand and grabbed the back of Peggy's body protector with the other as she broke the surface. She choked, spat and twisted out of my grasp.

"Let go of me!" she screamed. "We have to get the horses loose!"

The carriage was submerged, but I could feel the top of the seat with my boot. I kicked off to swim forward to the horses. "Swim to the bank," I shouted. "I'll get 'em." I didn't know whether Peggy could swim, but she was not young and the water was frigid. I didn't want to have to rescue her too.

I heard splashes behind me, and a moment later, a couple of spectators I didn't recognize swam past me to grab the horses' bridles. Shouting, others jumped in after them until people and horses roiled the water like an interspecies feeding frenzy. If someone was kicked under water or hit by the heavy center pole of the carriage, or if one of the horses broke a leg, this could be a tragedy, not simply a disaster.

I had to trust Peggy would be all right. Surely someone on the bank would drag her out.

The horses' heads broke the surface of the water ahead of me but immediately sank again. I sucked in a deep breath and dove. The water was murky, but those white manes floated ahead like ghosts. I swam to the pair of singletrees that attached the horses to the carriage. I could see someone doing the same thing on the far side of Golden.

The horses fought us, but their kicks had little force under the water. They were attached to the cart by quick release carabiners designed for just such emergencies. You couldn't cut the horses out of their rig. It's impossible to saw through either Biothane plastic — the newest material for harness — or thick leather, and certainly not under the water. Cutting them loose wasn't an option.

We had to free them from the singletrees first, then from the strap that held them both to the long pole shaft between them.

I managed to get both carabiners on Ned's side free, then surfaced to see men holding both horses' heads above water, before I pulled myself forward by grabbing the nearest handful of pale mane. Someone had already unhooked the pole strap, which meant that although the horses were free of the carriage, they were still coupled together.

Releasing the coupling rein that held Ned to Golden meant they could swim forward on their own. A pale hand came out of the murk and unhooked Golden from the far side.

I grabbed Ned's bridle. Once he was

released from reins and carriage, Ned kicked forward. I felt his hoof brush my knee. Golden would be free by now as well. I trusted that whoever had unhooked him would aim him toward the shore.

Ned tossed his head, thereby lashing me across the bridge of my nose with about two feet of wet mane that felt like a cat o' nine tails. "Ow!" I yelped and sucked in a mouthful of pond water. I swung my right leg over his back, startling him even more, and turned him toward the bank.

Where was Golden? I risked a glimpse behind me and saw him swimming close behind Ned. All around me people swam with the horses. I recognized Jack Renfro, the Tollivers' huge groom, hauling Golden along like a barge towing a john boat.

"We got 'em!" A gray-haired man I'd met at Friday night's exhibitors' meeting tilted his head back and let out a rebel yell. From the bank I heard shouts and applause. The horses shook their heads to free their ears of water, but otherwise, didn't react. They were used to spectators and just wanted out.

I saw Peggy sloshing along the shore still wearing her driving gloves, hardhat, and back protector as she attempted to climb down the bank toward us.

"Whoa! We don't need to rescue you too,"

16

Peggy's Gentleman Caller Dick Fitzgibbons said, grabbed her around the waist and swung her up the bank.

Horses are excellent swimmers, and our two were no exceptions. Hands reached down to grab bridles and help the horses find their footing on the bank. I dropped off. Dick hauled me up and reached down to grab Golden's bridle from Jack.

Peggy shook Dick off and ran to embrace the horses and me. "So much for getting around the course safely," I said and steadied myself with an arm on Peggy. "You okay?"

"I am now." Peggy stood between the two horses with an arm around each neck as they nuzzled her. Their white manes were green from pond algae. Their long outside reins and shorter inside coupling reins were still attached to their bridles. Ortega, Dick's groom, hooked lead lines to both bridles. Peggy and I unhooked the reins and dragged them out of the water. They felt as slimy as wet leather shoes.

"Could 'a been a damn sight worse," Dick said. He dropped his dry windbreaker over my shoulders. Someone had already draped a driving apron around Peggy, and I saw our other rescuers being tended to as well.

"But your poor carriage . . ." Peggy wailed.

"Screw the carriage," Dick said. "We'll drive the tractor down here as soon as the others get past the bridge. We'll winch it out in no time."

"But . . ."

"It's steel, Miss Peggy," said Jack Renfro. He patted her shoulder. "Water can't hurt it."

"The harness . . ."

"It'll be good as new after a powerwash."

Dick turned Peggy to face him. "We need to fix *you?* How are you?"

"I'm *mortified* is how I am." Peggy looked past Dick at the bedraggled group that had saved the horses. "You're soaked. I am so sorry."

Now that the danger was past, everyone around us, wet or dry, was laughing and clapping. "Thank you so much," she shouted. A chorus of "glad to do it"s and the like came back to us.

Catherine Harris, the official technical delegate to the show, walked up behind Dick Fitzgibbons with her hands on her hips and an expression on her face that would have melted lead. "Those horses could have drowned."

I'm sure Catherine realized intellectually that Peggy was not to blame, but in the final analysis, it's the reinsman's job to keep his team under control, even in the event of a nuclear disaster. A horseman's initial reaction in any accident is anger that horses have been put at risk. And we tend to take out that anger on whichever human being is closest.

Catherine took a deep breath. "Sorry, Peggy, Merry. Not your fault, but when I find whoever set this up, I intend to flay them alive."

She turned to her young assistant. "Troy," she said, "go bring me that ludicrous banner." She stormed off toward the bridge. "I'll teach the moron who did this to put horses in jeopardy."

Peggy caught my eyes and essayed a shaky smile. "At least she's got her priorities straight."

CHAPTER 2

Merry

If I ever found the idiot who thought opening a flapping banner across that bridge and howling into a bullhorn were appropriate methods to make an animal rights statement, I would do what the Chinese used to do to traitors. I would tie the fool's arms and legs to four big strong horses and gallop them off in different directions until he was yanked apart at the seams. No, I'd use oxen and walk them slowly. He'd take longer to die that way.

Catherine Harris would be a willing assistant. We'd known one another for years. My father Hiram actually taught her to drive when she was a teenager. She felt the same way about people who hurt horses as I did.

Through narrowed eyes, Dick stared into the thick copse of pine trees bordering the road, then nodded at two grooms who stood at the edge of the lake holding the Halflingers. "The Halflingers aren't going anywhere while we're here," he said. "Y'all, go see if you can find where that voice came from."

They ran into the woods and craned their necks to peer into the branches. "Damned voice didn't sound human," Dick said. "Probably using one of those fake voice things. Wouldn't want to be recognized."

"I see it!" Jack Renfro pointed toward a tall pine that stood among the trees edging the course. He started toward the trees, but Peggy put a hand on his arm and stopped him.

"Forgive me for saying this, but you are entirely too big to climb trees."

"Yes'm." He sounded disappointed.

"Leave it," Catherine called. "I want the police to see the set-up."

As soon as I heard the words "set up," I knew what to look for. I clutched Dick's jacket around my damp body and squelched over to the causeway in my wet paddock boots. Even though I had already started to dry, the breeze on my wet jeans and shirt made me shiver. I ignored the discomfort while I searched the ground just past the turn.

I found the trip wire for the banner almost at once. The wire was stretched just above fetlock level on a horse. Thank God it was thin enough to break easily when the horses hit it, although once they were cleaned up, we'd have to check for cuts around their ankles.

"Dick, come look at this," I said. The two broken ends of the trip wire lay on the damp grass and glinted in the sunshine. Each end was twisted around a stout twig driven into the soft ground on either side of the causeway. I knelt and spotted some kind of spring arrangement on the bridge. Break the wire and the banner would be released from the bridge rails on either side. Sort of like a horizontal Jack-in-the-box. I assumed there was some connection to synchronize the noise of the bullhorn as well, but somebody else could find that. Possibly someone was standing back in the shadows of the pines to cue the bullhorn. In today's world, they probably used a cell phone app.

Not my problem. I gave up shinnying up trees when I was a teenager and before I had a grown daughter.

Dick hunkered down beside me and looked at the wire without touching it.

"Peggy and I weren't supposed to be in the first carriage, but I suppose this wire thingie would have been triggered by whichever carriage was first," I told him. "An equal opportunity trap."

"The order of go was posted yesterday afternoon," Dick said. "Makes you wonder."

Dick pulled me to my feet. Peggy had stayed with the horses. I didn't think she could hear us, but she'd definitely know we'd found something.

"Anybody who triggered that banner and the noise would probably have wound up in the lake," I said. "The calmest horse would have spooked. And a pair would be that much harder to keep on dry land. Once Ned's foot slipped in the mud, we were toast."

One good-sized horse might have been relatively easy to release from a submerged carriage, but Halflingers, although they qualify as a draft breed, are the size of large ponies, and with two of them to free — I didn't want to think what could have happened to them.

"I'm not certain we could have saved a four-in-hand of short Welsh ponies," Dick said. "No matter how many people were holding their heads up, four horses wear a lot of harness, and it's not easy to find the carabiners under water. Those heads would have stayed under, and there would have been nothing we could have done for them."

He was right. Horses can snort, and they

can close their nostrils for a short period of time. I suppose that's from when they were faced with snow or sandstorms in their wild days. But they can't keep the water out of their lungs for long, and Ned and Golden had been dragged under again and again. An eighteen-hand draft horse might have been able to stand on the bottom and keep his head above water without assistance, but not these little guys.

"We might also have some drowned human beings," he added.

As usual we think of horses first and people second. Marathon cross-country carriages carry a minimum of two people, but they often carry a third person as well. In that instance the navigator rides up front with the driver while another person hangs off the back as a counterbalance. The big carriages may carry a fourth person. That would have meant three or even four people in the water.

Peggy is remarkably fit despite her age, and apparently she can swim, but dunking unprepared elderly drivers into a frigid lake might well cause a heart attack or seizure. Or drowning. Probably my drowning if Peggy ever heard me call her elderly.

"Come on, you two need a hot shower and dry clothes," Dick said. He threw one arm around my shoulders and one around Peggy.

"The horses . . ." I said.

Dick called over his shoulder, "Ortega, bring up the Halflingers as soon as you can, please, and give them a good bath. They're starting to smell like a dead alligator. Come along, Miss Peggy," he said to her. "We'll pull the carriage out after everyone else has crossed over the bridge." He called to Catherine, who stood on the bridge glowering down at the strip of canvas at her feet. "Catherine," he called, "may we borrow your ATV? I rode down with somebody else."

"Give me a minute, then I want to speak to Merry and Peggy before they leave. Can you two put up with being damp for a minute?" she asked us.

Of course we said yes.

"I need to alert the other judges at the obstacles to what happened here and ask them to check their venues. Who knows what else this lunatic left? Tack strips? Elephant traps?"

As a show manager, I'd often worked with Catherine Harris when she acted as technical delegate. She was in charge of following the national association rulebook and seeing that everyone else did as well. She took her job seriously and was very good at it.

Whoever had set the trap had better be long gone, because if Catherine caught him or her, there'd be hell to pay.

"We have to call the police," said a woman behind me. "What were these blockheads thinking? They could have killed *horses*." No one had so much as mentioned the possibility of killing *us*.

"What the hell kind of show are you running, Catherine?" A bass voice shouted from up the hill near the starting gate.

I knew that voice. Everybody knew that voice, as a matter of fact, and everybody hated it.

The equipage originally scheduled to start first, Giles Raleigh with his four-in-hand team had halted halfway up the hill. His big bay geldings weren't a bit happy that Giles had slammed on his brakes and stopped them so soon. They stomped and fussed while Raleigh's groom stood at the head of the team and struggled to calm them.

Raleigh tossed the reins to his daughter Dawn, his gator, jumped from the box and strode down the hill toward Catherine.

"Who told you to start down?" Catherine snapped.

"I got to the start. Judge nodded. I started. Obviously you need better communication with your underlings," Raleigh sneered.

Catherine glanced at Troy.

"I called, but he'd already left," Troy said. He sounded sulky. "Probably jumped the gun."

"Oh, God," Peggy whispered, slipped away from Dick and turned to intercept Raleigh. "Catherine's not to blame for my accident, Mr. Raleigh."

He turned his attention to Peggy. "Woman, if you can't keep your team out of the lake, you better take up knitting."

I dropped a hand on Dick's arm. Dick loathed Giles Raleigh. In another age, he'd have called the man out and skewered him with his sword to defend Peggy's honor. The spectators would probably applaud and provide Dick an airtight alibi.

Dick was taller than Giles, who was built like a fireplug with a gut, but he was also twenty years older and thirty pounds lighter. I doubt if Dick had ever been in a fistfight, and certainly not with a snake like Giles Raleigh. Raleigh would cheat.

Up to this point Peggy had seemed pretty apologetic. That is, until Raleigh attacked Catherine, who patently didn't deserve it. "Young man," Peggy said. Giles was in his fifties, but Peggy had been a college professor before she retired. I'd give her eight to five odds against King Kong. "Take out

27

your anger on the idiot who deserves it. A nasty practical joker landed my team in the lake."

"*I* was supposed to be first on course this morning," Raleigh said.

"How fortuitous for you that you were late," Catherine snapped.

For a man like Raleigh, there's always someone handy to beat up on when anything gets in his way. "The starter should never have let me on the course with the pileup down here," Giles said. I had to admit he was right about that, although I'd be willing to bet Troy was right as well. Giles had either jumped the gun or at least fudged his start.

Giles turned back to Catherine. "If I weren't such a damn fine driver, I might'a run my ole boys smack into that woman *and* her horses. Don't know many drivers good enough to stop a team of seventeen hand warmbloods halfway down a hill when they're rarin' to go." He glanced over his shoulder where his groom was just managing to head his team while his daughter Dawn struggled with four sets of reins. "Somebody was trying to drown *me* and my horses."

"Like, who'd want to do that?" Troy whispered.

"Yeah, Raleigh, why would anybody want to drown *you?*" That came from one of the spectators who'd jumped in the water to cut the Halflingers free.

"Lucky it was the two Halflingers that went into the lake and not that team you've been irritating to death all weekend," Catherine said. "Out of my way. I'm driving out to check the barrels before anybody else starts." She turned to her assistant. "Troy, you stay here and call the other course volunteers. Give them a heads-up to check for tricks. I'd be surprised if there are any. This is the best location to set up a trap like this — close to the trees and out of sight of the house. I'll be right back."

She floored the ATV, drove over the bridge and into the trees beyond. She hadn't planned to drive over to check the barrels herself, so she must have decided it was a good excuse to get away from Raleigh before she decked him. I didn't blame her.

Troy walked halfway down the bridge away from everyone else and keyed his walkie talkie to begin his round of warnings.

The woman who had given Peggy her driving apron stepped between Giles and Peggy. "We'd have rescued your *horses,* Giles. I'm not sure we'd have bothered with *you.*" She pointed up the hill. "Shouldn't you get on back to your team before they run over somebody? That daughter of yours has her hands full hanging onto them."

He glared, but turned on his heel and strode back up the hill to his carriage and team. "Dawn, goddammit," he called to his daughter. "What the hell are you playing at?"

I winced. If my father had ever spoken to me the way he spoke to poor Dawn, I'd have taken my whip to him.

Dawn was actually doing a fine job keeping Raleigh's big team from bulling their way down the hill, brake or no brake. His groom was having more difficulty heading them — that is, standing in front of them and hanging onto the leaders' bridles. All four bounced on their front hooves and tossed their manes. They were raring to go and furious that the crowd at the bottom of the hill was holding them up. Raleigh climbed into the carriage, elbowed his daughter off the right-hand driver's seat and took the reins from her. "Get on up here," he shouted to his groom.

"Daddy," Dawn said quietly. "We can't start until Mrs. Harris says we can."

"Hell, we'll never make the course time," Raleigh said and glared at Peggy.

She glared right back.

"Everybody's times on course are screwed up," Dick said. "If Catherine agrees, we might as well take a Mulligan, *if* we can get Raleigh turned around and back to the start."

At that point Catherine roared back across the bridge on her ATV and stopped beside Troy. "Did you check with the volunteers?"

"Yes'm," he said. "No trouble. Nothing suspicious. They've been out there since dawn."

"I saw nothing at the barrels either. The rest of the course is pretty open." She climbed down. "We're good to go. Let's get everyone moving."

"Catherine, give us a break," said the man who had unhooked Golden. I needed to find out his name and send him a bottle of Jack Daniels. "At least six people went into the water. We all need some dry clothes and a gallon of coffee."

"Peggy's obviously not driving, and none of the other carriages has started yet, so only Raleigh's carriage will have go back up the hill and start down again," Dick said. "We'll run late, but not that late."

Catherine nodded. "Agreed." She turned to the spectators with their ATVs. "Y'all back up and give Raleigh room to turn around and drive his horses back up the hill," Catherine said. "Raleigh, come back down as soon as the starter says you can." She turned to the spectators. "The next few carriages are already up at the top ready to start. Those of you who went in the lake should have enough time to get dry before you have to put to."

Dick's groom Ortega walked Ned and Golden onto the bridge so they'd be out of Raleigh's way as well.

It was a tight turn for Raleigh's big marathon carriage and foursome. I must admit Raleigh did it with dispatch and without running over spectators or ATVs. As soon as he started back up the hill, the damp spectators climbed on their ATVs and followed him. The dry ones hung around to watch.

Waiting on the bridge with Ortega, Ned and Golden had nearly dried. I doubted even a good bleaching with Silk and Silver would be enough to take the green out of their white blonde manes. "The sooner we get these horses on the wash rack," Peggy said, "the sooner they'll start looking like Halflingers again and not like green bullfrogs."

Actually, both Peggy and I looked a little green around the gills as well.

Finally satisfied that the show was back under her tight control, Catherine came over to us. "Now. Tell me what happened."

I pointed over her shoulder toward the turn onto the causeway. "Look back there. Close to the ground. See those two twigs? You can just see pieces of the trip wire that somebody strung between them."

She leaned against the railing. "I can't believe this was malicious. Maybe some teenager's idea of a prank."

"Big Jack Renfro spotted a bullhorn wired onto a limb over there," Peggy said and pointed into the trees. "The first horse that broke the wire would snap the banner up over the bridge. Then came the voice. That's no practical joke."

Catherine considered, then said, "Y'all had any problems with animal activists in north Georgia?"

"They seem to think we're not worth bothering with," I answered.

"I've heard of a few incidents at the University," Peggy continued, "but just lab rats and such. Nothing around here. Certainly no death threats."

"You think it's random nastiness?" Catherine asked. "Teenagers?"

I glanced at Peggy. "We agreed to go first this morning when Giles Raleigh was late.

33

This really might have been meant for him."

Peggy said, "My husband used to say, 'Never volunteer.' Now I know why."

"Troy rode over the whole course at dusk last night with his girlfriend." She lifted her lip slightly when she said "girlfriend." Catherine didn't like her.

Maybe she and Troy weren't sleeping together after all.

"If the wire had already been in place, Troy and Morgan would have set it off." She glanced at her watch. "It's only eight-thirty. Someone started early to mess up my show. As if Giles Raleigh weren't enough trouble." She sighed. "Why didn't his mother do the world a favor and expose him on Grandfather Mountain at birth?"

CHAPTER 3

Merry

In the end Catherine decided not to call the cops. As she said, "Can you see them sending a team of CSIs up that tree to fingerprint a bullhorn and an oak tree? They'll say it's a prank that went too far. We're behind schedule as it is."

After we spoke to Catherine, Peggy and I walked along the causeway. Deep gouges in the mud bank alongside the causeway showed where Ned's hooves had slid down followed by the four furrows of our cart wheels.

Peggy peered over into the murky water. "I can't even see the cart. They'll never get it out."

"Sure we will," Dick called cheerfully. "Y'all go on up to the stable, get you some coffee and a hot shower." He grinned at Peggy and pointed to the muddy trail. "If it were later in the year, I'd say one of the resident alligators had slipped down the bank."

"Alligators?" Peggy yelped. "Nobody mentioned alligators."

He patted her shoulder. "To the best of my knowledge, there aren't any." He glanced behind him. "Not lately, at any rate."

"Oh, you!" Peggy stalked off up the hill toward the starting line. I trudged after her as she whispered, "I can't face those people. How embarrassing. I couldn't control my horses."

We stepped off the path to allow one of the last ATVs to drive past us with a wave.

"See?" I said. "Nobody gives a hoot. They're just glad everyone's all right."

"Can we find out who went into the water to help? I want to do something for them."

"Most would probably love a bottle of Jack Daniels. I'm sure the volunteers will know. Watch out!" I grabbed her arm, and we dove into the trees as Raleigh's four Dutch warmbloods hurtled down the hill for the second time. His heavy carriage lurched from side to side and nearly sideswiped the pines. As he passed us, he swung his whip wide across his body to the left side. The movement of air actually lifted Dawn's bangs. Raleigh grinned at me.

I felt the lash brush my shoulder. "Sorry,"

36

he said, then over the rumble of the wheels and the thud of hooves I heard him laugh.

"I am going to kill that SOB," I said. "He's a menace to the gene pool."

"Did he hurt you?" Peggy asked.

"Barely touched me. That's not the point. He was marking his doggoned territory like a boy dog. He's never forgiven me for not overruling the vet at Southern Pines who told him his horse was lame. As show manager that was not only my right but my duty. The technical delegate backed me up."

"That wasn't Catherine, by any chance?"

"Actually, it was."

"You should tell Catherine how he's behaved. She'd have a conniption."

We'd reached the top of the hill out of the way of the drivers. Looking back, I could now see that there was a ton of room on either side of Raleigh's carriage all the way down to the lake. Raleigh had flicked his whip at me on purpose, but there was no way to prove that.

I shook my head. "Poor Dawn. Did you see that apologetic look she threw me? I'd hate to have him for a father."

"She seems like a nice woman," Peggy said.

The show was being held on the Tollivers'

big farm an hour or so from Mossy Creek, where the training farm I inherited from my father, Hiram Lackland, is located. That's why Peggy and I had chosen it for her first big show. We'd have to pay for only two nights in a cheap motel and could use the inside of our big trailer as stabling for Ned and Golden.

Many shows won't allow that, but because this one was small and stabling was limited, Juanita and Harry Tolliver had decided on a case-by-case basis whether to allow the trailers as stalls. We had come in well within the parameters.

This also gave us an opportunity to promote my own first, small, fun show at my Lackland Farm, scheduled for next weekend. In the year I'd been running the facility, I'd never attempted a driving show, although I brought in professional trainers and well-regarded regional amateur drivers several weekends a year to train our local drivers.

This show should bring in drivers from farther away who had not yet seen Lackland Farm.

"After this morning, I'm beginning to wish we'd never advertised our show next weekend," Peggy said.

A show is only fun for the attendees, not

the hosts. Peggy and I were already nervous wrecks over what could and would go wrong. This morning's incident underscored my worry.

"We have the food and the volunteers lined up. If there's plenty of food, horse show people will put up with anything."

"Even protestors?" Peggy asked.

"We won't have protestors. Not at a little show like ours."

She didn't seem convinced.

Even a small carriage show is much more complicated than the average jumping or dressage show. First, there are carriages — something you don't attach to the average jumping or racing thoroughbred unless you want to die an early death. Then, instead of a single rider on a single horse, carriages carry extra people.

Harness tack is complicated, and the complexity increases logarithmically with the number of horses put to a single carriage. A pair is more than twice as difficult to put to the carriage as a single horse and takes three times as long, and a four-in-hand is more than four times more complex.

Many people travel with several carriages ranging from two-wheeled runabouts to big four-wheeled coaches, so horse trailers are bigger, more unwieldy and need extra space to park. Some have eighteen-wheelers specifically built for driving equipment and teams.

Add the palatial living quarters in some of the ritzier trailers, and you can run out of parking space right quick, not to mention the pickups and Mercedeses and BMWs and Land Rovers parked around them like baby chicks snuggling up to their hens. Then there are the spectators and their cars and trucks. And the Porta Potties and the food stands and the people selling everything from horse portraits to jewelry to hats.

I know this because I am a horse show manager for hire. The headaches involved in running even a small show are the reason my hair might be snow white under the color rinse I'll keep on it until I die.

Most of the carriage people are great.

Then there's the teensy minority like Giles Raleigh. I considered suggesting he take up scuba diving in a tank filled with ravenous sharks and sea snakes. Or maybe nude rattlesnake wrangling. While bad temper flat wears me out, Giles seemed to thrive on it.

So far I hadn't seen an application from Giles for our fun show. Please God that meant he considered us beneath his attention. If only.

He only bothered to turn on the charm

when hitting on some unsuspecting woman, selling a piece of real estate for an inflated price or conning a mark into investing.

I had tried to find a parking place away from his eighteen wheeler horse and people palace at the Tollivers' show. Unfortunately, I'd wound up right next door. Our tack-room door was right across from the door to his living quarters. I had avoided him successfully until this morning.

What really drove me nuts was that he said he *intended* to sleep with me. How's that for a slick seduction technique? I'm a divorcee, so I should be grateful for his attentions, right? Wrong.

If I went to bed with him, he'd win. He could check me off his list and tack my pelt to his trophy wall. Raleigh will do anything — lie, cheat, and steal — to win. I suspect he's dreadful in bed. Not that I want an up-close-and-personal, definitive answer to that question. Eeew. Not in this lifetime.

The last time he grabbed my tush at an exhibitors' party, I warned him that the next time he touched me, I'd kill him.

He deserved it. If some seventyish gentleman with bright blue eyes and a ravishing smile took me in his arms for a dance and whispered in my ear, "Dahlin', you prettier than a newborn Angus calf," then nuzzled my neck and suggested we repair to the nearest bedroom, I would smile and accept the compliment, knowing he didn't mean the proposition, probably couldn't perform, and had been married to an adored wife for forty years. That's a *good,* good ole boy.

Nasty, southern good ole boys are like Giles. They are not gentlemen, even if they came to Georgia with Oglethorpe. They *mean* that remark about going off to the nearest bedroom for what would undoubtedly be "wham-bam, thank-you ma'am." And expect you to be eternally grateful to them afterwards.

Neither Peggy nor I could conceive why Sarah Beth, Raleigh's trophy wife, had married him. He was rich, but she'd had a successful career as an interior designer in Atlanta before she met Giles. I wondered if she'd ever been happy in the marriage. One hot afternoon beside the dressage arena, she whispered to me, "You know, Merry, I used to love horses. Giles has even taken that away from me."

I could have cried. Horses have saved my life, my sanity, my bank balance, and my ability to love. I don't have to ride them or drive them — just having them in the barn and in my life keeps my endorphins pumping.

My mother says that some people are born psychopaths, some choose psychopath and some have psychopath thrust upon them. I had no idea which category Giles fit into. Surely somebody loved him at some point. I used to think his daughter Dawn loved him, but although she was acting as his gator, she seemed to be ignoring him otherwise.

After we passed Raleigh, Peggy and I went to get dry clothes and towels out of our truck and hunt up the shower in the Tollivers' stable.

"I hope they have a big water heater," Peggy said. "I'll flip you for who goes first."

As I opened the door to our trailer, Sarah Beth opened the door to *their* trailer and leaned out. "I've been watching for y'all. Get yourselves in here right this minute. Y'all need some coffee and a hot shower."

"You've heard about our dunking?" Peggy asked.

"Who hasn't? I want to apologize for Giles. He shouldn't have spoken to you like that. I know how he gets when he's driving. Do you have dry clothes here or do you have to drive back to the motel?"

"We have several sets here, as a matter of fact," I said. "It's fifteen minutes back to the motel, so we came prepared."

"We just didn't expect to take a dive in the lake," Peggy said. "But we're covered in mud. We'll mess everything up. We were planning to shower in the stable."

"I've got more hot water, and I definitely have coffee. Get your fresh clothes while I heat up some hot chocolate. That's even better. Our shower is more private than the shower in the barn. Where are your Halflingers?"

"Dick Fitzgibbons's groom is looking after them." I saw Peggy shiver. "Okay, Sarah Beth. You have a deal." I shoved Peggy forward. "Warm this one up while I get dry outfits."

When I got inside Raleigh's trailer, I heard the shower running. In most living quarters attached to horse trailers — even the big ones — the shower is barely large enough to raise your arms to wash your hair. Raleigh's had a real bathroom. I shoved Peggy's fresh clothes inside the bathroom door and took the mug of hot coffee Sarah Beth handed me. "You're a life-saver, but won't Giles have a fit if he finds me here?"

"Screw Giles," Sarah Beth said. "Or not. Preferably not."

Uh-oh.

Sarah Beth had been trophy wife thin since I'd known her, but now she looked positively cadaverous.

I don't agree with the prevailing theory that you can't be too thin or too rich, although some of the rich-rich folks I know would benefit from a hefty dose of penury. But there is a limit on thin and she'd gone way past it. Something was wrong.

If anyone could find out if Sarah Beth was having health problems, Peggy could. People confide in Peggy. Not because she looks nurturing and motherly. Believe me, she doesn't. She's nearly as tall as I am with muscles like tanned leather strips. She taught at the college level until she retired and moved to Mossy Creek, Georgia, and has not lost her ability to terrify the average liar into blabbing the truth.

Until my father, Hiram Lackland, discovered her aptitude for driving carriages, she seemed content to cosset her four cats, read tons of murder mysteries, enjoy the Mossy Creek, Georgia, Ladies Garden Club and her grandchild Josie.

Now, I couldn't do without her as my second-in-command at the farm.

I stuck my nose into my coffee cup as though I hadn't heard Sarah Beth's comment about Giles. Peggy may invite confidences. I, on the other hand, generally run from them. Peggy saved me by coming out

45

of the shower.

"Lord, I *may* live," she said and accepted a mug of coffee. I slid out of the banquette, picked up my clothes, and left her to deal with Sarah Beth while I showered.

By the time I came out after my shower I felt human again, even though my short hair was still damp.

"Sit," Sarah Beth said. Something about her was different. She seemed to have undergone a backbone implant. I wondered what she had told Peggy.

"Sorry to scrub and run," Peggy said and slid out of the banquette. "But we really need to check on the horses, and I want to find out if they've managed to winch Dick's carriage out of the lake yet. Dick talks as though it's a piece of cake, but someone's going to have to dive in and attach a cable from the tractor to the rear axle. That lake is cold, not to mention murky."

"Dick will handle everything. I suspect he'd rather you stayed out of the way," Sarah Beth said. "He's such a sweetie. He taught me the difference between a real southern gentleman and the man I married." With no warning, she burst into tears.

Uh-oh again. I'm not insensitive. I'm simply incompetent when it comes to nurturing anything with fewer than four legs.

I'm terrified I'll make things worse. Thank God Peggy takes up the slack.

Peggy sat back down and stroked Sarah Beth's shoulder. "Honey, can we help?"

Sarah Beth shook her head without raising it from her hands. "Nobody can help me."

"Did that man hit you?" Peggy asked.

Again the head shake. "He doesn't have to hit me."

"Divorce the bastard," I said. See what I mean? No gray areas. Always cut to the chase. "God knows he's committed adultery enough times."

Peggy rolled her eyes at me. Surely Sarah Beth knew about her husband's serial infidelities.

"I can't."

Peggy mouthed, "Drop it" at me. I would have divorced him long since. I divorced Vic, after all. Okay, so maybe I took my time about it, but I eventually did it.

"Sometimes I think the only pleasure he gets in life is hurting other people," Sarah Beth pulled a paper napkin out of the holder on the pop-up banquette where we sat. She wiped under her eyes carefully so as not to smear her mascara. "You know what I'm talking about. What on earth does he have against *you*?" she asked me.

Peggy gave the kindest of the answers I could have given. "Uh, remember last year when one of the vets at Southern Pines called his black gelding lame and wouldn't let him compete?"

"Oh, Lord, yes. I thought he'd have a coronary right there."

"Since I was show manager," I said, "Giles thought I should overrule him."

"You can't do that," Sarah Beth said. "Can you?"

"No, I can't, but even if I could, I wouldn't have. The gelding was moving short on his off hind leg. A full day of showing and racing around a marathon course could have done real damage. Giles swore he was being discriminated against to give the other competitors an unfair advantage. I told him to take the horse back to his stall. When the gelding went sound the next morning, he called me everything except a child of God."

"Why you and not the vet?"

"Giles had a few choice remarks for the vet as well, but you can't ball out a vet with impunity. That can get you set down and fined. Anyway, Giles said I was incompetent and couldn't manage my way out of a paper sack."

Sarah Beth nodded absently. "So that's why."

"Why what?" Peggy asked.

Sarah Beth slid out from behind the banquette and pulled a couple of sheets of paper out of a drawer under the computer desk. "I think you should read this," she said and handed it to me.

The top sheet was a list of top rated shows in the United States for the next year, listing the names, telephone numbers, emails and mailing addresses of the committee heads for each. The second sheet was a letter set up to mail merge with the list on the first page.

My heart began to race after the first sentence. By the second paragraph I felt as though I had a fever, and by the end I was so stunned I simply sat down and gabbled.

"Give me that," Peggy said and took it from me. "That bastard," Peggy whispered. "This is libelous."

"He's telling everyone that you're incompetent, that you're responsible for the runaway last year at The Meadows that damaged all those trucks and trailers," Sarah Beth said. "I was there. I know you risked your life to save that stallion."

"I thought a few of my show contracts for next year were slow in arriving," I said. "A couple of people haven't returned my calls." I closed my eyes. The accident had been a

49

bad one, but I had in no way been responsible, as the show committee judged at the time.

"It gets worse," Sarah Beth said. "He keeps making these snide little remarks to people about your father's death. How convenient it was for you to inherit the farm free and clear . . ."

"How the hell does he know *that?*"

"If it has to do with real estate in the state of Georgia, Giles knows all about it. Particularly around Bigelow and Mossy Creek. He's big pals with the governor and his cronies."

Mossy Creek, Georgia, where the training farm I'd inherited when my father, Hiram Lackland, was murdered, has as its motto, "The town that ain't goin' nowhere and don't want to." A view not shared by Governor Bigelow, nephew and archenemy of Mossy Creek's mayor, Ida. His country place is in Bigelow, most of his family lives in Bigelow, and he is definitely the big dog in the neighborhood.

Except in Mossy Creek, where he is either ignored or treated like a bad-tempered Yorkie.

Since moving to Mossy Creek to take over my father's farm, I have come to share their view of the world. I suspect you have to be third or fourth generation Creekite to be considered a native, but they certainly try to make me feel at home.

I've never felt at home anywhere before. My mother and I dragged around with my father from training job to training job until they were divorced. By the time she remarried, I was incapable of putting down real roots. Then we moved around every time my husband — now my ex — Vic got a new job, but that's the paradigm I grew up with. Whither thou goest, etc. It had been tough on my daughter Allie, but she learned to make friends fast, a trait that has stood her in good stead as a starting broker in New York.

Even though I had no mortgage to pay on the property, horses and land cost a lot to maintain, plus I was building a log house on the farm so I didn't have to live in Peggy's basement apartment in Mossy Creek.

Training carriage horses and managing horse shows on the weekends kept me solvent. Giles Raleigh was damming up my income stream.

"Has he sent any of those letters out yet?" I asked.

"I'm not sure. He doesn't use email, but he may have gotten one of his secretaries to email these people. Plus he talks to people when he shows, and he knows everybody."

"Please try to find out if you can without bringing down his wrath on your head," Peggy said. "May I keep this?"

Sarah Beth nodded. "I'll run off another copy before he comes back from the marathon. He won't know I gave that one to you."

Peggy nodded and stood up. "Come on, Merry. We need to get out of here before the Cyclops catches us in his cave." She patted Sarah Beth's hand. "None of my business why you can't leave him, but if you change your mind and need a place to stay, I have an extra bedroom. Don't put it off too long. Men like that escalate to physical violence fast."

I thought Sarah Beth was going to burst into tears all over again, but she only hugged herself and nodded.

As we walked back to our trailer to drop off our soggy clothes, Peggy said, "It's chilly today, but have you ever seen Sarah Beth wear short sleeves, even in the Georgia heat?"

Actually, I hadn't, but the only time I notice what people wear is when one of the carriage ladies comes up with a supremely outrageous driving hat.

Ladies' driving hats are a cottage industry.

They can cost hundreds of dollars, and are often trimmed with bird feathers, multiple ribbons, silk flowers and tulle. The brims are usually moderate, however, so they can't be caught by a sudden gust of wind. They are also generally pinned on with their grandmother's antique hat pins. Even the calmest horse will rear and bolt if one of those creations lifts off for a test flight in front of him.

"What do you want to bet there are bruises on Sarah Beth's arms?" Peggy continued.

I stopped dead and wheeled to go back to their trailer. "If he beats her, she has to leave him. Now. And call the sheriff."

Peggy grabbed my arm. "You can't force her."

"Why doesn't she just kill him? Beaten wife defenses work pretty well these days."

"Not in Georgia they don't. And not if you kill a man who pays off enough politicians and judges running for office to buy half the Georgia legislature."

I opened the tack room of our horse trailer so hard the metal door slammed back with a clang that spooked a pair of VSEs tied to the neighboring trailer. VSE stands for Very Small Equine — miniature horses and such. "Then *I'll* kill him. After I remove his ability to procreate with a dull hoof knife."

"Let's pull his fangs before we remove his genitalia," Peggy said. She stuffed our wet clothes into the laundry bag and hung it up in the corner of the trailer tack room.

"Nothing we can do about the rumors he's spread about me, but maybe he hasn't sent those letters out yet. Maybe we should let him go ahead, then nail him for libel." I slammed the door shut. "Otherwise, he can always say he never intended to send them."

"I think libel is written and slander is spoken," Peggy said absently. "Whatever he's implying about your father's death is definitely slander. God, what a day." She leaned against the saddle rack. She looked tired, but I'm sure I did as well. I, however, wasn't on the edge of tears as she seemed to be. I'd never thought anything or anybody could embarrass Peggy, but driving into the lake had truly upset her.

She took a deep breath and shoved away from the saddle rack. "I want a hat. A honking great hat with ostrich plumes and cabbage roses and tulle all over it."

This sounded more like the old Peggy. "Of course you do," I said. "You'll get over it."

"I mean it, Merry. I drove my dressage test yesterday wearing a neat, unassuming black fedora from Stein Mart. After the disaster today, I deserve a real driving hat."

"*I* don't wear one."

"I'm driving, you're just the groom. You can wear your hard hat or your tweed cap. I'm the one people look at."

After the accident this morning, she had *that* right. She'd started off the weekend knowing almost no one. Now everybody knew *her.* Even the grooms nodded and grinned as we passed. Obviously, news of our accident had made the rounds.

I caught the set of her chin. Uh-oh. Peggy in this mood would not deviate from her path if faced with a live brontosaurus. At the moment, that path led right past the stable to the area on the lawn where the tack vendors' trailers were parked alongside the vendors who brought their own display tents. She jumped down from the trailer tack room and started up the hill at an extended walk.

I tried to head her off. "Peggy, be sensible. Why not buy yourself a nice pair of silver driving horse earrings?" I waved at the jewelry lady. I don't generally wear jewelry, but I had several of her pieces. They were charming, and all horse and carriage themed. "At least take a look."

"Maybe later. Right now, I deserve a *hat.*" She made a sharp right into the big tent under the banner that said, "Driving Divas."

"Hey, Merry," said Marguerite Valmont. Marguerite is her nom de plume — literally since she dealt in feathered hats. She was born Gertrude Gary from Indianapolis.

Before I could introduce them, Peggy said, "I want the biggest, craziest hat you've got."

"Oooooh-kay." Marguerite rolled her eyes at me, but smiled at Peggy and waved her hand at the twenty or so hats on stands around her. The showroom looked like an explosion at the 1910 Fifth Avenue Easter parade. Women today don't get much chance to wear big, extravagant hats, so the driving ladies compensate by wearing fedoras, picture hats, cartwheels and toques in silk, velvet, or Panama straw in every color of the rainbow.

Not satisfied with the hats alone, the driving ladies prefer hats decorated with silk flowers and feathers and tulle — sometimes all at once. Many a pheasant or a peacock sacrificed plumage to them, as did a few herons and emus. Theoretically the hats were chosen to complement the driver's formal ensemble. In reality the hat often came first. Then the outfit was chosen to fit in.

Marguerite's hats were elegant, elaborate, and expensive. I hoped Peggy knew what she was doing.

"Sit down," Marguerite said and sat Peggy in a tiny chair in front of a Baroque mirror. "Why don't we try on a few? Let's see. You have that wonderful silvery hair. What color is your driving jacket?"

"Blue," I said.

"Greeny-blue," Peggy added.

Marguerite reached around Peggy and lifted a teal blue picture hat from the hat stand. It was silk, nearly three feet in diameter, and sported peacock feathers nested in tulle along one side.

Peggy plopped it on her head.

"Hey! Not like that. Calm down. Take some deep breaths. I promise you we'll find you the proper hat."

"Oh, shoot, I'm sorry." Peggy's shoulders slumped. "This has not been the best day of my life."

"I heard. Look at it this way. Nobody's hurt, horses, people and harness are all in good shape."

"I look like an incompetent lunatic."

"If you promise to settle down, I'll fit you with the right hat, show you how to wear it, and regale you with some of my worst driving moments. Deal?"

Peggy nodded. "Deal."

"Merry," Marguerite said, "go away. Groom a horse or something. Don't come back for at least an hour."

"But . . ."

"Trust me."

So I left them alone and went over to the refreshment tent, where I gorged myself on Diet Coke and sausage biscuits.

I wasn't kidding about the prices of driving hats. Men generally wore tweed caps or bowlers in informal driving, top hats in formal classes and hard hats in marathons. Straightforward. Sort of. But as with most customs involved in carriage driving, top hats for gentlemen drivers differed from top hats worn by liveried grooms and coachmen.

Theoretically, both men and women could always wear hard hats in any class without penalty. In practice, except in marathons where both hard hats and body protectors were required, lady drivers tended to channel Queen Mary — not the bloody one, but the one who married George the Fifth. The fashion went back to the glory days where wealth and social standing were measured by the carriage and team.

A lady driver between classes might be wearing unzipped paddock boots with her driving apron stuffed into the waistband of her slacks, and a plaid shirt with the sleeves rolled up. But she'd also be wearing a hat for which a half dozen bantam roosters and at least one cock pheasant sacrificed tail feathers. I prayed Marguerite would somehow keep a lid on Peggy. A relatively simple lid.

Stuffed with sausage, I wandered back up the hill toward the tents and spent a few minutes lusting after the latest driving jewelry I wouldn't wear and couldn't afford, and looking at paintings of horses that would look wonderful in my new house if I could afford them. Which I couldn't.

As I neared Marguerite's tent, I heard her say, "Just like that. Perfect! That hat will stay on in a hurricane." I closed my eyes and said a prayer to the hat god.

As I entered the tent, I saw it was a blue hat, but not the one she'd plumped on her head before I'd left. This one was a lighter teal with French ribbon that matched the colors in Peggy's driving jacket, and only a few small feathers. No tulle.

"It's wonderful," I said. "Marguerite, I should have trusted you."

"Apology accepted," Marguerite said with a grin. "I was showing Peggy how to pin it on so it won't go flying off in the dressage arena and scare the horses." She pulled an elaborately painted hatbox from under the dressing table. "Remember, Peggy, remove

the pin first, then lift the hat straight up —
don't go yanking."

"I don't want to be around for this part,"
I said.

"What part?" Peggy asked.

"The credit card part."

Once the hatbox was carefully stowed on
the back seat of our truck, I could tell Peggy's mood had definitely improved.

"My mother always said that having the
proper clothes for a sporting event is half of
winning it," Peggy said with a satisfied grin.

"Then you'll be a champion."

Chapter 4

Merry

Since we'd been eliminated from this event because of our little debacle in the marathon, Peggy and I found the volunteer coordinator and offered our services if they needed us during the afternoon classes. The high fun classes like turnout, carriage dog, and scurry were scheduled after lunch. The marathon would be completed by then.

For many competitors, that meant a change of carriage to something fancier and more in keeping with Victorian traditions. The ladies pinned their fancy hats on and donned their jackets, the men their top hats, and everyone brought out the aprons to cover their legs. I won't go into all the regulations. Just take my word for it that competitive carriage driving has rules on top of its rules.

I have to admit I was annoyed, but not surprised, that Raleigh was leading after the marathon. He didn't do well in his after-noon tests, however. You can bully horses just so long. Then they simply refuse to listen to you.

Peggy and I were straightening up our tackroom in the trailer, when we heard the thud of hooves and the jingle of tack com-ing much too fast from the dressage arena. A moment later, we heard Raleigh's voice.

"Call yourself a groom?" he shouted. "You couldn't groom a poodle. Get the hell off my carriage. Where the hell is Brock? Brock, dammit! Get over here and take care of these horses."

"Daddy . . ."

So Raleigh was yelling at Dawn, his daughter, again.

"Shut up, just shut up. Get out of my face. You'll be damned lucky if I don't cut you out of my *life* as well as my will. I've got more options than *you* now. Tell that polo playing gigolo if he expects to live off you, go take a job at Walmart."

Raleigh's stable manager, Brock, a lanky guy who looked like a cowboy, ambled up to the side of Raleigh's carriage. He didn't seem bothered by Raleigh's tirade, but then, he was undoubtedly used to them.

"Goddammit, Brock, I pay you to look

after my horses, not to lounge up here in the shade."

Peggy reached across me and slammed the door to the trailer tack room. It didn't completely cut off the sound of Raleigh's voice, but deadened it a tad.

I really wanted to listen. If a little schadenfreude — enjoying your enemy's discomfort — makes me a bad person, then I'm a bad person. I felt sorry for Dawn and Brock. Most of all I felt sorry for the horses. Raleigh deserved a couple of well-placed hooves right in the gut.

He'd be hell on wheels at the exhibitors' party.

CHAPTER 5

Merry

Some exhibitors' parties are held outside or in stables. A few are real dress-up affairs, though by the time the day is over, usually competitors are too tired to do more than throw on a clean pair of jeans. What most of them want is a drink — generally alcoholic — lots of good food and a chance to rehash the day's driving with their frenemies. The parties don't generally last far into the night. People are tired, and competitors are facing the cones competition on Sunday morning. If you're weaving from bourbon the night before, you certainly won't be any good at weaving through cones the next day.

This party was halfway between barbecue and pheasant under glass. The Tollivers' house wasn't old as southern mansions go. Nouveau-Tara style, it was built in the mid-twenties before the Wall Street crash and passed down the generations. Some of the land was sold off over the years, but the Tollivers still raised prize Limousine cattle and Rhinelander horses for driving and riding on the thousand or so acres they had left.

There's an old story about a Texas matron who said she didn't own but ten acres of land. They called it Downtown Houston. The Tollivers owned a little less city acreage. They called it downtown Atlanta.

You'd never know that if you met either of them on the street. Juanita mucked stalls and cleaned tack right along with her grooms. She did usually wear thick gloves, however. Her six-carat engagement ring tended to catch otherwise, and she made certain her Patek Philippe watch could stand up to immersion in horse liniment. She'd once told me she thought Rolexes were tacky.

Happily retired from banking and now a full time farmer, Harry Tolliver shot skeet, drove his horses, played with his golf clubs and his grandchildren, and generally enjoyed himself. He'd lost a step or two the last couple of years, and his weight and blood pressure worried Juanita, but he refused to give up his early breakfasts at the local café with the other good ole boys.

Surprisingly, Giles sauntered onto the Tollivers' patio in full charm mode.

Peggy narrowed her eyes at him and whispered to me, "What's with the shake and howdy?"

"Probably improved his mood by dismembering the last remaining specimen of some endangered species on his way over here from his trailer," I whispered back as he approached us.

"Good evening, Peggy, you dry off yet?" He guffawed, bent over her hand, and might even have kissed it if she hadn't snatched it out of his way.

"How kind of you to inquire, Mr. Raleigh." Anyone other than Giles would have frozen solid from her breath.

"Oh, come now. Call me Giles. And how are you this evening, Merry? Hope I didn't upset you two fine ladies this morning. Sometimes my alligator tongue overwhelms my hummingbird brain when I'm on a marathon. Please accept my apologies."

My first thought was that he was drunk out of his gourd. But he was known as a bad drunk, not an eloquent one. Had he been hitting Sarah Beth's tranquilizers? He was too calm to be on cocaine or crystal meth. "Um-hm," I said, but he'd already brushed past us and wiped us from his memory bank. Both Peggy and I turned to follow his progress through the crowd.

"Catherine, don't you look lovely this evening," he said, and leaned over to give her an air kiss and a whisper in her ear. Prurient, probably. Offered to take *her* to bed.

Catherine Harris, still in technical delegate mode, flinched and gave him a stare that would have pickled okra in the field.

"You and I have to sit down and have us a long chat this weekend," he said. He turned and held out his hand. "And I must have a talk with that fine young man Troy I've heard so much about. I'm sure you rely on him *heavily.*"

"Ooooh," Peggy whispered. "Nasty."

Giles swept on, nodding to left and right. It was like watching a monarch process through a palace garden party. The monarch being Ivan the Terrible or Genghis Khan.

Troy hadn't heard Giles's remark. He was too engrossed with the tall, elegant post deb he was staring at. She was indeed beautiful, but I didn't like the way her eyes kept sweeping the room like a submarine periscope. Not wary, exactly, but alert.

"Do you see Sarah Beth?" I asked Peggy. "Is she here?"

"Maybe she's spending time fixin' herself up. If she doesn't show soon, we can fix her a plate and take it down to her."

"Good excuse," I said. "Hey, Dick. You do clean up well."

Dick Fitzgibbons leaned over and kissed Peggy's cheek. He didn't bother to kiss me, but I already knew he had a thing for Peggy and she had a thing for him. He considers me more like a daughter, anyway.

"What's with Raleigh?" he asked. "Did he just evict a bunch of nice old people from their retirement homes?"

"He's certainly happy enough," Peggy said. "Those yellow feathers sticking out of his alligator jaws worry me. And Sarah Beth's not here. I'm going to walk down and check on her right now instead of waiting."

"I'll come with you," I said.

"No. Stay here and keep an eye on Raleigh. If he's cheerful because he's been knocking her around, I don't want him running off before I can call the cops." We separated at the buffet table. Peggy filled a plate for Sarah Beth while I filled one for me.

The barbecued ribs were to die for, and I watched Raleigh surreptitiously while I gnawed. I lost him when he went to the bathroom, and once I saw him down at the end of the terrace texting on his cell phone. Most men over thirty don't have the thumbs to text, but he was grinning and tearing up that keyboard on his iPhone or his Droid or whatever it was. Something top of the line, no doubt. Must be cancelling somebody's construction loans for fun.

CHAPTER 6

Peggy

The lights were on in Raleigh's trailer, but nobody came to the door for the longest time after Peggy knocked. Finally, she heard soft footsteps and called out, "Sarah Beth, honey, I brought you a plate. It's Peggy. Let me in."

She opened the door, and Peggy spotted no obvious bruises. So, if he beat her, he'd been clever enough to leave bruises where they didn't show.

Sarah Beth's red ringed eyes, however, said she'd been crying. Peggy didn't wait for an invitation, but let herself in and set the plate on the counter beside the microwave.

"That's sweet of you," Sarah Beth said, "but I'm really not hungry. I think I'm getting a cold." She sniffed.

"Cold my Aunt Fanny. What did he do to you?" Peggy slid the plate toward her. "You aren't as big as a minute. You got to eat. Smell these ribs and tell me you're not hungry."

Her eyes got huge. She stared at Peggy, clapped her hands over her mouth, dove into the bathroom and dropped to her knees over the toilet without shutting the door. Actually, there wasn't room to shut the door. Her feet stuck out into the little hallway. If she'd had anything in her stomach, she'd already thrown it up, because all Peggy heard were dry heaves.

Peggy grabbed a dishtowel hanging from the stove handle, ran it under the cold water, wrung it out, and knelt down to wipe Sarah Beth's forehead, then laid it across the back of her neck. She wasn't certain whether she was looking at the beginning of DTs, a big fat hangover at seven in the evening, or some kind of medication. Maybe an overdose Sarah Beth decided to get rid of. Possibly she really did have some kind of stomach flu. Peggy prayed they weren't dealing with a bruised liver or ruptured spleen from Raleigh's fists.

"Please," Sarah Beth choked out, "put the plate in the icebox. I can't stand the smell."

That's when it hit Peggy.

Okay. She stashed the food and sat down

beside Sarah Beth in the narrow aisle. "How long?"

"How long what?" She avoided Peggy's eyes.

"How long have you known you were pregnant?"

Her head whipped around, and she gaped. "Pregnant? Why on earth would you think that? I've just got a twenty-four hour virus."

"Puh-lease. In my years teaching college students, I have seen far too many co-eds dive out of my classes and found them throwing up in the loo."

"Maybe they were just bored sick," she said. "Oh, what an awful thing to say."

"I may have been brutal, but I was never boring. From my lectern I had the perfect view of that deer-in-headlights look you all get before the projectile vomiting starts. So that's why Giles is strutting around on the terrace exhaling testosterone. You just tell him?"

"Oh, my God, he doesn't know!" She grabbed Peggy's hands so hard Peggy thought she'd break her arthritic pinkies. "He *mustn't* know. Promise you won't tell him."

"It's your job to tell him, not mine. Come on, Sarah Beth, even if he doesn't want a baby at this late stage in his life, once he knows, he'll be thrilled to death."

"No, he won't." She dropped her face into her hands. The towel draped around her neck started to slide.

Peggy caught and rearranged it. "Look, can we get up off the floor or are you going to hurl again?"

Sarah Beth grinned sheepishly. "Nothing left to hurl." She unfolded in one long piece. Peggy, on the other hand, struggled to her knees and had to use the edge of the cabinet to get all the way up. Her knees popped like Orville Redenbacher's.

Sarah Beth slid into the banquette, folded her arms and put her head down. "Throwing up wears me out."

"Auntie Peggy's tried and true antidote — hot tea with lemon and lots of sugar, soda crackers and half an apple."

"Nothing, please."

"Shut up. I'll take the plate I brought when I leave. If you don't want those ribs, I most certainly do."

Peggy filled the teakettle, lit the propane burner and set the water to heat, found a mug in one cabinet and a big box of Saltines in another. No apples. She did, however, find lemon juice in the small propane refrigerator along with a cold six pack of Pellegrino. She opened one of the bottles and handed it to Sarah Beth. "I know you don't want this, but if you don't keep hydrated, you really *will* be sick. It's not good for the baby either."

"Good." But she took a long drink of the water. Peggy suspected her mouth was as dry as kitty litter.

"Here." She handed Sarah Beth the box of crackers. "Eat at least a couple." The kettle whistled. Sarah Beth jumped a foot. If she hadn't been clutching the bottle of water so tight it would have flown out of her hand.

Peggy said and removed the kettle. "Teabags?"

"First drawer. Is there any Chamomile left?"

There was. "Good choice." Peggy added lemon. "Got any honey?"

She shook her head, so Peggy spooned a couple of tablespoons from the sugar bowl on the table. Sarah Beth made a face when she took the tea, but cradled it between her palms as though grateful for the warmth, blew on it and took a sip. "I'm sorry," she said. "You're missing the party."

"I hate parties. I'm only in it for the ribs. Those I've got thanks to you."

Sarah Beth managed a small smile. "I am a terrible person."

"Oh? In what way?"

"I don't want this baby. I've made up my mind. I'm not going to have it."

Peggy nodded. She had heard the same thing from a number of girls, some of whom had their babies, some of whom did not. Some of the girls who went through with the pregnancy kept their babies, some put them up for adoption. Peggy could not possibly judge them, since she had never been in that situation. She and Ben had produced one daughter. For both of them, Marilou had been sufficient. "None of my business," she said. "It is, however, Raleigh's business."

"No, it's not. It's my body and my choice."

"He won't see it that way." Peggy didn't either. But it wasn't her baby, and she wasn't married to Giles Raleigh. Thank God.

Sarah Beth clutched the mug so tightly her knuckles went white. Peggy hoped the crockery was thick. "He will never know unless you tell him. Promise me you won't."

"Of course I won't, but I still think *you* should. Not only are there ethical considerations, but legal ones as well. I know you and Raleigh are having problems . . ."

"A baby is not going to cure my marriage."

"Counseling might. This might be the

impetus to get him to consider going with you. Listen, Sarah Beth, your biological clock is close to chiming the midnight hour. If you *ever* want a child, you better think long and hard before you get rid of the only one you may ever conceive."

In an instant Sarah Beth morphed from waif to Valkyrie. "How dare you? I thought you were my friend. Get the hell out of my trailer!"

For a moment Peggy thought Sarah Beth was going to throw the cup. Hormones and misery.

Peggy slid out of the banquette and started for the door.

"And take your damn ribs!"

So she did.

As she walked back up the hill toward the party, Peggy heard the three-piece combo playing dance music from one end of the terrace. What on earth was she going to do with the ribs? She was ravenous, but couldn't see standing deep in the shadows and scarfing down ribs with one hand while trying to hold the paper plate with the other. She wound up sitting in the front seat of Merry's pickup in the dark like a lost soul cast into the darkness, while she worried about Sarah Beth.

If Raleigh didn't know he was about to

become a father, then what on earth was he so doggone cheerful about?

Chapter 7

Sunday morning
Merry

If we'd thought the early morning mist was bad Saturday morning before the marathon, it was *worse,* a London pea souper, at six-thirty Sunday morning. The thick pine forest that edged the dressage arena beside the stables held the fog tight among its needles. It swirled across the arena and left heavy dew that wet my supposedly waterproof paddock boots to the ankle.

I'd given Peggy leave to sleep in and have a leisurely breakfast with Dick at the motel before she caught a ride over to the Tollivers' place with him. I am so used to getting up at dawn to feed horses that I can't sleep in even when I'd like to. And since I didn't drink at last evening's party, I didn't have a hangover to contend with.

I'd agreed to help the volunteer committee set the cones course in the dressage arena. The third phase of the event after the marathon and dressage consisted of an obstacle course in which each carriage threaded its way through a corkscrew puzzle of tall orange traffic cones. Not the usual cones you see on the highway, however. These were cut at a slight angle that turned them into Leaning Tower of Pisa cones. A white ball topped each cone. If a horse or carriage hit one of the cones, the ball fell.

The cones, like the hazards course, were set just slightly wider than the carriage running the course — smaller carriage, smaller ponies or horses, and the cones were set closer together. For the large four-in-hands like Raleigh's, the cones were set at maximum distance apart, but still only a few inches wider than the carriage itself.

The horses had to maneuver through very tight turns at the highest speed they could manage. The carriage with the fewest balls down and the shortest time on course won.

I fed and watered Golden and Ned and picked the overnight manure out of shavings in their cushy trailer stalls, then wrapped my windbreaker around me tight and walked down to the dressage arena. After last night's party, I wasn't surprised to find I was the first to arrive.

Tacked to one of the light poles I found

the course designer's outline of where the pairs of cones should be set. One set of volunteers were to pick up as many cones as they could tote and drop them in the general area, then a second set of volunteers would measure distances precisely and set the balls on top of each cone.

The area was surrounded by pine forest on three sides, open on the side facing the parking area and the stables. The arena itself was delineated by steel cable stretched through pad eyes on the tops of steel spikes that were driven into the ground every eight meters and at each of the four corners.

Fancy dressage arenas are often bounded by low white PVC fences, but this one was actually part of the Tollivers' pasture most of the time. The cable and spike arrangement was inexpensive and easy to set up.

The rubber cones were heavy and cumbersome. Setting them was frustrating and tedious. That's why the committee started early. Not as early as me, apparently.

I hefted a couple of cones and walked across the arena toward the trees on the far side. Squish, squish. Like walking across a marsh through clouds.

Without even the sound of a hoof, a phantom horse loomed up out of the mist and stopped a foot from my face. I squealed and dropped the cones. He snorted, tossed his head and did a little dance but didn't back away.

The mist parted for a moment and I saw why. I wasn't facing one horse, but four — one pair harnessed in front of the other. And pulling a big carriage.

Without a driver.

I held up my hands. "Whoa, sweetie," I crooned and walked up to the left lead horse, who seemed glad to see me.

When I took hold of his bridle, he nuzzled me and deposited a wad of half-chewed grass on my shoulder. His harness mate nickered a soft greeting.

Why on earth were they wandering around this early in the morning in full harness without a driver? I recognized Raleigh's team. Where was *he?*

"Raleigh?" I called tentatively. The whole situation was eerie. I couldn't leave the horses to go look for Raleigh. On the other hand, if he'd fallen off the box and was hurt, I couldn't *not* look for him.

The reins had been looped over the whip holder in the carriage so that they wouldn't drag and get caught in the wheels. If Raleigh had fallen or been thrown, he wouldn't have had time to do that. But why on earth would he leave his team unattended? At a show, that was grounds for instant elimination.

The horses weren't lathered as though they'd run away and tossed Raleigh off. Their backs were damp, but from the mist.

I couldn't wait for another volunteer to show up to head the team. I needed to hunt for Raleigh right this minute. If he was hurt, minutes counted. Surely this wasn't another attack of the lunatics from the bridge. This must be an accident.

I could feel my heart in my throat and that heat on the skin that means adrenaline is pumping big-time. I closed my eyes and remembered my mother lying on the ground under the wheels of a similar carriage that I'd been driving even though I'd been forbidden to. My stupidity had nearly cost my mother her life, and kept me from driving for nearly twenty years. So, believe me, I knew what could happen when someone fell off a carriage that size. But if Raleigh had fallen, where was he?

Behind the carriage I saw the parallel snail tracks the wheels had made through the wet grass. "Stand," I said to the horses. A well-trained carriage team wouldn't move until I released them.

The wheel track behind the carriage led away from the trailer area toward the far corner by the woods. Even now, with the fog lifting, I had to keep my eyes on the ground. Otherwise, I couldn't see more than a couple of feet in front of me, although I looked behind me occasionally to check my location.

I was spooked. Raleigh would never abandon his team willingly. Moreover, why would he have put to at the crack of dawn in the first place? The cones class didn't start until nine. He might not be scheduled to drive until noon. Nobody needed that much warm up.

I tripped over him.

He sprawled face down in the farthest corner of the arena.

The spike anchoring the cable at that corner should have been driven deep into the dirt.

Instead it was driven into the nape of Giles's neck.

I sat down hard and clapped my hands over my mouth. He had to be dead.

Didn't he?

I started to shout for help. Then I didn't.

The fog seemed to steal not only sight but sound.

Anybody could be standing behind a pine watching me. For that matter, someone could be standing in the open six feet away in the fog. I wouldn't see them and probably wouldn't hear them. Then I felt warm breath on the back of my neck. I yelped and scrambled away on my backside.

Startled, Raleigh's lead horse, the one who'd dropped grass on my shoulder, snorted and butted me with his nose. The team pulling their driverless carriage was standing practically on top of me. I made it to my feet and backed out of range. Either they weren't all that well trained to stand, or they'd come looking for the nearest human being that could climb onto the carriage and take the reins.

I am generally calm during a crisis. That ability to turn off emotion is what makes me a good show manager, so I took hold of the coupling rein that held the leaders together and quietly led them away from the bundle of flesh that had been Giles Raleigh. When they were far enough away, I gave them the "stand" command again, this time with more authority in my voice. "Do not come find me," I said. Then I forced myself to go back to Raleigh.

The last thing I wanted to do was touch him, but I had to know if he had a pulse. I knelt beside him, touched the pulse point under his throat with two fingers, felt around. Nothing.

Since the stake driven up into his skull was still in place, there was almost no blood. The cable still ran through the pad eye and held the stake near to the ground. Raleigh must have been lying on the ground or kneeling when he was struck. Could his carriage have run over the spike, yanking it from the ground then left it lying point up? Raleigh fell out of his carriage and onto it somehow? Next to impossible, but better than the alternative, that someone had driven it into his head.

"What the hell?" I heard a male voice somewhere out in the arena, loud enough to penetrate the fog. "What the Sam Hill are you guys doing out here by yourselves? Where is Raleigh?"

"Over here," I called. "It's Raleigh. He's hurt." Actually, I was as sure as I could be that he was dead, but I wasn't about to tell my erstwhile rescuer that.

Georgia Bureau of Investigation agent Geoff Wheeler propped his feet on his dusty coffee table, blew on his mug of black coffee, opened the Sunday *Atlanta Journal* and pulled out the comics section. He bit into his third jelly doughnut from the box of Krispy Kremes. He might just finish the box.

He should be contentedly watching a non—blacked out Atlanta Braves game and drinking a couple of beers. He should have Merry Abbott curled up on the sofa beside him.

He considered driving north to Mossy Creek and *her* sofa, only he'd probably fall asleep at the wheel and wind up in a ditch. His plane had landed in Atlanta too late to call her last night, and when he'd tried this morning he'd gotten her voice mail — "gone to a horse show. Please leave a message." She'd left a number for emergencies, but she probably wouldn't return his call until she got home to Mossy Creek, if then.

Life had been a damn sight less complicated before he'd met Merry. He could go off on a deep cover assignment and not feel the isolation. He could enjoy working down south or on one of the barrier islands and not wish for an assignment around Dahlonega or Bigelow.

He'd met her a year ago when her father was murdered outside of Mossy Creek. He'd been instantly attracted to her, but involvement with murder suspects was definitely against Georgia Bureau of Investigation rules.

And Geoff was a stickler for rules. He had to be. Break the rules, and some defense attorney would have your ass for favoritism and get your airtight case tossed out. Juries did not enjoy wondering about the credibility of a police witness.

Once Hiram Lackland's murder had been solved, they'd tried to get together, and even managed a couple of romantic dinners in Bigelow, the county seat for Mossy Creek. Most of the time, however, either he was off on assignment in South Georgia or she was at a horse show.

Geoff wanted more. Much more. He'd thought Merry did too. If they could find the time. At least the next time they met, she wouldn't be a murder suspect. He wouldn't have to hold back.

He nearly choked when his cell rang as he wolfed down his fourth doughnut. He swigged a mouthful of coffee, still hot enough to singe the roof of his mouth, and lunged for the phone on his kitchen counter.

He checked the ID. Unknown caller. Not Merry, then.

Sunday calls were never good, even thought he was officially off duty. He caught it as it started to go to voice mail. "Hello, Geoff? Agent Wheeler? This is Peggy Caldwell from Mossy Creek."

His heart sped up. Had something happened to Merry? He hadn't heard from

Peggy since she'd sent him a Christmas card and an invitation to a Christmas party he hadn't been free to attend. "How badly is she hurt?"

"I beg your pardon?" Peggy said. "Oh — Merry's not hurt. I'm sorry if I gave you that impression."

"Then why . . ."

"Can you come? I think she's about to be arrested for murder."

CHAPTER 8

Still Sunday —
Merry

Sheriff Nordstrom had set up an interview room of sorts in the lounge of the Tollivers' palatial stable. I felt as though I'd been sitting across from him for days instead of hours. So far I was too exasperated to be frightened, but that would come. The law may be "a ass," as Dickens's Mr. Bumble said in *Oliver Twist,* but it is still the law. It can arrest people, toss them into jail, and send them to prison.

"Yes, I was sitting on the ground beside Raleigh when Harry Tolliver found me," I said. "I was feeling for a pulse."

"Not driving that stake through his neck?"

"No, sheriff," I tried to keep the edge out of my voice.

This Nordic giant sheriff looked as though he belonged in Minnesota, not Georgia. If he started giving me problems, Peggy would call him a Storm Trooper if we were lucky, and the Gestapo if we weren't. I doubted that would endear either of us to him.

"Tell me again how you found him," Sheriff Nordstrom, probably no relation to the store, said patiently.

"I found his horses," I said. "I only started looking for Raleigh after I realized they were without a driver."

"And when you discovered him, what did you do?"

"We've been over and over this," I said and massaged the tight spot I get in the left side of my neck.

"Humor me."

"I knelt down to see what was the matter. I figured he'd been tossed out of the carriage and was unconscious."

"When did you realize he was dead?"

"When I saw that spike." Boy, did I want to believe that Giles had fallen on it, but I didn't suggest it. I really wanted the sheriff to come to the conclusion that Giles died in an accident.

"Then what?"

"The lead horse harnessed to his carriage darned near stepped on me. I got up and backed the team and the carriage away from the — from Giles. That's when Harry Tolliver found the horses and then me."

"You were on the ground again."

I nodded. My head hurt so badly it was about to come off my shoulders. I hadn't had so much as a cup of coffee. I was hungry, thirsty, and had a caffeine deprivation headache that was going to get worse if I didn't get a big dose of it soon.

"I couldn't just walk away from the man," I said.

"Did you try to remove the spike?"

"Are you kidding? You never pull the instrument out of a stab wound. If you do, you risk letting loose a torrent of blood."

"Not if he was already dead. Blood ceases to flow when the heart ceases to pump."

"At that point I was hoping he still had some spark of life in him. I didn't want to cause him to bleed out."

"And you know this how? You a nurse? Have a medical degree?"

That was a new question. I suppose I shouldn't have said anything about the puncture wound bleeding, but I was tired. "Sheriff, I breed and train horses. They hurt themselves a lot. Occasionally one of them will run into a sharp branch or a broken fence post and drive it into himself. My vet taught me many years ago never to remove any foreign object that might be keeping an artery or a major vein from blowing. So, no,

I did not touch the spike. Or the cable or anything else around him, for that matter."

"But you touched the carriage?"

I closed my eyes and ran back over my actions. "Raleigh uses — used — Biothane harness. It's as shiny as patent leather and should take fingerprints well. Let's see — I grabbed the leader's bridle. I touched the coupling rein."

He raised his eyebrows.

"That's the rein that secures the two front horses together. I saw the reins were looped over the whip holder, but I didn't touch them. You shouldn't find my fingerprints anywhere else."

"You and Raleigh had a big fight yesterday, right?"

I'd already gone over this several times. I proceeded to tell him again about our dunking in the lake and Raleigh's reaction to it. "Everyone at the party last night will tell you he was charming to Peggy and me. I thought he was a jerk, but that's no reason to kill him."

"We have a witness who overheard you threatening to do just that."

"Not recently." Had I actually threatened to kill him after we left Sarah Beth? "If I did, I wasn't serious. Everyone says stuff like that."

"Uh-huh."

I didn't volunteer any information about his trying to curtail my manager's jobs at horse shows. If it came out, it came out. Nothing I could do about it. But I wasn't going to bring it up and give Nordstrom more ammunition against me.

"Sheriff, I've been much more forthcoming than I probably should have. I'm hungry, tired, and I have a headache. I have to get home to my other horses, so Peggy and I can load up and head back to Mossy Creek."

"Nobody said you could leave the area."

"Nobody said I had to stay, either. I have horses at home that need looking after. Unless you have additional questions or plan to charge me with something, I don't think you can force me to stay."

"I could hold you as a material witness."

I didn't know whether he could or not and didn't want to find out.

"We're interviewing everyone . . ."

"Then letting them go home," I said. "I heard what you told your deputies." The only difference between most of them and me was the size of our bank balances and the political influence many of them could wield.

"One final question. Who might have

wanted to kill Raleigh?"

Lots of people loathed him, but loathing didn't usually escalate to murder. "In all honesty, I didn't know the man that well."

"But you didn't like him? Maybe hated him?"

I shook my head. "I don't hate, sheriff. It takes too much energy. I seldom go further than dislike."

"You planning on leaving the state anytime soon?"

"Not for six weeks. Peggy and I will be driving at a couple of shows, but they're both in Georgia. Next weekend I have a two-day carriage show and clinic at my place in Mossy Creek. The next time you plan to speak to me, please give me some warning so I can have my lawyer with me."

"You think you need a lawyer?"

"Sheriff, everybody involved in a murder investigation needs a lawyer."

I said goodbye to him, opened the door, and walked right into Geoff Wheeler's chest.

He grabbed my shoulders, held me at arms' length, and said, "What the hell have you done this time?"

I shoved away from Geoff and cracked the back of my head on the frame of the door. My headache went up a couple of notches. So did my blood pressure. *"Me?"*

I heard footsteps behind me, then Nordstrom's voice. "Geoff Wheeler? Where the hell did you come from?"

Geoff eased me aside and behind him before he stuck out his hand. "Hey, Stan. I promise I'm not intruding on your territory. I was in the neighborhood and picked it up on the scanner."

I knew that was a lie. So, I supposed, did Stan the Man. Short for Stanislaus?

"You know this wo— lady?"

"Met her and Peggy Caldwell on a case last year."

Stan held the door open as an invitation to Geoff to enter. He did and closed it in my face. Oh, lovely. Once the sheriff heard about my father's murder in Mossy Creek last year, he'd arrest me on general principles. I went to find Peggy, certain that she had called him to come rescue me.

CHAPTER 9

Sunday
Geoff

"Why are you really here?" Stan asked Geoff.

"Kind of a long story."

"I have time. Actually, I don't, but tell me anyway."

So Geoff told him about Hiram Lackland's murder. "Peggy Caldwell and Merry Abbott were completely innocent, if major pains in the neck."

"Uh-huh," Stan said, looking at Geoff curiously. "So when Mrs. Caldwell called you at home, you drove straight here?"

Geoff held up his hands. "I would never get in your way."

"Oh, please, please, please, get in my way," Stan said. "You have any idea who these people are? Who the deceased was? Who the Tollivers are? I was about twenty minutes from putting in a call to the GBI anyway."

"What have you done so far?"

"Damn all. The pediatrician who passes for a medical examiner in this county came out, took liver temp, and said the guy was probably killed within an hour of when he was discovered. We took pictures, walked the grid around the body, and carted it off to the local funeral home, which has the only facilities around here for corpses. Doc Agostino wants us to send Raleigh to Atlanta for a proper autopsy."

"Did he remove the stake?"

Stan shook his head. "We had to cut the cable running in through it to get it loose. We left about six feet on either side in case there was trace. Had to transport him on his stomach."

"How much force would you estimate would be needed to drive that stake home?" Geoff asked.

Stan shrugged. "No idea, but if you're asking whether a woman could have done it, a strong one maybe. Like your girlfriend."

Geoff rolled his eyes. "She's not my girlfriend."

"See, what I can't figure out," Stan said, "is how the killer got him down on the ground in the first place. Nobody would kneel down and let somebody drive a stake through the base of his skull."

"No chance he could have done it himself?"

"Suicide? Accident? I don't see how, but I'm willing to be convinced if the medical examiner in Atlanta tells me it's possible."

"I've been around these people enough to know they do not get off the driving box for any reason on show grounds. So why would Raleigh get down, wrap his reins around the whip holder, and walk off? Bad enough to leave a single horse, but a four-in-hand?"

"A cry for help? The pinewoods come right up to the edge of the arena on that side. Anybody could stand in those woods at that time of the morning in a heavy fog without being seen. I just found out about some kind of animal rights prank yesterday morning. Banner, lot of noise. This doesn't seem like the same sort of thing, but we're checking it out. So far, nothing."

"Any footprints?"

Stan shook his head again. "Thick pine needles do not take prints. No handy fibers caught up in the needles either."

"Huh."

"So," Stan said. "Now that you're here, how do I make you all official so we can get your CSI team down here?"

"Make the call. Let them know I'm staying. No telling how long it'll take the CSI van to get here."

"At least you *have* techs. We have ten deputies to police the entire county, and I'm the only one who's even *seen* Quantico."

"Make the call," Geoff repeated and stood. "Call Chief of Police Amos Royden in Mossy Creek if you want a run down on Peggy and Merry. They can be a handful, but the only reason I can think of that Merry Abbott might consider killing someone is if she caught him hurting horses." He stopped with his hand on the door. "Raleigh didn't hurt his horses, did he?"

Stan guffawed. "Not to the best of my knowledge. Man, you ought to see your face. You're dead serious, aren't you?"

"I just came back from an assignment in the Caribbean," Geoff said with as much dignity as he could muster. "That's why my face is red. Sunburn."

"Riiiiggghhhht."

He threaded his way through trucks and trailers until he spotted Merry's white dually and its attached horse trailer. He didn't see Merry, but Peggy stood on the step of the tack storage area hanging a set of harness on one of the hooks inside.

"Need a hand?" he asked.

She took a deep breath, closed her eyes,

and said, "Thank God, you came." She stepped off the trailer and hugged him. Surprised, he hugged her back.

"I don't think Stan Nordstrom is going to arrest Merry," he said when she'd released him. "Not at the moment. Where is she, by the way?"

"Borrowing a set of VSE harness and a small cart. It folds flat, so we can stow it under the marathon carriage. You can help slide it in and help put the carriage cover on."

"What's a VSE?"

"Stands for Very Small Equine," Peggy said and shook her head. "Miniature horses. Worse. Miniature donkeys."

"Like Don Qui?" Geoff said. He flashed back to Don Quixote, Merry's miniature donkey that had tried to stomp and bite him at every opportunity.

Peggy leaned her hip on the side of the pickup. "Merry is teaching Don Qui to drive."

"You're kidding, right? When did she develop the death wish? Sorry, bad choice of words."

"She read up on the breed. Apparently, they have a reputation as kind, easy-going animals . . ."

Geoff snorted.

"And she says if he's going to continue to eat her grain, he's going to have to pay his way by training students."

"Training them to do what? Bail out of a carriage at a dead gallop?"

"I know, I know," Peggy said. "But she is bound and determined. So we're borrowing a miniature Meadowbrook cart and small harness from Juanita Tolliver. Her grandchildren have outgrown their VSEs and graduated to Welsh ponies, so she's not using it at the moment. We've been longeing and long-reining him since February, but we don't have a small cart."

He glanced up.

"Here she comes. Don't say a word about Don Qui. She doesn't want anyone to know until she's certain he'll be trustworthy to a cart."

Merry had draped the VSE harness around her neck, and balanced the little two-wheel cart behind her. Built of natural wood, it wasn't much bigger than a dog cart. She walked between the shafts in front as though she were a horse and pulled the cart behind her.

Since the Meadowbrook cart was entered from the rear, both left hand and right hand seats folded down so driver and passenger could climb through, open up the seats, and sit behind the dashboard and between the two wheels. With the seats down, the cart stood no more than three feet from the ground to the top of the wheels. It probably weighed less than a hundred pounds, but it was cumbersome for a human being to pull. It was one of the few carriages that could be folded flat, so that it would fit into the back of a van.

When she reached the open door of her trailer, Merry began to collapse the cart. Both Geoff and Peggy hurried to help her. Her face was streaming with sweat despite the cool breeze.

She glared at Geoff, and said, "Take this harness off me before I trip over the reins and break my neck."

He reached for it. "Please might be nice," he said.

"I'm not feeling polite. Not after you disappear for months and then barely say hello before you accuse me of murder."

"Hey," he said and draped the harness over his own neck. He reached for one of the shafts, but she shook him off. "I was undercover. I couldn't call you, and I didn't accuse you."

"You demanded to know what I had done *this* time. Like I was some sort of serial killer. I'm sure Thor the Wonder Sheriff took note."

"He's letting us go. Don't pick on the man," Peggy said.

A big rig with living quarters nearly as large as Raleigh's passed them in a fug of diesel fumes.

"And we're not giving him time to change his mind," Merry said. The center ramp on the trailer was already down. Inside, Geoff could see another, larger carriage with its shafts already secured to the roof of the trailer.

"Is that thing going to fit?" he asked.

"If you'll help me get it inside, it'll slide backwards between the four wheels of the marathon cart with the shafts beside it on the floor," Merry said. "I've already measured."

Easier said than done, but he shooed Merry out of the way and managed to slip the cart into position. When she finished tying it down and stood, she brushed against him. He felt as though she'd jabbed a cattle prod into his chest. From the way she bounced away, he suspected she'd felt the same charge, but she carefully avoided looking at him.

Women didn't have a clue how soft their breasts felt. His ex-wife Brittany had been practically flat chested. She called it model-thin. He called it cadaverous, but not where she could hear him.

Merry, on the other hand, might have muscles on her muscles, but she was definitely soft where she should be. He'd fantasized about her all over the Caribbean on his undercover assignment, but the fantasy didn't come close to the reality.

She slipped the heavy duck cover over the marathon carriage, pulled it down to the ground over the wheels, fastened it around the shafts, shooed him down the ramp ahead of her, then lifted and fastened the ramp before he had a chance to help. "You sticking around to help the sheriff?" she asked him.

"For the moment. He'll want to talk to you again. If I get officially pulled in, I'll need to interview you as well." Then it hit him. She was a suspect in a murder case again. That put her out of bounds again until he'd solved it. Damn and blast.

"Do I have to come back here?" she asked. "It's an hour from Mossy Creek."

"Depends. We may wrap this up fast."

"But you don't think so, do you?" Peggy said.

He shook his head. "Not unless somebody confesses. That's not going to happen. From what I hear, there's no shortage of people who disliked the guy."

"If that were the criterion for killing him, you'd be looking at a modern day *Murder on the Orient Express*," Peggy said. "You know, the Agatha Christie mystery where all the suspects joined together to kill the guy."

"That may happen in one of your mysteries, Peggy, but not in real life," Geoff said.

"So I guess we won't be seeing you again," Merry said, still avoiding his eye.

"I'll drive over to Mossy Creek to interview you."

"Gee, thanks for the favor. Peggy, are Golden and Ned secured?"

Peggy nodded. "Checked and double-checked, not to mention impatient to get home."

"Me too. Come on, let's mount up." She walked up to the driver's side and climbed into her truck.

Peggy leaned over to him and whispered, "Thank you for coming, Geoff. When you come to Mossy Creek, you can stay with me. I'll take you to another garden club meeting." She actually winked at him, climbed into the truck and waved out the window as the rig passed him. He watched it drive slowly down the long driveway toward the road. Then he went back to Stan.

He'd definitely volunteer to interview Merry and Peggy again in Mossy Creek but damned if he'd ever be tricked into attending another one of Peggy's garden club meetings. Those women were dangerous.

Chapter 10

Sunday afternoon
Merry

"We didn't offer our condolences to Sarah Beth or Dawn before we drove off," Peggy said.

"And have them accuse me of killing Raleigh?"

Peggy handed me a Diet Coke — one with caffeine for my headache. I drank half of it in one long pull. "Did you call Geoff Wheeler and ask him to come rescue me?"

"Maybe," Peggy said. She sounded guilty. "All right, yes. And you see how fast he got there. The man likes you, Merry."

"He likes *you*. He thinks I'm a pain in the butt."

"But not a murderer. The police always think the person who found the body is the killer."

"And it's never true, is it?"

"In real life, it often is."

"I did not kill Raleigh," I said.

"Of course you didn't! Perish the thought."

With each mile farther from the Tollivers' farm I relaxed a bit more. We'd picked their relatively small show close to Lackland Farm, so Peggy could drive her pair with less pressure from a horde of other equipages. She'd also see what it took to run a carriage show. Ours would be on a much smaller scale, pleasure classes Saturday with a separate carriage clinic on Sunday. We didn't need as many volunteers, but the jobs were pretty much the same.

"What I don't understand," I said as I pulled out my big aluminum gooseneck trailer out to pass a pickup truck doing thirty-five in a fifty-five zone, "is why Raleigh was out there at dawn with all four horses harnessed. Even if he decided to get a head start on his warm-up, he would have rousted his groom out of bed to get the horses ready and Dawn to act as groom on the carriage. It's not that simple to harness four big horses alone."

"You don't think he might have let them sleep?" Peggy asked, then answered her own question. "Nah. He'd have taken great delight in dragging them out of bed before dawn."

"So maybe he did," I said. "Who's to say he didn't have someone with him?"

"Someone who killed him, then went happily back to bed and left you to find him?"

"I wonder how closely the sheriff and his posse checked the woods beside the arena? Maybe there were footprints or a piece of cloth on a branch. Maybe another of those dumb banners."

"If they didn't check, Geoff will," Peggy said with satisfaction. "He doesn't miss much."

I shuddered and covered it up by chug-a-lugging the rest of my Diet Coke. "I didn't say this before because I figured everyone would think I was crazy or hysterical or trying to spread the guilt around . . ."

Peggy turned as far as her seatbelt allowed. "I won't. What?"

I eased on the brakes and brought my big truck and trailer to a standstill at a crossroads with a four-way stop. People who don't drive trailers, particularly rigs with live animals in them, have no idea how hard it is to stop one or how long a distance it takes. I have signs all over the back and sides of my trailer reading "Lackland Farm" and "Caution, show horses." That doesn't always do the trick, so I'm extra vigilant.

"Merry," Peggy repeated, "tell me."

I looked both ways, four way stop or not, and eased across the road. "When I found the carriage and nearly fell over Raleigh, I had the strangest feeling somebody was watching me."

Peggy made a sound.

"I'm not talking about the horses either. You know I normally have as much ESP as your average earthworm, but I'm fairly positive someone was standing out of sight in the trees on the far side of the arena."

"You didn't see anyone?"

I shook my head and slowed down to give half a dozen turkey buzzards time to fly off the road and away from the dead armadillo they were cleaning up. They waited until the last possible moment, staring me down, then flapped off. "Not consciously. It's probably nothing," I said.

"Did you tell the sheriff or Geoff?"

"Lord, no. I nearly didn't tell you."

"If you'd been a few minutes earlier you might have seen the murder and gotten killed yourself."

"I heard the trees rustle, but that was probably the wind. I couldn't prove anyone was there."

"But can the killer be certain of that?"

We were driving slightly under the speed limit down a straight stretch of two-lane highway. This time on Sunday afternoon there was almost no traffic. The morning churchgoers were home and the evening prayer meeting goers hadn't started yet.

My truck has big side mirrors that stick out far enough to see around the trailer to what's coming up behind. One minute when I checked, there didn't seem to be anyone behind us. The next a big, honking SUV seemed to shoot out of nowhere. He must have been doing eighty.

"That fool behind us is flying," I said as he passed the trailer's rear door and came up in the left lane. I slowed down to give him plenty of room to pass. The driver could be drunk, hyped up, or texting. I am always wary when I trailer horses.

That wariness probably saved our lives.

He'd barely passed my front fender when he swerved hard into my lane and slammed on his brakes. Peggy screamed. I swerved right and stood on my brakes to avoid him.

I didn't have time to scream before the maniac in the SUV took his foot off the brakes and laid rubber down the road doing at least a hundred. By then the damage was done.

"Hang on!" I yelled and took to the shoulder. If I tried to stop, we were sure to flip both truck and trailer.

So I floored it. Thank God the shoulder was fairly broad and relatively flat. For one terrible moment I felt the rig tilt to the right, then the big diesel gave me all it had. "Come on, baby," I prayed as I fought the wheel, concentrating on one keeping us straight. If I pulled back onto the road too fast, we'd careen off the other side.

I have no idea how long it took to get us back on the road and under control. Probably no more than a minute, but it felt like a lifetime. It very nearly was.

When we were safely back on the road and headed down the right lane, I tapped the brakes. Up ahead on the right, I spotted an abandoned seafood restaurant with a big parking lot half overgrown with meadow daisies. I managed to slow down enough to make the turn. The rig bumped into the lot and came to a shivering stop.

We stared straight ahead without uttering a sound, then I said, "My headache's gone."

"What a breakthrough," Peggy whispered. "Let's email the AMA we've found a surefire cure."

"Shut up."

"Get out," she said. "We have to check the horses."

"Can I walk on my knees? I don't think I can stand."

Silently, slowly, carefully, we climbed out of the truck. The air bags hadn't deployed, but then we hadn't actually hit anything.

We opened the door on the left side of the trailer. I was terrified we'd find both horses hanging from their halters with their necks broken.

Ned had managed to pull his halter off. It hung, still tied to the trailer by its lead rope. He regarded us balefully, but he seemed unhurt.

Golden was tied and annoyed about it, but he'd stayed on his feet.

"I don't see any blood," Peggy said as she ran her hand down Ned's legs.

I checked Golden. "None here either. Possibly some pulled muscles. We can check when we get them home."

Across the partition, the two carriages had shifted no more than an inch to the left. One thing I'd learned from my father was how to tie down carriages so they don't shift. The harness, however, lay in a python's nest on the floor of the compartment. "Leave it," I said.

We closed everything up and walked back toward the trailer in silence. "Can you drive?" Peggy asked.

"Of course," I said. Then I walked over to the edge of the parking lot and threw up.

Not that there was much to get rid of. I still had not had breakfast or lunch, and it was mid-afternoon.

In the truck, Peggy handed me another Diet Coke and took one herself. I was way beyond spitting cotton. This had to be how people lost in the desert felt just before they died. I had experienced the dry mouth of fear before, but never this bad. We sat and drank in silence.

When I reached to turn the key in the ignition, my hand shook.

"Sure you can drive?" Peggy asked. "I can probably manage this thing in a pinch with you to coach me."

"I've had all the terror I can handle today, thank you. Did you get the license number of that car?" I asked.

"I pray with my eyes closed."

We pulled into the road at a snail's pace and drove that way for several miles.

"Make and model?" I asked after I'd gotten up to something close to the speed limit.

"Black SUV."

"Everybody has a black SUV," I said.

"I think it was black. The windows were tinted. I didn't even glimpse a silhouette when it passed." She thought a minute, then shook her head. "Could have been dark blue or green or even maroon. Something dark, at any rate. I think the license plate was covered with mud. Crazy hunter out poaching and drinking? Big joke running a horse trailer off the road?"

"You really think that?"

"The name of the farm is on the back of this trailer," Peggy said. "They knew who we were. They knew we had horses."

"Uh-huh."

"I thought we were dead," she said.

"Me, too."

"The minute we get home, I'm calling Geoff."

I glanced at her. "To tell him what?"

"What we both believe. Somebody just tried to kill us."

Twenty miles later, I asked, "Can we stop in Bigelow and pick up some cheeseburgers and fries? My stomach's growling louder than the diesel."

We took up half the parking area at Wendy's. Peggy went in while I stayed with the truck. No matter how tired we were, we had to drive out to the farm, unload the horses, check them over, feed and turn them out to pasture for the night. The carriages and harness were fine where they were. I could lock them in the trailer.

Keeping an eye out for another attack of the killer SUV, I drove one-handed and practically inhaled the cheeseburger and fries.

In the foothills north of Mossy Creek close to Lackland Farm, I had to slow down to make the curves without knocking the horses off their feet. This would have been a much more dangerous place to try to force us off the road. On the left, a narrow shoulder gave way to a precipitous wooded drop off. We'd have rolled up in a big ball. On the right, a narrow shoulder gave way to a wooded hill that climbed steeply to the top of our plateau. We'd have been crushed against the hill.

"Why not go after us here?" I asked. "Wait. I can answer my own question. He couldn't count on being able to get away from us here. He'd have to slow down for the curves too."

By the time we turned in between the two boulders that marked the driveway leading up to Lackland Farm, the shadows were deep under the trees and in the valleys, although at the top, the sun was still shining.

One of Louise Sawyer's grandsons, Pete, who was pre-vet at UGA, was barn-sitting for the weekend. He'd been working part-time between spring semester and summer school, knew the horses, and was completely trustworthy. With the horses in pasture and no training going on while Peggy and I were away, all he had to do was feed, water, and check to be certain none of the horses was hurt or colicking. He had our vet's number on speed dial and knew when to call it. Pete also had the emergency cell phone number I used at horse shows. He hadn't needed it.

Driving the big rig up the narrow, winding gravel road that led to the plateau where the farm was located required careful maneuvering, but eventually I turned around in the parking area and backed the rig into its regular spot. The food had given me a second wind.

Ned and Golden were so glad to be home that they trotted straight into the stable and waited in the aisle while we opened their stall doors.

"Bless Pete," said Peggy, as she peered into the boys' stalls. "He's filled their water buckets and put out their oats and hay."

He'd also left me a note on the white board beside the clients' lounge telling me that everything was okay and that the other horses had been fed and watered.

I walked out to the pasture where the other horses — and one miniature donkey — waited to be greeted. The water trough was clean and full, they were all munching hay, and nobody was bleeding or limping. Even Don Qui seemed glad to see us. He let loose a series of outstanding brays.

When Ned and Golden finished eating, we didn't bother to halter them before we opened their stall doors to let them into the pasture for the night. They were eager to greet their friends. Everyone bucked and snorted, then wheeled and took off running with manes flying and tails in the air.

"God, I love horses," I whispered as I watched them gallop away.

Peggy dropped her arm across my shoulder. "Me too. Thank you."

"What on earth for?"

"Letting me be a part of this."

"How about I let you be a part of driving us back to Mossy Creek? I've reached my limit." I handed her the keys to my aging pickup. I don't normally drive the big diesel truck unless I'm hauling a trailer. Since I still lived in the garden apartment under Peggy's house, we'd driven out to the farm together on Friday morning. Tired as we were, we didn't even unhitch the dually from the trailer.

Tonight I was glad I would not be alone on top of Hiram's hill, but tucked safely inside Peggy's Tudor revival cottage only

118

minutes from the Mossy Creek police station.

When we parked in Peggy's driveway, she handed me my truck keys, opened her door and said, "I'll call Chief Royden and tell him what happened to us on the road."

Amos Royden is chief of police of Mossy Creek. Not the jurisdiction for either the murder or the near miss on the road. "What would be the point?" I followed her to the bottom of the steps leading to her kitchen.

"He needs to know about Raleigh's murder and our involvement," Peggy said.

"That I'm a suspect? That I may be arrested?" I unlocked the door to my apartment and stood with my hand on the knob. "He'll love that."

She leaned over her rail and said, "You don't think Geoff or that sheriff person will call him first thing tomorrow morning? Or even tonight?"

"Right now I don't care." I was beyond bone tired. I pretty much shut the door in her face. Then I stood under a hot shower until I turned pruny.

That SUV might have been after me alone. Peggy and the Halflingers would simply have been collateral damage. Only Peggy wasn't collateral *anything* to me, nor were Golden and Ned. If someone was after

119

me, then let them come after *me* and not the people and animals I loved.

I brushed my teeth and ran a comb through my wet hair. Surely nobody at the show would take the chance of hurting horses to get to me. Would they?

I planned to lie awake and stew over finding Raleigh's body and our narrow escape. Instead, I climbed naked into bed, pulled the duvet over me, and slept instantly.

CHAPTER 11

Monday morning
Geoff

"You going back to Atlanta?" Stan Nordstrom asked Geoff over coffee and sausage biscuits at a local café.

"Not yet. My people in Atlanta are checking Raleigh's business and personal affairs. They don't need me there."

"I hear Raleigh was a womanizer. Maybe his wife got fed up with serial infidelity."

"Why kill him *then* and in the open? Fog or no fog, somebody might have witnessed the whole thing."

"Your girlfriend, maybe?" Stan wolfed down his third sausage biscuit and held up his cup for the waitress to refill.

"She'd tell me." Geoff hoped that was true. "I doubt the wife is strong enough to drive a stake through his head. She's one step this side of a skeleton."

"I'm damn glad to be rid of this can of

worms," Stan said. He paid the bill and stood at the counter gossiping with the manager, while Geoff headed out with the intention of driving to Raleigh's farm. He was glad to be on his own to question the suspects without Stan looking over his shoulder.

Geoff had noted that while Stan didn't quite pull his forelock when they'd spoken to Raleigh's widow on Sunday, he'd definitely gone easy on her, and on Raleigh's daughter, Dawn, as well.

Geoff wanted both women to *think* he was going easy on them, too, as long as possible. In his preliminary interview yesterday, after they'd been notified of Raleigh's death, neither had requested a lawyer. Good.

An hour later, he pulled into Raleigh's driveway between elaborate wrought iron gates hung between white four-board fences that stretched out of sight in both directions. He parked in the gravel turnaround in the front of the house. When he knocked, a uniformed maid opened the double front door and took his card.

She nodded him in and left him standing in the cavernous front hall without a word or a smile. Definitely no sign of tears for the death of her master. No red eyes or trembling lips.

She was no more than twenty, he guessed, and pretty, although beginning to plump up. Latina. No wedding ring. Possibly no green card either, but that wasn't his problem. Knowing Raleigh's reputation, he wondered whether she'd been one of Raleigh's conquests, willing or not.

He assumed she was going for her mistress. He used the time to check out as much of the house as he could see.

In *Gone with the Wind,* Tara was actually fairly small and simple for an antebellum Georgia plantation house. Raleigh had therefore modeled *his* house on Ashley Wilkes's Georgian mansion, right down to the double staircases in the front hall.

Sarah Beth Raleigh had been an interior designer in Atlanta before she met and married Raleigh. It showed. The house looked as though it had been plucked from a *Southern Living* or *Architectural Digest* photo shoot, complete with a head high arrangement of fresh flowers on the round table in the center of the foyer. Depending on how regularly they were replaced, a year's worth would cost a fortune.

He bet money that the provider of the flowers would send a substantial spray to the funeral with an appropriate message of condolence. He supposed it was too early to deliver condolence arrangements, though they'd start showing up once people read Raleigh's obituary.

Although the credenza in the front hall looked like an old family antique, Geoff would have given eight to five it was an expensive reproduction. Through the arch on his left a double parlor ran the depth of the house. On his right a dining room held a mahogany table and twelve tall chairs. Everything looked brand, spanking new from the heavy silk drapes that pooled on the floor to the freshly-polished silver epergne on the sideboard.

There was none of the shabby genteel elegance in houses owned by generations of the same wealthy family. He'd been in enough of those homes over the years. Those pieces were generally easy to spot, like the chip on the left corner of the plantation secretary where junior broke his tooth when he was seven, the fraying edge on the museum-quality Heriz in the living room, the marks of kitty claws in the Moroccan leather of a library sofa. Photos of children and pets in silver frames — not necessarily recently polished — that sat haphazardly on top of the baby grand piano, usually Steinway, Baldwin, or Bechstein, with keys yellowed from the touch of generations of fingers.

Raleigh's house, on the other hand, was perfect. And soulless. Like an upscale funeral home. Surely there was at least one room where these people actually lived.

Sarah Beth came down the stairs to meet him. God, the woman was thin! She reminded him of his ex-wife Brittany. She wore a black cotton turtleneck and black silk slacks. Her streaky blonde hair and makeup were flawless. Her eyes were neither red nor swollen, but these days that could mean she used good cosmetics and prescription eye drops.

Like the house, she was built for show. He had yet to discover whether she was soulless as well.

She extended her hand palm down. For a moment Geoff wasn't certain whether she expected him to shake it or kiss it. He shook. It felt frail and boneless. "What do I call you?" she asked. "Agent Wheeler?"

"That's fine." As formal as possible for as long as possible. If he needed to get chummy later to convince her he understood why she'd killed her husband, the contrast would be greater.

"I hate speaking in the living-room," she said and walked down the hall between the two staircases. "I'm having coffee served in my morning room."

He followed her into a relatively small room at the back of the house with French windows opening out onto a perfect garden. This must be where she did what living she could. It was as over-decorated as the rest of the downstairs, but the chintz-covered sofa and chairs looked comfortable, and the soft peach toile on the walls and at the windows looked feminine and cheerful. Beside the sofa sat a big basket full of some kind of needlework.

A white computer desk with printer sat in the corner. Good Feng Shui to sit with her back to the wall and her face to the door? Or did she want to be certain she was not caught unawares?

After they had settled themselves with excellent coffee brought on a silver tray by the maid, she asked, "What can I tell you?" Still no demand for a lawyer. Good.

"Why was your husband driving his team in the fog at six-thirty in the morning?"

She caught her breath. "I really have no idea. I didn't even know he'd gotten out of bed, much less that he'd put the horses to." She looked down. "I took a sleeping pill Saturday night. I had a migraine. That's why I didn't go to the exhibitors' party."

"Would you mind pushing up your sleeves?"

She jumped as if he'd struck her. "What on earth for?"

"Please. Is there any reason not to?"

She stared at him for a moment with her mouth open and her pulse beating in her throat. Then she shrugged and shoved her left sleeve up to her elbow. She took a deep breath, then shoved back the right. "When I get migraines, sometimes I get dizzy. The kitchen in the trailer is so small, sometimes I bounce off the counters."

"I see." He let the silence between them lengthen. "Hard to conceal bruises on your arms. Makeup tends to clump in your arm hairs."

She tried a laugh, but it came out more like a wheeze. "I really am clumsy. Ask anyone."

"Mrs. Raleigh," he said gently, "I've been a cop a long time. I am an expert on bruises. I know fingerprints on skin when I see them. Should I get a warrant and bring in a female officer to check you over, or would you rather just tell me?"

"You can't do that, can you?"

"Yeah, I can, but I'd rather not. Let's be hypothetical. If that officer were to take off your sweater, would she find more bruises?"

She lowered her eyes and began to cry silent tears.

"I'll take that as a yes," he said.

She shook her head but without looking up at him. "I swear he never hit me. It's just that sometimes he grabbed on to me a little hard. I bruise easily." Now she met his eyes. "I didn't kill him."

Geoff nodded. "If you fought back when he beat you, any good lawyer will get you off on self-defense."

"I've seen *The Burning Bed* and read all the books. If I waited until later and then killed him, it's first degree murder."

"Did you?"

"No. I told you, I didn't even know he'd left the trailer. I was still in bed when they came to tell me what happened."

She'd certainly seemed to be in bed. Stan said she'd answered the door of the trailer wearing slip on shoes and a silk robe, but she could have raced back from the murder and climbed into bed before Merry found Raleigh. Nobody had checked her shoes or the hem of her robe to find out if they were damp. By the time the CSIs checked, everything was dry and her shoes were clean.

"Why not divorce him?" Geoff asked.

This time the smile she gave him was so feral he nearly choked. "If I stick it out another year, I get three million dollars when I leave. Call it severance pay. I intended to stick it out whatever happened."

"Even if he kept, as you say, grabbing you?"

"He would not have kept — grabbing me."

"Men do." Even now she refused to admit her husband had actually hit her, although Geoff would have bet his pension that he had.

She hesitated, then seemed to make up her mind. "All right, he hit me. Not often, but I decided to make it stop." She nodded at the corner of the room over the door. "Nanny cam. I knew sooner or later he'd go for me in here. A couple of weeks ago he did. My lawyer has the tapes and a letter that says if anything happens to me, if I wind up in the hospital or die, those items go straight to the district attorney. With a backup copy to the Federal agents, in case the Georgia Department of Justice is as corrupt as everybody else Giles knew and owned."

"Your bruises are new."

"I just told him about my protection on Friday night. Unfortunately I told him after he shoved me. He was livid. He stormed out to go beat up on somebody else."

"Physically?"

"Or psychologically. He must have caused somebody some pain, because when he came to bed he was cheerful." She pulled her sleeves down and wrapped her arms around herself.

"Why was he angry at you?"

She rolled her eyes. "I was handy. He thought his dressage scores should have been higher. As though it mattered."

"Why did you marry him? I thought his reputation with women was well known."

"Not to me. I'd just moved to Atlanta from Richmond to work for McCallum's. Wealth and power are very sexy, but I didn't marry him for his money. I fell in love with him. When he wants something, he can be *so* charming. The night he asked me to marry him, he took me for a moonlight drive in the carriage to an arbor where he'd set up a picnic with champagne and foie gras . . ." She caught her breath. This time when she raised her eyes to look at Geoff they were full of tears. "He said I'd disappointed him."

"Did he tell you why?"

She shook her head.

"When did he say that?"

"The first time he hit me. He actually cried when he calmed down. He swore he'd never do it again and claimed everybody always disappointed him. If you disappoint somebody, how can you ever get past that?"

"It would seem someone decided to stop trying to get past that and got rid of the problem."

"Not me. I don't have the nerve or the strength."

"So, if you didn't kill him, who did?"

She twisted her hands in her lap. "I truly don't know."

"He had an argument with your step-daughter Dawn at the party Saturday night. Any idea what that was about?"

"Probably Armando Gutierrez, a polo player. She wanted to marry him. Giles told her he'd cut her off without a cent and fire her from the company if she did. He was pulling strings to get Armando's green card pulled so he could be deported to Argentina."

That added two suspects to his list. "Was he successful?"

"I don't think so. Not yet. But he had very powerful friends."

"How do you and your stepdaughter get along? You can't be much older than she is."

This time she smiled. No wonder Raleigh was besotted. The woman was Angelina Jolie Catherine Zeta-Jones gorgeous. "I am actually four years older than Dawn. She's twenty-six."

"Do you get along?"

"Most of the time. She has a perfect right to marry Armando. He's a hard-working professional horseman. He loves her. I tried once to talk to Giles about it." She touched her cheek as though remembering a slap. "I didn't try again."

"Did your husband think Armando was a fortune hunter?"

"He thought every man who came near Dawn who wasn't a multimillionaire was a fortune hunter. Giles desperately wanted an heir to his empire. Since Dawn was an heiress, she was expected to marry the putative heir with his own fortune. Until she does, and produces at least one son, Dawn does the scut work, Giles makes the decisions."

Interesting that she kept speaking of her husband in the present tense. "Thank you for speaking to me so frankly, Ms. Raleigh." He stood. "Now, do you know where I can find your stepdaughter?"

"I'm sure she's at the stables. The horses still take priority, so she tries to work from home whenever she can."

"Did Mr. Raleigh have a home office?"

"Obviously he couldn't work in here." She waved a hand at the peach toile. "He has a private study upstairs."

"I'd like your permission to search it."

"Don't you need a search warrant?"

"Not with your permission." He saw her stiffen.

"I don't think I can give it."

When he raised his eyebrows, she said, "I don't know what he had in there, Mr. Wheeler. You might find something that could hurt the family but had nothing to do with his death. I'm not even certain the house is still mine. So I guess you better get that search warrant."

Geoff nodded, although he knew no judge would sign a search warrant for what would essentially be a fishing expedition. Any search warrant would have to show probable cause to look for a specific item in a specific place. Not gonna happen as things stood.

"I understand." He did understand, but he was still annoyed. "It would, however, be in the family's best interests not to destroy or conceal anything that might turn out to be useful in solving the crime. The state of Georgia takes obstruction of justice very seriously."

"I'm not a fool. I locked the office first thing when I got home Sunday evening. That sheriff took Giles's keys. I have the only other one." She came off the couch in one elegant move, started toward the door of her office and asked too casually, "What would you look for?"

"His will."

She caught her breath, but kept walking.

He'd rattled her. Maybe *nothing* was hers since Raleigh's death. So long as no one knew about the disposition of Raleigh's assets, she would remain the lady of the manor. It was a manor worth fighting for.

"Do I need a lawyer?" Her hand went to her throat and grasped the gold chain at the neck of her sweater.

"Do you think you need a lawyer?" he asked.

"Actually, I do." Suddenly cold and formal. "Please call my attorney in Atlanta, Agent Wheeler." She reached into the pocket of her slacks, pulled out a business card and handed it to him. "This is his number. If you want to talk further, make an appointment. The next time we speak, he will be present." So she'd had her lawyer's card all ready to hand him.

He could only accede gracefully. "Certainly. Of course, that will mean you'll have to come to me. Thank you for seeing me, Mrs. Raleigh. I'll see myself out."

At the door, he turned back to her and

said, "I'm sorry for your loss."

As he closed the door behind him, he swore he heard her whisper, "I'm not."

Dawn Raleigh might be four years younger than her stepmother, but she looked five years older. Her chestnut hair was short, and she wore little or no makeup. If she'd had on lipstick, she'd chewed it off rough lips. Her skin was starting to show the results of too much time in the sun. Not only were there crow's feet at the corners of her eyes, she had shallow parenthetic lines on each side of her mouth. Frown lines. She was handsome enough, and had a lean, taut body, but she wouldn't be launching a thousand ships anytime soon. She had, however, inherited her father's piercing blue eyes. When she spotted Geoff, the mouth lines deepened and her nostrils flared.

"Can't you leave us alone to mourn?" She handed the leather horse collar she held to a stable hand. "Clean it properly this time, please, Manuel," she said. "Then hang it with its harness. Gracias." She turned on her heel and walked toward what looked like an office door.

He followed her into a handsome paneled room that was part library, part office, and part lounge, with a stone fireplace in one corner, and a galley kitchen across the back. "Is that what you're doing?" he asked. "Mourning?"

Those blue eyes blazed at him, then she smiled. She might not be Helen of Troy, but her smile transformed her handsome face into something approaching real beauty. "Actually, I'm celebrating. Ding Dong, the wicked warlock is dead." She sat on a battered maroon leather couch and motioned him to an equally battered club chair across from her.

Ah, *here* was where at least one member of the family lived. Sarah Beth had her peach morning room. Dawn had this room.

"If you don't mind, I have a few questions for you."

She waved a hand. "Ask away. I didn't kill him. I have nothing to hide."

"Not even your attitude?"

"Not even."

"Or your fiancé?"

The smile vanished. "You leave Armando out of this, cop. He's on his way back from Wellington as we speak. You know where Wellington is?"

"South Florida, by Palm Beach."

"Right. He's been refereeing a tournament in Wellington all week. Plenty of people can vouch for him."

"Good. I'm always happy to mark somebody off my list. I will, however, need to speak to him personally. Does he speak English?"

"Probably better than you do. And Spanish, and Portuguese."

"Are you going to marry him?"

"As soon as this mess is over with, you bet your ass. He's going to train polo ponies, and I'm going to take over the breeding end of the business."

"So you inherit the farm?"

"Of course I do. Unless Daddy changed his will recently, Sarah Beth gets a bunch of cash, and probably the condo in Atlanta. Maybe even the house on Jekyll Island. But the farm was always going to come to me."

So she thought she knew the provisions of her father's will when Sarah Beth swore *she* didn't. Geoff made a mental note to check with that lawyer quickly.

Stan said he'd heard that at the show Raleigh threatened to disinherit Dawn. Maybe he was always threatening, but never made good on his threat. If she thought that this time he was serious, however, she might have wanted him dead before he could do it. She was her father's daughter. She'd fight for what she wanted.

Without evidence of anyone besides Raleigh in the dressage arena before Merry, he and Stan Nordstrom had been working under the assumption that Raleigh had been driving his horses alone.

Merry had told him that putting to a four-in-hand of high-strung warmbloods wasn't easy.

Raleigh could have done it, but so could Dawn and a number of other people. What if Raleigh hadn't been the one to harness the horses and put them to the carriage? What if someone else had been driving them? If Raleigh had seen his carriage and team loom up out of the fog, with Dawn or someone else on the reins, he'd have hot-footed it across the arena to find out what the hell was going on.

Maybe two people were involved in the murder — one to decoy Raleigh with his own carriage, one to waylay him at the edge of the woods and kill him. Armando's alibi had better be solid.

Merry said the fog dampened sound. Even if Raleigh had shouted, the sound might have been swallowed up, or simply ignored.

Could Dawn have done the job alone? If she'd taken his team without permission, Raleigh might have dragged her off the box in a rage. He was big and tough, but even big men overbalance. She might have tripped him so that he fell face forward. If she had the stake ready and waiting, she could have driven it into his brain before he'd had time to react.

He wished Arnie at the Atlanta medical examiner's office would finish the autopsy. Even with a high profile case, the results might not be in for days, possibly a week. Tox screen and DNA results would take longer.

If Raleigh had been drugged, or if there'd been blunt force trauma, he'd have been easier to get down on the ground. The ME hadn't noted bruising on the skull in his initial exam, but if the skin wasn't broken, and there was no blood, he wouldn't necessarily have seen anything at the scene. The bruises wouldn't show up on the skull until he'd removed the skin.

"Agent Wheeler?"

He looked up, realized he'd let his mind wander. "Sorry. I'm told you assist in your father's development company."

She snorted like an annoyed mare. "Assist, my ass. I have a Wharton MBA, and I've been going to the office with my daddy since I could walk. I don't *assist*. I *run* the business, and I plan to continue running it."

"I thought you were going to run *this* place."

"That too. Most of the time I can work from here. When necessary, I drive to Atlanta. One thing my daddy could do was pick staff. My barn manager Martin Brock handles the day-to-day operations, oversees the staff, and has for fifteen years. Daddy fired him at least once a week, but knew he couldn't get along without him. They go way back."

Changing tack, hoping to catch her off guard, he asked, "Why do you think your father was such a bastard?"

"I beg your pardon? Is that a proper question?"

"Everyone I've met says he was an SOB, including you. Has he always been like that? Must have made for an interesting childhood."

She sank back, put her booted feet onto the coffee table — a polished slab of old-growth walnut tree — and thought for a minute. "People who knew him when he was just starting out say he was always tough and willing to do anything to get what he wanted, but he wasn't mean, not the way he got later. We used to have good times, family times. Then when I was eight, momma got breast cancer. She was dead in six months. I don't think Daddy ever got over it."

"He loved her?"

"Yeah. I think he maybe actually did." She waved a hand. "I don't know if he'd have kept on loving her if she'd lived. It's easy to love a memory, but nobody ever measured up to her. He was too damn mad at her for dying to grieve for her, so he nailed every female who'd lie still long enough. Trying to replace her, I guess. My first unofficial stepmother lasted less than six months."

"Where is she now?"

"In Hawaii on a sugar plantation with a richer man than Daddy and three kids. Daddy didn't legally remarry until Sarah Beth."

"Why did he marry *her?*"

Dawn laughed. "Have you *looked* at her? She's sweet and smart and good-natured, and until he got ahold of her, she was happy. That's another thing, he liked to go for women who were happy, at least on the outside. Women in good marriages or relationships. Then he'd love 'em and leave 'em as miserable as possible. That was my daddy. Good ole Giles."

"You have excellent insights," Geoff said.

"My MBA is in finance. I had a double major at Emory. Business admin. and psychology. Four point oh in both, by the way. I hoped I could figure out my life and fix it, then make my own fortune. So far it hasn't happened, but I'm working on it with Armando."

"I'd like to speak to Mr. Brock. Do you know where I could find him?"

"Sure. He's in the carriage barn." She stood. "Far end of the stable. Trust me, if Brock wanted to kill Daddy, he'd have done it years ago."

Martin Brock was tall, thin, and looked as though he worked out. He had a shock of gray hair, weathered tan skin, and the easy grace of a cowboy. Geoff guessed he had to beat women off with a stick.

"Mr. Brock," Geoff called. He extended his hand as he walked to meet the man. "I'm Geoff Wheeler of the GBI. Can we speak? I have a few questions about Mr. Raleigh's murder."

"Can't it wait? I'm busy. I got axles to repack."

Geoff raised an eyebrow and gave a pointed glance at the two men kneeling on a plastic tarp beside the front wheel of a marathon cart. "I imagine they can do without your supervision for a couple of minutes," he said.

"Oh, hell, come on." He strode off through a door in the back wall. Inside was a small office, not as big nor as plush as the office where he'd found Dawn, but strictly utilitarian with file cabinets, a big laptop, printer, and combination fax. Except for driving bits hung from hooks on the walls, there was nothing horsey about the room.

Brock sat behind his desk in an office chair that looked as though it had given up stuffing to the local mouse population. Geoff took the hard chair on the other side.

"Ask away, but make it quick. I don't know a damn thing about Giles's murder. Makes my life a damn sight more complicated."

"How so?"

"Dawn and I respect one another, but we're not exactly bosom buddies. If that Armando guy decides to take over running the place, I could be out of a job. And that includes the guesthouse I live in. Jobs like this don't come easy. So, if you're looking for motive, I don't have one."

The man was tense, as if waiting for a blow to fall. And there was fear behind his eyes. What was he afraid of? Losing his job and his guest house? Or going to prison for murder?

"Miss Raleigh says her father fired you

regularly. Several people heard you arguing on Saturday at the marathon."

Brock pushed his gray hair back with gnarled fingers. Geoff had noticed that most horse people, including Merry, had at least a couple of twisted fingers that had been broken and healed crooked.

His heavy hair fell back across Brock's forehead. "You must 'a heard we fought all the time. Whenever he was pissed at something — which was pretty much all the time — he took it out on the closest person. That was usually me. We both learned over the years to ignore him."

"We?"

"Him and me. After he cooled down, we never mentioned the fight again."

"Ah. So things were fine between you?"

"As fine as usual. He was in a good mood Saturday night."

"I heard he fought with Dawn at the marathon."

Brock shrugged. "That was nothing. Thing is, except for that, he was real cheerful. Now, *that* was scary."

"Any idea why?"

Brock shook his head. "Must have screwed somebody over. That generally made him happy."

"How hard is it to harness the four-in-hand alone?"

Brock blinked at the change of subject, but after a moment's thought, he said, "Not hard. Complicated, maybe, but whatever Raleigh was *personally,* he could handle a horse."

"How would you go about it?"

Brock tipped back in his chair and templed his hands over his flat belly. "Lemme see. We were using the stalls at the end of the stable farthest from the house. Nobody close to us. That's the way he liked it. Nobody had any reason to go down there. We laid everything out and prepared the carriage on Saturday, so it was standing ready for the horses to be put to."

"Also at the far end?"

Brock nodded. "If I was gonna do it alone, I'd fasten the harness on the horses in their stalls."

"Dangerous?"

"Not if you know what you're doing and don't leave harness loose to be stepped on. Then you lead the horses out one by one — wheelers first — that's the pair closest to the carriage — and put them to. Cross tie them so they don't go wandering off while you put the leaders to, attach the traces, pole chains, coupling chain and reins. Usually you have somebody heading them to keep them from moving off, but those horses are trained to stand on command like all good carriage horses. He'd unclip them from the crossties, gather the reins, settle himself in the driving seat and tell them to walk off."

"How long would it take?"

Brock shrugged his shoulders. "Half, three-quarters of an hour, if none of the horses was feeling uppity. It was barely dawn and kind of foggy even in the aisle outside the stalls, but you could see all the hooks and buckles all right up close."

"So it was feasible that he was alone, that nobody saw what he'd done."

"Uh-huh. Though Lord only knows why he would 'a done it. Makes no sense whatsoever in my book."

"Could he have been meeting somebody?"

Another shrug. "Maybe. He used that carriage to impress folks. New woman he wanted to lay, banker he wanted to screw out of a line of credit below prime, somebody looking to buy a horse or the whole team — who knows? I sure don't."

"Was the team for sale?"

Brock snorted. "All horses are for sale all the time for the right price, but he hadn't said anything and he loved those ole boys much as he loved anything."

"Would he be likely to impress a woman at six-thirty in the morning in the fog?"

"Good a time as any. Not easy to get it on in the front seat of a carriage, but, take it from me . . ." Brock tossed him a grin. "It can be done."

"You know anybody with a new grudge against Raleigh? Anyone looking for revenge for a horse or business deal that had gone sour?"

"About business, I don't know. That's Dawn's area. Haven't sold any horses lately. Most people know enough to have any horse they plan to buy well vetted, X-rays and all."

"Any particular vet?"

"We generally use Gwen Standish, but a buyer can bring in any vet he likes."

"You ever hear he might have bribed her or any other vet to pass a horse that was marginal?"

Brock's chair hit the floor with a thump. A moment later he guffawed. After he calmed down, he said, "Gwen Standish weighs maybe ninety-five pounds on her best day, but if Raleigh or anyone else ever offered her a bribe, they'd wind up sitting on their butts nursing a black eye or a broken arm."

"What about other vets?"

"Can't say. If Raleigh was honest about anything, it was his horses. He wasn't above offering a commission to a trainer to recommend one of his horses to a client for more than its value. Most buyers expect that. It's standard to pay a trainer to find you a horse. Raleigh just added a tad from his end as well."

"You ever do that?"

"Everybody does it. Part of the game. Why do you think they call it horse-trading?"

"Anybody find out he'd been scammed and get mad?"

"Told you, not recently."

Geoff stood and shook Brock's hand. "I'm sure I'll have more questions, but at the moment that's all I can think of. I'd appreciate a list of buyers and sellers from say, the last six months, and vets other than Dr. Standish that were used for pre-purchase exams."

"Should I ask you to provide a court order?" Brock asked.

"If you like. I can have one faxed to you before the day is out." Now, that one, a judge *would* sign.

"Let me check with Dawn and Sarah Beth. If they say it's okay, then it's okay."

"Good enough." As he followed Brock out of the office, he asked casually, "Just to cover all the bases, where were you on

Sunday morning at six a.m.?"

Brock stopped and glared at Geoff over his shoulder. "Asleep in my motel in town. And, before you ask, I was alone. I didn't have to be at the show until seven, and I could make it in ten minutes."

Geoff nodded. "Thanks." He handed Brock a business card. "I'm using a fax in the office of the chief of police in Mossy Creek. Here's the number when you have that list ready for me."

As he maneuvered the Crown Vic between the white fences that lined the long drive-way, Geoff worried. He hadn't considered Raleigh might have planned to seduce a woman at that hour. The nearest woman was none other than Merry Abbott. Com-mittee assignments had been posted outside the stable, so Raleigh would know Merry was helping to set up cones and in what area she'd start. He also might know she gener-ally got up very early to start work.

She said Raleigh'd been charming on Saturday night. Maybe because he'd laid his plans to waylay her on Sunday morning. If Geoff knew Merry, she wouldn't scream even if Raleigh jumped off that box and took her down. She'd assume she could handle anything he threw at her. It wouldn't occur to her that he'd try anything seriously

149

sexual in such a public place. First she'd laugh it off. If he frightened her badly enough, she'd fight like hell.

But she wouldn't scream for help. Not surrounded by the carriage crowd. How embarrassing would that be?

Would she grab the nearest weapon, the steel stake, to defend herself?

That didn't compute either. She'd have kicked him, scratched him, bitten him, and *then* she might have screamed. She would not have carefully driven a stake through his skull, then hunkered over his body until Harry Tolliver found her. If anything like that had happened, she might not tell Stan, but Geoff knew damned well she'd tell him.

CHAPTER 12

Monday morning —
Merry

I had barely squeezed lemon into my second glass of iced tea when my cell phone rang. Police Chief Amos Royden. Great. If Mossy Creek's bush telegraph works fast, cop telegraph must spring across the galaxies at warp nine. I clicked it on.

"What have you and Peggy got yourselves into this time?" he snapped.

"And good morning to you, Chief. Why do we get blamed when things *happen* to us?"

"You are a lightning rod, like that character in *L'il Abner* — the one with the dark cloud over his head all the time. Maybe *Carrie*? Or that kid in *The Exorcist* whose head spun around?"

"We were simply *there*, Amos."

"You *simply* stumbled on the corpse of one of the most connected rich men in

151

Georgia. Generally hated by all, incidentally, to add a little more fuel to the fire."

Peggy was giving me "what is he saying" signals. I turned my back on her.

"How'd you find out?" As if I didn't know. Initials G.W.

"Had a conference call last evening with Geoff Wheeler and Stan Nordstrom. Stan wanted to arrest you on the theory that whoever finds the body is probably guilty, and where there's smoke there's fire."

"What smoke? What fire?"

"That thing got a speaker setting?" Peggy whispered.

As a matter of fact, it did, but I'd forgotten it. I clicked it on. Wasn't all that loud. Peggy leaned over practically on top of it.

I drank half my glass of iced tea in one long pull. I was suddenly terribly thirsty.

"Amos," Peggy said. "Merry certainly had no reason to kill him, nor did I."

"You can discuss that with Geoff. He'll be here before suppertime."

"Oh, for . . ." I said. "Why isn't he up at Raleigh's farm talking to the less-than-grieving widow and the daughter with the attached polo player?"

"He is. He's coming down here from there. Raleigh's place is less than an hour away. Asked me to make him a reservation

152

for tonight at the Hamilton Inn because he'll be too tired to drive back to Atlanta."

I heard a faint snort of derision from the other end of the line and an answering snicker from Peggy. Good thing we weren't on Skype because my face was undoubtedly flaming.

"Well, if he shows up around four, I'll be out at the farm doing the afternoon feed," I said.

"I thought we weren't driving today," Peggy said after I stuffed the phone back into the pocket of my jeans.

"Not Golden or Ned, but if I have the energy, I thought I might give Don Qui another lesson. He's missed three days now and will probably act as though he's never seen long lines or a bridle. No reason you have to come out, but I have to unsnarl, clean and hang all that harness, polish bits and hames, unload and clean both carriages, clean the shavings out of the trailer, clean manure out of stalls . . ."

"Stop! Of course I'll come. I do not want to be here when people start calling to hear what happened yesterday, and you have no business working Don Qui alone. Finding one body out there is enough." Her hand flew to her mouth. "Oh, Merry, what an awful thing to say."

"But true," I said firmly. I would never be over my father's murder out at the farm, but no way would I let Peggy see that. "Have you looked at the news?"

"I'm avoiding it. If it's gory, it's a big story," she said. "In other words, if it bleeds, it leads. Ghouls! Whoever invented the idea that the public deserves to know everything about everything and everyone all the time should have been drawn and quartered."

After a moment spent stirring her already stirred coffee, she said, "So far, the media has concentrated on the Raleighs and the sheriff, but it wouldn't surprise me to see a couple of news vans out at the farm."

"If they drive onto my property, they'll drive off with rumps loaded with rat shot."

"You will say 'no comment' and shut the stable door on them."

"You really don't have to come," I said, hoping that she'd hear the plea behind my words.

"Nonsense. I work there too, remember?"

"Has Marilou called?" Marilou is Peggy's stuffy daughter who thinks her mother should sit by the fire and read mystery novels. I knew the minute she heard about Raleigh's death she'd pounce on her mother to tell her she was in danger and to quit the farm at once. She'd been horrified when I'd hired Peggy to help me part-time. It's turned into pretty much full time except for garden club days, but I think Peggy is happier working with the horses than she's been since her husband died and abandoned her in Mossy Creek.

"What do you think? Marilou called first thing this morning. Did she ask how well we did in the show? Noooo. She started to say something about 'allowing me' to drive, but she stopped herself in time."

Good thing.

Trying to control the whole world must give Marilou ulcers. Poor thing, she can't even control her mother. Now Josie, Peggy's granddaughter, has fallen in love with the farm, the horses, and driving, in no particular order. She and her little friends were the reason I wanted to train our recalcitrant donkey, Don Qui, to pull a cart.

I felt certain that with the proper training he could be safe to drive, but he wasn't noted for behaving himself. Miniature donkeys are some of the kindest, hardworking equines in the world. Look at all the carts they pull, the huge loads they carry on their backs, the human hulks they haul up Santorini, the milk carts they take to market. Don Qui was, if anything, smarter than his equine cousins. There was no reason he should remain a psychopath all his life for lack of a little friendly discipline.

In the meantime, the kids were driving Golden, my Halflinger, who was completely unflappable and loved children. The odd thing was that Don Qui took to them as well. He could be nasty around adults, but perhaps since children were more his size, he considered them allies.

We generally took both our cars, and thank goodness, there were no TV trucks or reporters at the end of Peggy's driveway waiting for us.

I paid Peggy a pittance for fifteen to twenty hours work a week, but she often worked longer than that. The farm Daddy left me was too much work for one person, and Peggy was the only help I could afford, so I was darned glad for every minute she could spare me.

When I was growing up, Daddy had plenty of help. He'd made an excellent living driving and training for wealthy sponsors who either had elegant training and stabling facilities of their own, or kept their horses in plush boarding barns with lots of staff. Daddy hadn't been responsible for staff salaries, but in a sense they'd worked for him. As his kid, they'd let me hang around with them, taught me about the horse business, and usually kept me from doing anything too outrageous or danger- ous.

Until the day I'd driven a carriage over my mother's leg and damned near killed her. That's when I gave up horses. Then my mother divorced Daddy. After that, I'd seldom seen him.

After Daddy retired from competition and moved to his new farm outside Mossy Creek, he divided his time among restoring carriages, working to get the farm on its feet, and training and driving horses sent him by a few old clients. I don't know whether he felt lonely or relished the free- dom.

In the year I had been running the place, I had taken in enough young horses from clients and managed enough horse shows to keep the place solvent so long as I didn't spend much money on frills. Peggy was not a frill — she was a necessity.

My townhouse in Lexington, Kentucky, had taken six months to sell, but made a modest profit even in the recession. Since it had been mortgage free, it gave me enough money to build my log house at the farm.

That was the good news.

The bad news was that the building pro- cess was taking much longer than I had expected. However, now that the drive up to the site had been graded and regraveled at a cost that nearly gave me heart failure, and now that the spring mud had abated, I expected everything to go much faster. It had to.

I wanted to be in my own place by Labor Day, because driving from Mossy Creek and up my father's hill was hair-raising in the fog, ice, and occasional snow that hit North Georgia in the fall and winter. The rest of the year we dealt with sudden, humongous thunderstorms that knocked out power and made the roads impassable. I couldn't afford to get stuck in Mossy Creek where I couldn't look after the horses.

Not that I wouldn't miss Peggy, but having my pasture right outside my kitchen window would be a blessing. I also wanted my stuff that was stored in a rent-a-shed place in Bigelow. How do you live without your books?

I had no one else to stay at the farm at night. When a horse colicked or needed care around the clock, I slept on a cot in the clients' lounge. Lord knows I've done it often, but I've never gotten used to it.

A stable at night can be one of the most peaceful places on earth. It can also be eerie. Sometimes in a dark stable at night I feel as though I am the last human being on earth. If Peggy was right and our near accident on the road back from the Tollivers' had been a deliberate attack, might that person try again to hurt us? Or the horses?

More likely they wanted to do *me* damage. If so, I'd avoid staying late by myself if possible. If it couldn't be avoided, I'd be well armed.

CHAPTER 13

Monday morning
Merry

During the previous winter, I'd traded Hiram's old tractor in on a slightly larger, newer model, so we could pile the manure into the front loader, drive it directly to the new manure pile, and dump it far enough away from our barns so we had neither odor nor flies.

While I'd been still reeling from my daddy's murder last year, Governor Bigelow had sent his aide de camp to harass me into selling Hiram's farm, which abutted land the governor and his cronies owned. As I recall, that little weasel Whitehead said something about leaving my grief behind and making a fresh start somewhere else with my profit. Insensitive jerk. Wherever I am, I'll carry my grief forever. How could I give up the place that had made my father happy?

I'd been so mad at the governor, I moved the manure pile right over against his boundary line fence. If he and his cronies ever decided to build their fancy residential homes on that hill, they might have a few odors and horse flies to deal with.

Then in early February, all the Mossy Creek Garden Club ladies had descended on us and carried off the whole pile to use in their gardens. You'd have thought I'd donated a million dollars to the Mossy Creek Garden Club instead of a load of crap. If they won the annual Garden Club Feud-off with the Bigelow Garden Club, they'd promised me fresh vegetables all year and all the Mimosas I could drink. I'd taken them up on the vegetables, but nixed the Mimosas. Those sweet little ladies make an absolutely lethal Mimosa.

Now Peggy and I were building up a new pile for them to use in the fall.

While we mucked, Peggy worked on me to tell Geoff about our near miss on the way home from the Tollivers'.

"The SUV didn't even graze us," I said.

"It tried to make us kill ourselves," Peggy argued, as she hefted a bucket of manure into the front loader. "Someone chased us."

"If we'd hit the SUV in the rear, they'd have gone off the road too and probably smashed worse than us. Dumb way to kill someone." I dumped another full bucket. "There, that's it. Clean stalls for one more day."

"Whoever was in the van took off before we could hit them. They weren't in danger. We were." She leaned her fork against the side of the stall. "Can I drive the tractor?"

Peggy had become a tractor-driving fool since I'd shown her how the front loader dumped. She hauled herself aboard and turned the key. The tractor grumbled to life. She lifted the front loader and trundled out, dumped the manure and headed back.

She parked the tractor behind the stable, climbed down, and took up the argument. "That driver stabbed his brakes just long enough to bring on his brake lights and force us to brake behind him. He had plenty of time to speed up before we connected with his rear end."

"We can't identify the driver." I counted off on my fingers. "Nor the color of the van. The glass was tinted. We don't know how many people were inside. No license plate number. No make or model on the SUV. I'd feel better if we had more to give Geoff. But you're right. He needs to know."

We spent the rest of the morning doing chores, then ate a scrappy picnic lunch. The day was glorious. Cool with a breeze but not a wind, clouds that ambled across the sky rather than scudded.

After we put our feet up on some hay bales in the aisle for an hour or so, I stood up and said, "It's time."

"Oh, Lord, are you sure?"

"No time like the present."

"Shall we bring Heinzie up to keep him company?" Heinzie was Don Qui's Friesian sidekick, a black giant with the soul of a kitten. While Don Qui no longer brayed non-stop whenever they were separated, he preferred to keep the big horse in sight. He'd finally accepted knowing Heinzie was in his stall or in pasture, but not for long.

In the year I'd had him under my care — if not my command — I had taught Don Qui to wear a halter and a lead rope without fussing. I had even taught him to accept a driving bridle with a bit, so long as I gave him a sugar cube along with it, but he might get a tad antsy when I put the full driving harness I'd borrowed from the Tollivers on his back. He wouldn't much enjoy having the crupper buckled under his tail either. I had to be extra careful not to get any tail hairs caught in it. Like getting a human pony tail caught in a scrunchie, catching tail hairs in the crupper hurt.

Today Don Qui stood calmly cross-tied on the wash rack with Heinzie in his stall across the way. In the months we'd been working him, the little donkey had finally learned to enjoy being groomed and petted.

The first step in training a horse to drive is to ground drive him. That is, to walk far enough behind him so that if he kicks he can't connect with any portion of your anatomy, with the reins in your hands and the ends connected to the bit, and with another person to the side holding a long line snapped to his halter to stop him if he attempts to bolt. That would be Peggy's job.

In a driving harness the saddle lies across the horse's back, buckles under his belly, and has loops that carry the carriage shafts along the horse's sides. The saddle also attaches to the breeching, which goes over and down the horse's rump to give his rear end something to push against while he's in draft.

The horse sits back against his breeching going down a hill, making a turn, or backing up. A horse doesn't only pull with his shoulders. The harness allows him to use his whole body to spread the weight of carriage and passengers.

The language of driving can run from complex to silly. For example. Driving people say the horse is being "put to." They assume you know put to *what.* When he's in harness, they say he's *in draft,* whether he's a Welsh pony or a Clydesdale.

Don Qui jerked awake when I tightened the girth around his middle. He turned his head as far as the cross-tie allowed, glared at me and let forth a resounding bray in my ear. He made as much noise as the steamboat Robert E. Lee announcing its arrival in port.

"Keep feeding," I whispered to Peggy as I continued to buckle the harness.

"Should I bring Heinzie?" Peggy asked.

"Leave him in his stall for the moment, until we see how Don Qui reacts. This may be the shortest lesson in history."

Amazing that such a little guy could be such a handful. Despite a ragged ear heroically gained in saving our lives, he was beautiful as miniature donkeys go. He had a sleek mouse-colored pelt with the cross of dark hair across his withers. Legend says that one of his ancestors carried Mary and the baby Jesus to Egypt, for which service his descendants have forever borne the sign of the cross.

Don Qui's *ancestor* may have been a saint. Somehow those genes got diluted through the generations before they got to him.

165

He allowed Peggy to lead him into the enclosed dressage arena, although he looked around several times for Heinzie. I could already feel the tension in him. This was the first time we'd ground-driven him when Heinzie was out of sight.

I gathered the reins and sauntered casually behind him as I stayed well out of range of his fast little hind hooves.

"If he freaks, just let him go," I said.

"You sure?"

"And get out of kicking and biting distance. Fast."

"It's a deal."

"Walk on," I said quietly. He didn't move. "Don Qui, walk on."

If anything, he planted all four feet even deeper in the arena sand. No Heinzie, no forward movement.

I shook the reins. "Walk on. Peggy, grab his halter and see if you can urge him forward."

She gave me an uncertain look, but she grasped the halter and tugged. He tugged back. Then he sat down.

"Stand up!" she snapped.

"Wiggle his bridle. Hold out a piece of carrot so that he has to reach for it," I suggested.

That ploy was met with pure donkey

disdain. "Should I get Heinzie?" Peggy asked.

"No way."

After ten minutes of cajoling, Peggy was losing her temper. I wasn't. I'd handled worse. But once battle is joined with an equine, the human being is committed to win or to lose forever. So, even if we were still right here tomorrow morning, Don Qui would move forward before we quit. One or two steps would be plenty, but he *would* move.

Non-drivers hear the word "whip" and freak out. A driving whip is not for punishment, however. Horses don't mind the slight touch — more of a tickle — of the whip on shoulder or croup. Sitting behind the horse, drivers don't have the luxury of giving the horse signals with legs and seat the way a rider does. The whip acts as our means of communication. And Don Qui definitely needed to learn to speak carriage horse.

"Bring me a dressage whip," I told Peggy. Most of our whips were long enough to reach a much larger animal's shoulder from a carriage. If I tried one of those on Don Qui, the end would land somewhere north of his nose.

The look she gave me and the moan she made reminded me of Lurch, the butler in the Addams family television series. She did as I asked, however.

"Now get outside the arena and shut the gate," I said.

"Are you sure?"

I nodded. "I may join you in about thirty seconds." I touched the soft lash of the whip to Don Qui's fat little butt. "Don Qui, walk on."

His ears wiggled, but nothing else moved.

"Okay, Don Qui, walk on." And I popped him. Not hard, but enough to shock him out of his sulk.

He levitated. In one movement he came off his rump and into the air with all four legs, then kicked out with his hind end higher than my head and took off.

One would think that a woman as big and strong as I am could stop a little, bitty donkey. Don Qui, however, must have mastodon genes hidden somewhere inside his DNA. He did an excellent imitation of a ski boat at full throttle, and I skidded along behind him braced back at a forty-five degree angle like a skier.

But I didn't let go.

He ran and bucked and snorted and kicked and ran some more. "Don Qui, whoa!" I shouted. I was running out of breath trying to stay on my feet.

"Doggone it, whoa!"

He had bucked in a relatively straight line down the center of the arena, and because his legs were so short, he didn't cover any great distance. I knew that as he came up to the far end of the arena, he'd have to turn, or jump out of the arena and run straight into the fence beyond.

Or stop. Which is what he did. I damned near ran into his rear end, not a wise thing to do under the circumstances. We stood there huffing and puffing. "Whoa. Good boy," I wheezed, and put my hands on my knees, leaned over and dragged a few breaths into my lungs. "Stand." He might not need to stand, but I sure did.

I'd long since dropped the whip. It lay in the dirt somewhere along our line of travel. I tugged on his left rein to turn him, clucked to him, and asked him quietly to walk on.

Amazingly enough, he did. He'd made his point.

Peggy came into the ring, walked to his head, clipped on the lead line, and held his halter while I took the driving reins off. We petted him and loved on him, told him what a beautiful, intelligent boy he was, and fed him sugar cubes until he was on the edge of a sugar-induced coma, then walked him between us back to the barn. We were both dripping with sweat.

"When are you joining Ringling Brothers?" Geoff Wheeler said from the shadows in the barn doorway. "I'd definitely pay to see that again."

"You want us to join you at Clown College?" I asked.

He moved aside so that Don Qui and I could get past him.

"Sorry, I left my big red nose at home."

"Kept the big shoes, I see."

"Geoff," Peggy said from behind me. "I am so glad to see you. We have so much to tell you. Someone tried to run us off the road on our way home yesterday. I think they were trying to kill us."

While I washed Don Qui down with tepid water, Geoff lounged against Heinzie's stall door and listened to Peggy's story more or less politely.

"Peggy," he said, "there's a bunch of good ole boys who think running a big horse trailer off the road is great sport. You have nothing to show it was personal."

"Not personal? How could it not be personal? There's a sign on the back of the trailer that reads 'Caution, Horses' in *big* letters with the name of the farm."

"Probably wouldn't have mattered to Bubba if you'd been hauling Durocs or

Black Angus. Or chickens. Think what fun they'd have had if you'd decanted a couple of thousand Rhode Island Reds on the highway."

"They didn't wait around to see if we went over," I said quietly. Geoff always picked up on the first sign of female hysteria. "And Bubba usually drives a pickup, not a big, shiny SUV with mud covering the license plate."

"The only mud there was on it, by the way," Peggy chimed in.

"So say that they were actually out to get you. Why? You might be hurt, but you have airbags."

"The horses don't," I said. "And airbags wouldn't have helped much if we'd flipped over on our side."

"Airbags that didn't deploy because we kept going and didn't hit anything," Peggy said.

"The horses might have been killed or so badly wounded we'd have had to put them down." I shuddered. I've never had to do that, but on long trips, I keep not only an extensive first aid kit for horses, but syringes of Acepromazine to sedate an injured horse and enough barbiturate to kill one. And a gun in case the drugs take too long.

"You say horse people will do anything to

avoid hurting horses, so who do you know who'd risk the horses to get at you?" Geoff asked.

"Maybe after you drive a steel stake through somebody, hurting horses isn't such a whopping leap," I said.

"And preferable to spending the rest of your life in jail," Peggy added.

"If all this is true," Geoff said, "then someone thinks you either saw something or know something dangerous. What?"

I led Don Qui to his stall and tossed him some extra hay. "I have no idea. I have to get these guys fed. Can we talk later? Amos said you were spending the night at the Hamilton Inn."

"And having dinner at Mama's. How 'bout both of you join me?" Mama's was one of Mossy Creek's excellent restaurants. Geoff had learned to like it on his last visit to Mossy Creek to clear up my father's death.

The last thing I wanted was to have to clean up and stay awake during dinner, but the food would be good, and I wouldn't have to cook it or clean up after it, a winning combination in my book. We agreed. I'd had fun at our last dinner together in Bigelow before Geoff up and bailed on me. Tonight we would go back to our favorite

172

topic for dinner conversation — murder. And my involvement in it.

"I'm going to help Merry feed and turn out," Peggy said. "You go on down and check in to your hotel. Meet you for dinner sevenish?" she asked.

He nodded.

"I'll walk you to your car," Peggy said and slipped her hand under his arm.

Uh-oh. She wanted to talk. Privately.

CHAPTER 14

Peggy

Peggy hooked her arm through Geoff's as they crossed the gravel parking lot to his car. "I'm certain the SUV thing was intentional."

"What's Merry not telling me?" Geoff asked. He leaned against the hood of his Crown Vic, carefully avoiding the antenna farm that announced he was driving an unmarked police car.

Peggy shook her head. "I don't think she's holding anything back on purpose. Maybe she glimpsed somebody or something in the woods after she found Raleigh's body."

"Hell, anybody would feel unseen eyes on them in an open field sitting beside a corpse. No ESP required."

"What about Raleigh's family?" Peggy asked. "Surely they're more viable suspects."

He shrugged. "Not a well-liked man, Mr. Raleigh. His nearest were not his dearest, nor was he theirs. Motive, however, is the least important part of a murder. Cops don't have to prove motive if they have forensic evidence, which in this case, they don't."

"But don't juries want to know why somebody got offed?"

Geoff laughed and shook his head. "Offed? You been watching too many cop shows, Pretty Peggy. See y'all at dinner."

Peggy hugged herself against the chill breeze that always arose on top of Hiram's hill in the late afternoon. She stared after Geoff as he negotiated the turn and disappeared. Geoff hadn't said as much, but officially, at any rate, that meant Merry was still a suspect.

Merry finished filling the water trough by the pasture gate, ran her hands down her back and walked over to Peggy. "I might need to spend the night here in case somebody tries to hurt the horses." She walked over to the stack of logs and roof trusses at the corner outside the pasture. They were supposed to be made into her log house.

Eventually.

"I'm sick of sleeping on that cot in the clients' lounge, when I have to stay here at night," Merry said. "Why can't they finish my house so that I can sleep in a real bed?

At the rate they're going, I won't move in until after Christmas."

Peggy knew how much Merry wanted to move into her new cabin, but she would miss having her in the apartment downstairs. She didn't have to sabotage the construction, however. The contractor was doing a great job of missing deadlines on his own.

'You'll be moved in by Labor Day," she said and patted Merry's shoulder. She was surprised at how tense her muscles felt. "It's the site prep, the gravel, the grading, the footings and slab and so forth that take the time. All the rain we had in March didn't help either."

Peggy pulled her to her feet. "Come on. You'll feel better after a shower and a good dinner." As they walked to their vehicles, Peggy said, "Sooner or later you're going to have to talk to Geoff. Might as well be tonight. As to the horses, where *you* are is where the trouble will come, if it comes. The horses should be all right. They are every night. *You* are safer in your apartment."

"Every night doesn't follow a murder. Which at least one lawman thinks I probably committed."

"Geoff doesn't really think you killed

anyone. He's trying to be — I don't know — circumspect. You know he likes you."

"I thought so for a while. Now that I'm involved in another murder, he's treating me like just another suspect."

"Only until he finds the killer."

If he was keeping Merry at arm's-length again, the way he had when he was investigating her father's murder, he was just being silly. There was a limit as to how closely he adhered to the GBI regs about personal interaction with suspects and witnesses. Time Merry told him to stop being a stuffed-shirt and get a grip.

Peggy would leave them after dinner to talk it out. "See you at home," she said and drove off. In her rear view mirror she saw Merry climbing into her truck, sagging with exhaustion.

Dammit, Peggy thought, as she whipped around a corner too fast. Life was too short to miss a chance at love. One day her newly-retired husband Ben had been digging in his flowerbeds, enjoying their new home in Mossy Creek. The next he was dead, and she'd never stop missing him, wishing they'd had longer.

Once they found one another, she and Dick Fitzgibbons had seized the day. Why couldn't Geoff and Merry?

177

Neither of them had a significant other. Well, Merry didn't. Geoff might have a dozen girlfriends in Atlanta pining for him. They'd both had bad first marriages. These days, nearly everybody had at least one. Family? Geoff had no children. Merry had her daughter Allie, who never visited, not even at Christmas. She went skiing instead. Merry had joined Peggy's family for Christmas dinner.

Peggy's daughter Marilou might be a control freak, but at least she was there and cared about her mother. And Peggy had a grandchild, her darling Josie.

Christmas afternoon, Merry had spent alone with the horses. That's where she always went when she was unhappy or lonely or upset. They didn't talk back or ask questions.

Merry couldn't — or wouldn't — leave her horses for long. Geoff was always working in Atlanta or elsewhere. Long distance relationships were tough. Both Merry and Geoff needed to rearrange their priorities. Both Peggy and Dick understood that.

At some point Merry had learned to avoid risking her emotions. She wasn't a physical coward, Lord knew, but she didn't like getting her heart bruised. She preferred to act as though she didn't feel emotional bruises, only physical ones. Responsible for the carriage accident that crushed her mother's leg, Merry had simply stopped driving, even quit horses entirely for several years.

She had distanced herself from her father after her mother divorced him, and only reconnected with him just before he died. She dumped her unfaithful husband. Geoff hadn't exactly hurt her. He'd simply disconnected without explanation.

In time Merry could overcome her fears. She had returned to horses, then to driving, made up with her father before his death, even forgave Vic. So there was a good chance she and Geoff could get back to where they were. She'd opened up Peggy's world to horses. Peggy wanted to open Merry's to a relationship with a real man.

Ten minutes later, she pulled into her garage as Merry pulled in the driveway behind her. Her knees ached as she climbed the stairs to her back door.

What the heck. Even a day as tough as this was more exhilarating than sitting in her recliner reading murder mysteries with four cats. The Mossy Creek Garden Club ladies still didn't understand why her gardening had dropped by the wayside. She didn't have the nerve to tell them that she'd never been all that fond of gardening in the first place. She preferred her manure straight from the horse.

CHAPTER 15

Monday evening
Merry

I'd managed to put off answering questions about Raleigh's murder throughout dinner at Mama's restaurant. Now, over coffee, I couldn't stall any longer. "You've read my statement, you've asked me the same questions over and over, and neither one of us has learned a doggone thing," I said. "Maybe someone was standing back in the woods watching when I found Raleigh, but all I can give you is a feeling."

"Sitting beside a corpse in the fog might generate weird feelings," Geoff said. "Didn't it occur to you that whoever killed him might be waiting to take you out as well?"

"Why? I was no threat, and I didn't see another loose stake. Surely if he'd brought a gun or a knife, he'd have used it on Raleigh. Can't have been easy to kill a man with that stake, even if he was unconscious and lying on the ground right."

"Not that hard, actually." Geoff pushed aside the plate containing the few remaining crumbs from his chocolate cake and picked up his coffee spoon. He stood it straight up with the bowl on the top. "The cervical vertebrae attach at the base of the skull." He leaned over and poked the spot where my hair stopped growing at the nape of my neck.

"Hey!" I jerked away.

"There's a groove right where the spinal cord rides under the skull. Not that hard to miss if you know what you're doing. No bone in the way, just a straight shot into the brain."

"Thank you, Dr. McDreamy," I said. "Does that mean that whoever did — that — had medical training?"

"Luck or good research would work."

"The show grounds were crawling with medical people. Doctors with plenty of disposable income, some of them married to their nurses. Then there's an on-site veterinarian, although she's not big as a minute. And the EMTs, of course. I'm not sure they'd arrived yet."

"Every female equine vet has to be strong," Geoff said.

"She is," Peggy said. "I'd kill to have her abs."

"Did any of those people have reason to get rid of Raleigh?" Geoff asked.

"He may have offended them all at some point, but probably not badly enough to get himself stabbed," I said.

"Did he offend *you?*"

"Absolutely, but if I stabbed every driver or groom who offended me, the sport of carriage driving would take a major hit."

Peggy had been listening to us without comment. Now she laid down her coffee spoon and asked, "Why was he out there at the crack of dawn with his four-in-hand? Isn't that the big question?"

"Warming them up," Geoff asked.

I shook my head. "Not that early. He wasn't scheduled to drive his dressage test until late morning. The fog was so thick I couldn't see his carriage and team until the horses nearly ran over me. Not the best atmosphere to warm up your horses. In the fog, he might have driven into the cable bounding the arena. That could have badly hurt his horses. So, how did someone know he'd be out there? I don't see how killing him could have been premeditated. Wouldn't the killer have brought a weapon to do the job? Using that stake was crazy."

"So you're saying a stranger spotted him in the dressage arena driving his horses, knocked him off the box somehow, rolled him over on his face and jabbed a six inch stake into his brain?" Geoff rolled up his napkin and set it beside his plate. "I don't *think* so."

"He must have arranged to meet someone," Peggy said. "But why then and there? Wouldn't it have been simpler to intercept whoever it was by the trailers or in the stable?"

"Seems better to me," Geoff said. "But what do I know?"

"Not much," I said.

"Back off, little lady, or I'll call Stan and tell him to arrest you on general principles."

"Fine with me, as long as you take over mucking and feeding and turning out the horses," I said. "I could use the rest."

"I could probably handle the horses, but not that little hellion with the long ears." He grinned at me. "What was all that about this afternoon?"

"If the hellion is going to continue to eat my grass and feed, and require shots and worming and have the farrier trim his feet and such, he's going to have to earn his living."

"As what? A Hit Donkey?"

"He's going to teach my young students to drive."

"You truly are crazy," Geoff said with a shake of his head. "If you can't hold him, how can they?"

"You ought to see him with my granddaughter, Josie," Peggy said. "The only thing I can figure is that he sees them as allies — just his size. He follows her and her friends around like a Labrador retriever. He even likes Li, Casey's little girl. She's too young to drive, of course, but he even endures having his ears pulled if Li's doing the pulling."

"But you're outside the size limit, apparently," Geoff said, grinning at me. "And you have to do the training."

"We will do fine," I said with much more assurance than I felt. "After his temper tantrum, he settled down and behaved like a normal equine."

"Bet he'll misbehave just as badly tomorrow — or whenever you plan to drive him again."

"Put your money where your mouth is, G-man," I said. "He may fuss, but I bet you he'll give in quicker and behaves himself longer."

"Even odds? Five bucks?"

"Five bucks." I could afford to lose five

bucks, and probably would, but I couldn't let Geoff rag on Don Qui. He was a hellion, but he was *my* hellion. He'd come a long way since we started working with him in January.

"Peggy can call the bet. If she agrees he's better, I'll give in gracefully," Geoff said. "If you wind up in the emergency room, I win."

"You got it."

As our waitress poured our second cup of decaf, Peggy said she was exhausted. Before I could stop her, she asked Geoff to drive me home so we could linger over our coffee. If that wasn't transparent, I don't know what is.

"I'll go with you," I said, and reached down to my purse.

Geoff put his hand on my arm. "How about I buy you a brandy down at the Hamilton Inn and you can tell me in detail how Raleigh annoyed you."

I glared down at his hand, but by then Peggy was scooting out the door.

Geoff lifted a finger for the check, but Earline shook her head, pointed at the door and mouthed, "On her tab."

He started to get out of his chair, then subsided. "So I owe you both another dinner."

"Not me, you don't. Does that constitute

a bribe within the meaning of the act?"

"Probably. If I have to arrest Peggy for murder, her lawyer will no doubt bring it up."

"That's not funny."

He blew out his breath. "No, it's not. Nothing about this whole mess is funny. Why did everybody hate this guy, anyway?"

CHAPTER 16

Merry

"I didn't hate him. I loathed him," I said as I slid into the booth in the bar at the Hamilton Inn. "Initially, I tried to put his nonsense down to alcohol or ego, but it was more than that. I finally came to the conclusion that he was so miserable that the only pleasure he got in life was to make everybody around him more miserable than he was."

"What did he have to be miserable about?" Geoff asked. He pushed my pony of B and B across the table. I took a sip and let the warmth sink down to my toes.

I don't drink often, but I have nothing against alcohol per se. Tonight, the liqueur was reaching places that hadn't really been warm since I spotted Raleigh's body. I could feel my toes uncurl.

"You'd think he'd be the happiest man alive," I said. "He was rich-rich, a mover and shaker in Georgia and beyond, had a beautiful wife, a brilliant daughter, a gorgeous house and barn, magnificent horses — everything a man could want. What's that old saying? Everything turned to wormwood and ashes in his mouth. I have no clue why. He just got a kick out of screwing everybody's life up."

"Yours?"

"He sure tried." I pondered about whether to tell him about the poison pen letters. The only other person who might mention them was Sarah Beth, the widow. Would she? If she felt threatened, she might. If she'd actually killed her husband and needed to spread the suspicion, she definitely would. I couldn't count on secrecy. I'd better get my story in first.

So I did. "Peggy has a copy of the mail merge letter he was going to send telling the show organizers — the driving clubs that sponsor the shows — what a terrible manager I am, that I allow unsafe conditions. He also intimated that I had something to do with my father's death."

"Mail merge? Why not emails?"

"I couldn't accuse him without letting him know Sarah Beth had snitched on him. God knows what grief he would have put her through if he'd found out."

Geoff got that quizzical look he gets sometime. "Say he did find out, put her through hell, and she decided she'd had enough. She told me she wouldn't divorce him yet, but admitted they weren't Romeo and Juliet. We have only her word that she was asleep when he left her that morning. Maybe she was with him. She told me he'd won her with a moonlight carriage ride. Could be she conned him into an early morning ride to make up."

"Raleigh would never get up at dawn for Sarah Beth."

He shrugged. "But he might for some other woman."

"Not me."

"I didn't imply it was you," he said, and lifted his snifter of brandy to salute me. He pointed to my empty pony.

I shook my head. "I can feel that one already."

"So, how about a walk around the square to clear your head?"

I wondered whether he planned to hold my hand. He didn't. I knew from when he investigated my father's murder, Geoff did not consort with suspects — not even a little.

"Merry, when this is over . . ." he said. "At the moment, I can't . . ."

190

He was uncomfortable. Good. I considered grabbing his hand, swinging him around and planting one on him right out here in public. Then I relented. "So solve the damned thing fast."

"I'm trying." He sucked in a deep breath. "So, if you didn't plan to accuse him of slander and libel, what did you plan to do?"

"Enlist my driving friends to speak to their show organizer friends and tell them the truth. If it came to a choice between listening to Pete and Tully Hull or Giles Raleigh, he didn't stand a chance. It was simply another attempt to make me miserable. As for the emails — a lot of these folks don't use computers, or they have secretaries that print them out. Emails aren't real to them."

"So what else did he do to you?"

We were passing one of the benches that lined the square when I realized I was even more worn out than I'd thought earlier. "Who said he did anything?" I sat and he sat beside me.

"Tell me."

I avoided his eyes. "He hit on me. A lot. And hard. *Mean* hard."

He kept his voice level, but I heard strain. "Attempted rape?" The corollary was unspoken, but there. Had I meant *rape?*

"How do you define *attempted?* A couple

of times he ambushed me and tried to hold me down and shut me up. Once I managed to yell for help. Somebody intervened. Once, I kicked him in the crotch. After that I tried never to be alone with him." I glanced down and saw that Geoff's hands were in fists. "He didn't single me out. I was simply another possible conquest. You know, newly divorced woman, should be grateful he was willing to *service* me."

"Did he actually use that word?" he growled.

"Yep. When I kept turning him down, he seemed to have decided we were in a contest he would win only when he had me naked and flat on my back."

"What about Saturday night?"

"He barely noticed me. Maybe he'd found some other woman to harass. When he was drunk — and that was often — he wasn't too picky."

"Don't sell yourself short. Any heterosexual with a minimal testosterone level would go after you like a hound dog after a pork chop."

In the shadows I couldn't tell whether his ears were red, but I'd seen them that way before when he'd been embarrassed.

"Come on, let's get the car and I'll drive you home," he said.

Ten minutes later, when he pulled the Crown Vic into Peggy's driveway, I didn't wait for him to get out, walk around the car and open my door for me. I like courtesy as well as the next female, but that particular courtesy has always seemed ridiculous to me. I was sliding out the door before he put the car in park.

He did, however, catch my wrist as I slid out. Peggy's driveway is secluded and dark and apparently private enough even for Geoff. "I have a lot more than the minimal amount of testosterone," he said.

My insides turned over and my heart went into overdrive. "Glad to hear it."

"When this is over, I intend to prove that to you."

I sank back onto the edge the seat. "Sooner or later, we have to talk about something other than murder."

"So we do. We have all sorts of hidden depths to plumb. Now we just have to find the time to explore them without a murder hanging over our heads."

I gulped like a landed trout, whirled around and bolted inside my apartment. Just before his engine revved and backed out of my driveway, I heard him laugh.

CHAPTER 17

Midnight
Merry

Maybe it was the B and B wearing off, or Geoff, but as tired as I was, I couldn't settle. Worry about the horses is a semi-permanent state for me.

Eohippus, the German Shepherd–sized ancestor of the present day horse, must have been a tough little critter to survive in the world of Saber-toothed tigers, but with size came fragility. Horses look tough and can be a handful, but they are babies about their health and psyches.

Ned and Golden had seemed no worse for their banging around in the trailer on the way home from the show yesterday, but horse bruises and lameness often take days to develop.

Whoever tried to wreck us had shown total disregard for the welfare of horses. I couldn't seriously believe any of the driving group could have been that cavalier.

The difficulty was that I had no idea why we'd been targeted. I'd narrowly avoided having my father's new stable burned down less than a year ago. That was one of the reasons I kept all the horses in pasture as much as I could. In a fire or a natural disaster like a tornado, they were better off being able to run away. But they were there and I was here — twenty minutes away. The last time I checked, even Don Qui, smart as the demonic little toad was, could not dial a cell phone to ask for help.

I felt uneasy, although I couldn't have said why. If I didn't drive out to the farm to see that the horses were munching their way across the dark pasture or sleeping peacefully under the trees, I wouldn't get any sleep at all.

I keep a big Glock loaded with half rat shot and half slugs, with another loaded magazine in the center console of my truck, and one of those gigantic flashlights in my glove compartment with a complement of extra batteries. I am careful to keep my cell phone charged as well, although it can't always get service on Hiram's hill. Still dressed from dinner, I pulled on my paddock boots, tied a cotton sweater around my waist, and headed out to the farm.

195

Peggy's bedroom is on the other side of her house from the driveway, and she has shutters on her windows, so I could sneak out without waking her. I knew that if she did wake, she'd demand to come with me. I didn't want to argue with her, and since I was probably being silly, there was no reason to wake her.

When my cell phone didn't ring before I was halfway down the block, I knew I'd made my escape. Good. Twenty minutes to the farm, twenty minutes to find and check the horses and the locks on the trailer, workshop, and stable, then home again, home again, jiggety-jig.

I didn't meet a single car on the winding two-lane road to the farm, nor were there any strange cars in front of the barn we used for a workshop and storage.

We'd removed the harness for cleaning and swept the shavings out of the stall areas in the trailer, but we hadn't dragged Dick Fitzgibbons's marathon cart and the miniature horse cart out. Locked inside the trailer was as good a place as any to store them. I might not attempt to put Don Qui to the miniature cart for a week.

The next step was teaching him to drag an automobile tire while I steered him with reins.

I parked my truck with the headlights pointed toward the pasture in hopes I'd spot the horses looming out of the darkness, but no luck. I'd have to go walk the pasture and look for them. Nuts.

At night, horses habitually stand perfectly still in the shadows, while they watch human beings search within five feet of them without seeing them. You have to wait for the swish of a tail or the stamp of a hoof to give away their position. Irritating.

I didn't actually expect trouble, but I slipped my Glock into the holster on my belt, stuck the spare clip in the pocket of my jeans with my cell phone, worked the big flashlight down the back of my jeans — a singularly unattractive sensation in the chill spring air — and climbed out to start my horse hunt.

The moon was at that point my grandmother called "the old moon in the new moon's arms." The sliver of new moon lay on its back with its horns up, while the outline of the last full moon could still be glimpsed between the horns.

That meant precious little moonlight. I could see billions more stars than I could in Mossy Creek, but they didn't do me much good.

And the temperature had dropped to the

dew point. When I aimed the flashlight on the grass, it turned into a carpet of diamonds. My left paddock boot had developed a leak. I could feel the moisture soaking my sock.

On my left loomed the big pile of logs and roof trusses slated for my house. On the right stood Hiram's workshop, behind it, the stable, and past the stable, the dressage arena. Beyond the border of my land to the north lay the heavily wooded property belonging to the governor and his cronies.

I knew my way around my own property pretty well even without moonlight to aid me, but I also knew I could stumble or run into a tree if I got cocky, so I kept the flashlight pointed toward the pasture.

"Come on, guys," I called, and whistled. I whistle loud enough to startle *me* at night. I listened. No answering stamp, no tail swish, no sound of approaching hooves. I swung the light in an arc shoulder high. Nothing.

I didn't want to go into the pasture to hunt for them. I wasn't afraid. They wouldn't stampede. Whatever books say, horses don't generally do that. They see better than we do at night, but they are still careful. And they absolutely, positively will not run into or over a human being or animal if they can possibly avoid it. Human beings feel squishy when stepped on. Horses loathe stepping on swishy stuff. I wasn't concerned that I'd be ground into the mud. But I'd be wet to the knees and cold.

Off to my left I heard movement, but it sounded as though it came from the far side of the pasture where the old farmhouse had stood before my contractor knocked it down.

The construction types had also cleared away the debris along with the decrepit house trailer where Hiram's handyman had lived. Then they'd scraped and re-graveled that back drive up from the highway. Since my front road up to the stable with its sharp turns and steep drop-offs was dangerous for the contractor's big equipment, they drove up the back road and across the geldings' pasture to my building site. I had to live with the ruts in my pasture until they were finished.

The only thing that remained of the original farmhouse was the root cellar. Bobby, my contractor, had been promising to fill it in and cover it with a concrete pad so we could park the tractor on it, but hadn't gotten to it yet.

As I walked across the pasture, my light glanced off the yellow road grader sitting at the top of the hill in front of the old cellar.

Since the guys were driving their equipment through the pasture, I warned them to be extra careful to secure the pasture gate on that side. I didn't want horses falling into the cellar or wandering off down the old driveway to the road below.

I heard another movement . . . dear Lord, it sounded as though it was on the far side of the gate! If they'd left the gate unfastened, I would flay Bobby alive.

My heart lurched and I sped up only to stumble and fall onto my hands and knees in the wet grass. The flashlight rolled five feet away from me. I lunged for it, clambered to my feet, and realized I'd twisted my knee.

Couldn't let a little thing like that slow me down. Hoping the kink in my knee would work itself out, I limped on until my light hit the gate.

It was open!

Only a gap of about six inches — not wide enough for a horse to slip through, but wide enough for a big horse like Heinzie to push open with his nose if he decided to try. The gate was always double latched — two chains with two latches, top and bottom. I checked late this afternoon. They'd both had been securely fastened. Now both were undone.

No horse did that. I stood with my back to the gate and swept my light in an arc behind me across the pasture.

About fifty feet from me the entire herd watched me silently. *Now* I heard a tail swish and a snort. I counted quickly. Even Don Qui was there. He might have been small enough to slip out. Instead, he stood between the Friesian Heinzie's big black feet and stared at me.

"Hey guys," I said softly. "What ya' doin'?"

In answer they turned as one and meandered off into the darkness.

Why was the gate open? If I hadn't heard a horse outside the pasture earlier, then what had I heard? A deer? Coyote? Too big for a raccoon or a possum. No panthers left in this area. Bear? They went through *fences,* not gates.

Animals didn't unlock gates. Human beings did.

I snapped off my light, moved to my left and stood perfectly still. I needed to give my eyes time to adjust. If someone had come up the back driveway while I was around to hear him, he'd taken care to walk on the grass verge, and not on the noisy gravel. I hadn't seen a light either.

I'd walked up and down that driveway lots

of times, but I wouldn't want to walk it at night without a light. "Anybody there?" I called.

No answer. If there had been someone over there, I wanted to believe they were long gone. But they could be hiding, waiting for me to leave so they could go back through my pasture, leave the gate open again, and do what? Burgle the place? Let the horses loose again? Burn down the barn?

I am a card-carrying coward. I do not go blindly into anything remotely resembling danger, so I pulled my Glock out of its holster and took out my cell phone. Shielding its light with my body, I checked the signal. Two lousy bars. Maybe that would be enough. Who to call? It wasn't really Mossy Creek police chief Amos Royden's jurisdiction, and the sheriff of Bigelow County didn't like me. I didn't want to wake Peggy, who would freak.

So I called Geoff Wheeler. I didn't know his room number at the Hamilton Inn, but I did know the number of the inn.

At first the clerk didn't want to ring his room because it was after ten p.m.

In a whisper that no doubt carried in the clear night air like a boom box, I finally convinced him it was an emergency.

Geoff answered instantly.

"I'm at the farm," I whispered. "Some-body's been here. I may be over-reacting, but . . ."

"Stay where you are. I'm on my way."

"Geoff, I'm . . ."

He'd already hung up. I hadn't told him I was at the far end of the pasture. He didn't give me a chance.

Now all I had to do was sit tight. I put my cell phone back in my pocket with the extra magazine of shells.

That's when I saw the light. Or the reflec-tion of a light. *Penlight, maybe?* Something small at any rate, shining off the far side of the road grader.

The intruder was still here, but with the road grader in the way, I couldn't see him. Inside I went dead still. If he wasn't doing anything wrong, then why hadn't he an-swered me?

Panic would get me and the horses hurt. I knew that as surely as I knew my own name. I willed myself to calm. I could stop him and hold him for Geoff. I was armed and carrying a big honking flashlight.

Course, he might be armed as well. These days, everybody is. I slipped through the partially open gate and hooked it behind me. I hunkered down, stuck my flashlight back down my jeans, and held the Glock in the two-handed grip I'd been taught.

So long as I stayed on the grass and off the gravel, I too could move almost silently. All I had to do was get the drop on him. With the pasture gate chained behind me, his only escape route was back down the driveway.

The road grader sat at the edge of the cellar excavation.

I listened, heard nothing, not even breathing.

I peered around the edge of the road grader. Nobody. I only realized I'd been holding my breath when I released it.

I should never have called Geoff. I'd probably stumbled over some poor hunter jacklighting deer. Could be a teenaged couple looking for someplace to smoke dope and make out, although a road grader would not be my first choice.

Whoever it was, was long gone. Probably scared worse than I was.

I leaned against the front edge of the road grader and reached for my cell phone. I might still catch Geoff before he dressed and came out to rescue me. I'd never live that down.

Then something smacked me hard across the back.

I stumbled forward. The Glock flew out

of my hand and down into the darkness in front of the road grader. Breathless and momentarily stunned, I tripped over the lip of the cellar and tumbled head first, down into the pile of sand and dirt on the cellar floor.

"Ow!" I yelped as my hands and wrists took the full force of my body.

Talk about a sitting duck! I groped around for my flashlight with one hand while I felt for the Glock with the other. The mud and sand felt as soggy as quicksand, but thank God it was just wet from sitting in the dew for three days.

"Whoever you are, get me out of here! All is forgiven if you don't leave me down here. I won't tell the game warden, your wife or your parents if you promise not to come back on my land," I shouted. Surely if he intended to kill me he would have done more than just tumble me into the cellar.

"I promise I won't tell your preacher either. Get me out!"

This time there was no attempt to disguise the footsteps. They ran down the driveway. One person in silhouette behind the flashlight. I couldn't tell whether it was male or female.

A moment later, a car engine started and gunned away. Since it was impossible to turn on that slope, he must have driven up the hill, turned the car and parked it heading down hill for a fast getaway.

Great! Talk about pitch black. I kept feeling for the flashlight — the Glock wouldn't do me much good at the moment.

I found it after what felt like a panicky half century. "If you're broken, I'll kill you," I promised. I snapped it on and breathed a sigh of relief when it lit.

The Glock lay nose down in the dirt two feet to my right. Did guns fire when their barrels were blocked with dirt? I had no intention of finding out.

I picked up the Glock and shook it barrel down to clear it.

That's when I heard the noise. I froze. Something was down here with me.

CHAPTER 18

Merry

I went very still. I hoped for a mouse or one of the brown pink-eared field rats that scampered away when I opened the feed room. I did not want to see a Norway rat the size of a Scottie. Or a possum or raccoon. Possums have nasty tempers, and tangling with a big raccoon can be deadly. The noise wasn't loud enough to be a cougar or a black bear. A deer would have hopped out.

Staying as still as I could, I swung the light carefully around the cellar.

The snake struck just as my light hit it. I felt as though a straight razor had slashed my wrist.

I howled, flung it away, and fired half a dozen shots so fast they sounded like a single burst.

Its head exploded. Thank God the rat shot had hit it. Otherwise it would have come at me again.

My wrist was on fire. I scrambled to my feet and backed up against the cellar wall while I threw the beam of light into every corner. Please God I wasn't in a nest of snakes. The walls were of concrete block, but the floor was dirt, now mostly mud. Except for the pile of sand I had fallen into, the floor was covered with wet leaves.

They weren't moving.

Only the body of the snake I had shot still writhed in the far corner

I shone my light on it from a safe distance. A good six feet long, but thin and black. Rat snake then, or speckled king. Not a thick-bodied copperhead or water moccasin. Not a rattler, pygmy or otherwise. Plenty of those in the woods in the wooded property behind mine.

Rat snakes weren't poisonous. One that size, however, gave a big, nasty bite that carried a ton of bacteria.

Suddenly every atavistic anti-snake nerve in my body went ape. I started yelling. I had the presence of mind to stick the Glock back into its holster, but I kept the flashlight clutched in my good hand. I could feel blood oozing from my right wrist down the back of my hand.

Where was Geoff?

How would he even know where to find me? I wrapped my sweater around my wrist and used my fingertips to pull out my cell phone.

Down in this hole surrounded by stone and concrete, there was no reception.

I had to get out now, rather than wait to be found. I scrabbled at the wall, but the dirt kept sliding out from under my feet and I couldn't catch hold of the lip of the cellar above me. I was crying and gulping, my heart racing — the opposite of what I needed, but I couldn't seem to help myself. So much for being cool in a crisis.

Then from across the pasture, I heard Geoff's voice. "Merry! Where are you, dammit! If you've let something happen to you, I swear I'll kill you myself. Merry!"

With my good left hand I waved the flashlight over my head like a klieg light at a Hollywood opening.

I heard Geoff's shout, then the squelch of his footsteps as he ran across the pasture. I could see his light bobbing with the movement of his body. "Where are you? You hurt? Merry!"

"Come through the gate," I called. "Don't forget to lock it behind you or the horses will get out."

"Screw the horses."

I heard the scrape of the chains and the squeal of the gate as he opened it.

Then, a second later, I heard the chains again. He'd fastened it. Good.

"Where are you?"

"Be careful. I'm in the old cellar. In front of the road grader."

"The cellar?"

A second later his light hit me square in the face. I sank down onto the sand and let my arms fall beside me.

"You hurt?"

"Not really. Just get me out of here. We'll talk up there."

"Your gun secure?"

"It's in my holster." Then I switched off my lantern and stuck it back into my jeans.

"Give me your hands," he said. "Plant your feet against the wall. I'll pull, you walk up the wall. Can you do that?"

I took off my sweater and tied it around my neck. No doubt it was badly blood-stained, but they say stain removers do a great job these days, and it was an expensive sweater.

My wrist still hurt like poison, but I tried to ignore it as I reached up to him like a baby reaching for its mother.

He grasped my wrists. I gasped with pain.

"What the hell? You sprained your wrist in

the fall?"

"Don't worry about that. Get me out!"

It felt like a millennium before I lay face down beside the road grader.

"*Whoa!* You're bleeding?" he asked.

"Big snake," I gasped.

"Sweet Jesus."

"Don't worry. King snake. Non-poisonous."

He aimed the light at my wrist. "You're seeping like a stuck hog." He took the light between his teeth, pulled out his handkerchief and wiped away the blood. "You sure it wasn't poisonous? We should take it to the ER with us so they can identify it."

"Neither of us is going back down into that cellar after a dead snake. I blew its head off, but I recognized it. Definitely not poisonous."

He managed a chortle. "Good shooting."

"I wasn't holding a tight pattern."

He hauled me to my feet. "Can you walk?"

"Away from here? I'll crawl if I have to, but yeah, I can walk."

"How'd you wind up down there? Trip and fall?"

I hesitated and then just said it. "Someone pushed me. On purpose."

"You're sure?"

I swung away from him. "I don't think it

was a loose horse. There was somebody here. I saw the light just before I landed in the cellar."

He opened the gate. We slipped through, and he latched it behind us.

"Both latches, please," I said.

"Yes, madame."

The horses loomed up out of the darkness. "And here you are again," I said.

They followed us step for step across the pasture, then huddled around the gate until Geoff bundled me into his car. "I'm going to bleed on your upholstery," I said.

He undid my sweater and handed it back to me. "Bleed on that. We're headed for the hospital in Bigelow.

"I told you . . ."

"The heck with what you told me." He handed me a pristine pocket handkerchief. "I am not taking chances with that bite. Wipe your face. What were you doing out there anyway? I left you at home on your way to bed, and an hour later you're half buried in a cellar with a snakebite and a clip of ammunition gone."

"It wasn't a full clip. I was worried about the horses." My voice sounded weak. God, I was thirsty.

"Don't you go into shock on me, Merry." He smacked me on my thigh.

"I'm *not* going into shock." I put my head back and closed my eyes. The next thing I remember was Geoff shaking my shoulder.

"Wake up, sleeping beauty, the doctor awaits." He stood at the open door. "You need a gurney?"

"Don't be silly." I slid out and almost fell on my face. He wrapped his arm around my waist and I flopped my snakebit hand across his shoulder. "I didn't mean to go to sleep."

"You snore."

"I do not."

He shoved me into a chair in the waiting room and disappeared.

I expected to have to sit for at least an hour and answer forty thousand questions about my insurance. I guess, however, that being a GBI agent has its perks. I was whisked into an examining room.

"Wow! How many teeth did that sucker have?" The young resident wiped the blood off my wrist and agreed the snake was nonpoisonous. "Big dude. No fangs. Course, it might be a coral snake."

"It was black."

"I'm kidding. You're lucky. He chewed a small vein, but not an artery."

Next he gave me a tetanus shot which I swore I did not need, then had me drop my jeans so he could shoot a big syringe of penicillin into my rear end.

When I lifted my turtleneck and unzipped my jeans, the doctor said, "Geez, what happened to your back?"

Until that moment, I hadn't realized it hurt like hell.

"Somebody shoved me," I said.

"Somebody cracked you with a two-by-four, more like," he said. "We need to get you up to X-ray, make sure you didn't fracture any vertebrae."

"Oh, come on! All I want is to go home with a big prescription for pain meds and antibiotics." I wriggled. "See. No broken vertebrae."

From outside the room, I heard Geoff say, "Shut up, Merry."

The X-ray seemed to take forever to read, and I was correct. No broken bones. Not even a cracked rib.

But I was hurting worse with every passing moment. "Please," I asked the doctor, "give me mega-legend drugs and send me home. I need a shower."

I fell asleep in Geoff's car again, but woke with a start when we pulled into my driveway.

Peggy's house was lit up like a Christmas tree.

"You called her from the hospital, didn't you?" I said.

The minute Geoff shut off the engine, the back door opened, Peggy flew down the steps and wrenched my door open. "Are you all right?"

I nodded.

"Then I'm going to kill you."

"Please kill me tomorrow," I said to Peggy as I unlocked my apartment door. "And grill *him*. He called you." I waved my good hand at Geoff. "Damn, my truck's still out at the farm." I glanced down at my watch. "It's four in the morning. I have to feed by six-thirty."

"Shut up," both Geoff and Peggy said.

"I'll do it," Peggy said. "I'll bring you some breakfast afterward."

I opened my door. Both of them followed me inside before I could shut them out. "I'm supposed to check with a doctor. I don't have one," I said.

"I do. He'll see you," Peggy said.

"You said you wanted a shower," Geoff said. "You do feel gritty. Can you get your clothes off?"

"Certainly."

"Got a baggy?" He pointed. "To keep your bandage dry." Without waiting for permission, he rummaged in my kitchen cabinet, pulled out a box of plastic bags and a roll of duct tape.

"Whoa! I can't get my clothes off with a baggy on my arm. Go away, Agent Wheeler. I'll manage." I stumbled toward the bedroom, then looked back at him. "Somebody really did whack me across the back? I really didn't imagine that?"

He nodded.

"And Geoff? Thanks again." I shut my bedroom door on them both.

CHAPTER 19

Merry

By noon when I woke, my entire body seemed to be a single throb. I stood under another long shower and took a deep breath before I looked at the damage. I'd been hit just above my waist, so I could check the bruise in the mirror.

And boy, was it a doozy. The doctor had been right to demand an X-ray. If I ever caught the person who hit me . . . As I rubbed horse liniment into my aching back, I realized I didn't want to think what would happen if Geoff or Peggy actually got a glance at it. I'd never be allowed to leave the apartment again.

I unwrapped my wrist, saw no sign of infection, slathered antibiotic ointment across the bite, then used my teeth to apply a fresh bandage and wrap the wrist with bright blue Vetrap, the stretchy wrap I use to bind the horse's wounds. Every horseman keeps a supply at home for minor sprains and such. Much better than people bandages.

I dressed and went upstairs to bang on Peggy's door.

When she opened it, all four cats eddied around her expecting me to love on them. When they smelled the horse liniment, however, they turned tail and disappeared.

"If it's not the idiot child," Peggy said. "Do come in. I have the straitjacket all laid out and ready."

"Don't start. I'm starved. Thank you for looking after the horses this morning."

"They're all fine. Everything is locked up tight, and I put a padlock on the pasture gate by the old cellar."

"You think I ran into a plain old thief or vagrant?" I asked.

"If not for our road rage incident, I'd say yes. As it is . . . How's your wrist?"

"Hurts, but not as badly as I thought it would."

"Be grateful it wasn't a poisonous snake."

I sank onto a kitchen chair and accepted a glass of ice tea. "I owe that snake a big apology."

"I beg your pardon?" Peggy sat opposite me.

"Big king and rat snakes keep the poisonous snakes away," I said. "They eat them. He was a good snake and I killed him." Maybe it was the cumulative effects of assault and drugs, but I felt downright maudlin when I thought of what I had done to that poor unassuming snake.

"Snake is snake," Peggy said. She reached across for the platter of sandwiches on the kitchen counter and held it out to me.

"Is not." I took one and ate half of it in two bites. I was starved. Fear does that to me. "That snake was in the cellar catching field mice and minding his own business. If it hadn't been so chilly last night, he'd have been able to slither away safely, but he couldn't move fast in the cold air. Must have scared the stew out of him when I hit him with that light. No wonder he nailed me. I owe him an apology for blowing off his head."

"Whatever you say." Peggy rolled her eyes.

"Do you mind driving me out to pick up my truck?"

"*Can* you drive?"

"I've had worse cuts and bruises than this falling off horses. I'm good to go."

"And stoked to the gills with pain meds," Peggy said. "You have an appointment with my doctor tomorrow. In the meantime, I can change your dressing."

"Already done. I've watched over enough horses with injuries. The wound is neither hot nor suppurating. No sign of blood poisoning or infection. I really don't need to see your doctor unless something changes before morning."

Peggy nodded. "We'll see. Geoff called to check on you. He's coming out to the farm this afternoon to help with evening feed and to look for signs of attempted burglary."

"Just what I need," I said.

"You may be surprised."

CHAPTER 20

Geoff

When Geoff walked into the stable that afternoon, he was amazed that Merry, whom he expected to be home in bed, had finished bridling and hitching that infernal donkey to her pair of long lines. Peggy rolled her eyes at him.

"Now I know you're crazy," he said. Merry's wrist was wrapped in bright blue Vetrap.

"You and I had a bet, remember? Five bucks that Don Qui would be marginally better today?"

"Oh, for . . . we can postpone the bet under the circumstances."

"If I let him slough off, he'll think he beat me. Can't have that. I have a full training schedule tomorrow and a couple of driving lessons with Creekites, so this afternoon is my only free time. If I don't keep moving, my back will freeze up."

Peggy made circles with her finger against her temple.

"If you're determined, why don't you let me handle those reins or lines or whatever you call them?"

Merry stared at him with her eyebrows raised almost up to her hairline. "What do you know about long-lining a horse?"

"Exactly as much as you think, but with this ass, all I have to do is stay far enough back from his rear end to avoid his hooves when he kicks, and hang on when he goes forward, right?"

"It's a bit more complicated than that."

"I offered," Peggy said, "but she turned me down flat, too. Merry, let him do it. You can walk beside him and give instructions."

Merry looked at them both, then down at Don Qui's fat little body already duded up in its shiny VSE harness and blinkered bridle.

She closed her eyes for a second and sighed. "Let me get him out in the arena and set up for you, then you can give it a shot."

That must have cost her, which meant she was further below par than he'd guessed. She gathered the lines while Peggy slipped Don Qui's halter on over his bridle and led him out to the arena.

When he saw Heinzie, his friend, standing by the pasture fence watching, he let forth a single bray, but whether he was complaining or showing off, Geoff had no way of knowing.

"I'll handle the whip," Merry said. Don Qui stopped in the center of the arena, allowing Merry time to play out the long lines and show Geoff how to hold them. "I'll give the commands. You guide."

Geoff realized at once that he'd lost his bet. Don Qui had either mellowed in twenty-four hours or figured that he wasn't being attacked from the rear. Maybe the difference was simply Heinzie's presence at the fence. He walked forward on command as though he'd been doing it forever. Until Geoff tried to turn him left on Merry's command. Geoff got the lines crossed and tangled, then hauled hard on the left line.

Don Qui took instant exception. He stood straight up on his hind legs, then plunged forward kicking as high as possible with his rear end. Startled, Geoff dropped the lines, and Don Qui took off at the donkey version of racing gallop with the lines flying behind. Merry took two hobbling steps after him before she gave up.

Geoff had run track in college and still ran to keep in shape, but the lines flying behind the donkey eluded his grasp when he reached for them.

Peggy stepped out in front of Don Qui with her arms up. "Whoa, dammit!"

As the donkey zigzagged to avoid her, Geoff caught one of the lines and hauled him around in a circle so tight he nearly fell over before he stopped. Donkey and man stood facing one another, both gasping from the exertion. Geoff turned to Merry, who stood in the center of the arena with both hands on her back and eyes tight against her obvious pain. Or the pain of losing the bet.

"So, who wins the bet?"

"Call it even," Peggy said. "Could have been operator error."

"Take your five dollars," Merry said.

"Buy me a drink tonight and call it even," Geoff said.

"I can't drink with all the crap I'm taking."

"Yeah, but *I* can."

"We can't quit yet," Merry said. "He has to get it right first."

That took a while. He had mastered going straight ahead, but seemed to have difficulty turning in either direction without bucking. Eventually, with Peggy holding the longe line and Geoff working the lines properly, he managed to circumvent the arena. Since it was eighty meters by forty, that was a creditable distance for a small creature.

By the time they finished, Merry stood in the center while Peggy and Geoff did the actual work. Everyone except Merry was drenched with perspiration, when she finally called a halt to the exercise.

"Remind me not to do this again," Geoff said they walked into the stable.

"No good deed goes unpunished," Peggy said. She looked at Merry. "You look a little gray around the gills. How badly do you hurt?"

"Bad enough. I need another dose of pain meds."

"How's your wrist?" Geoff asked.

"Not too bad. Feels as if I have fifty small paper cuts."

"Eeew!" Peggy said. She put Don Qui on the wash rack, and she and Geoff stripped him of his harness.

He looked over at Merry, his face suddenly serious. "I got info from Atlanta over my cell on my way out here. The Governor's fancy chums? One of them was Giles Raleigh. He owned a twenty per cent interest in the limited partnership that holds title to the other side of your mountain."

Merry sank back against the wall. "God,

no. I had no idea. The only one I've ever met, the one who tried to intimidate me into selling, is the governor's pet Jack Russell terrier, Whitehead. Giles never mentioned it."

"Do they still want to buy your place?" Geoff asked.

Peggy took the harness across to the tack room, washed the bit and hung it all up from its harness rack.

"Nobody's bugged me about it for a long time. Once the water report about the arsenic in the ground water on that side of the hill came out, and the construction of high-dollar vacation homes went to hell in the recession, I assumed they'd given up the idea of developing it."

"Or were hanging onto it until prices went back up," Peggy said from the doorway of the harness room. "So what happens to Raleigh's twenty per cent now?" She took Don Qui's lead rope and led him into his stall.

"Haven't seen the will yet," Geoff said. "Merry, what say Peggy shows me how to get these guys fed and watered and bedded down. You drive home and get some rest."

"Are you supposed to do chores for suspects?" she asked.

"She's not a suspect. You are."

"Okay, you got a deal." She held up a hand at Peggy. "Yes, I can drive. I'm not totally spaced out. If you don't mind, I'm going to nuke a diet meal and go to bed."

"Do you want me to feed *you,* Geoff?" Peggy asked.

"I owe *you* a meal, Peggy, not the other way around. Give me a rain check. I'm meeting Amos Royden at the Hamilton Inn. I need to bounce some ideas off him."

"Promise me you'll stay home," Peggy said to Merry. "Shall I spend the night out here?"

"With the pasture gate and all the doors secure, I think the horses should be okay. If we do get burgled, anything inanimate can be replaced."

Geoff toted and fetched while Peggy fed and watered, then watched her drive down towards the road before he climbed back out of his Crown Vic.

He had come to know this place fairly well during the investigation into Hiram's murder. He had thought at the time that with no one actually living on the place until Merry's house was built, it needed better security. He locked tack, feed, and clients' room in the stable, then shut the stable doors and chained them.

The big double doors to the old barn that Hiram had converted to his workshop were heavy, thick, and securely padlocked. A burglar would be most likely to go for the workshop. A junkie could fence power tools easily.

Finally he checked to be sure all the doors on Hiram's white dually and trailer were locked.

Someone could break in — there was always a way in if you had the time, the tools, and the desire — but he hoped the average burglar would pass the place by for an easier target.

The willingness of Merry's intruder to employ violence bothered him. He hadn't hesitated to use a two by four on Merry and toss her into that cellar. He might have clubbed her across the skull and killed her. He hadn't.

Geoff couldn't be positive the incident on the highway had been more than road rage or drunken rednecks, but the bruise on Merry's back didn't lie.

Assuming the two incidents were connected, then connected to what?

The road down the hill lay in shadow, making it even more hair-raising a drive. He took his time. At the foot of the hill, he paused between the two big boulders that marked the entrance before he turned left to drive back to Mossy Creek.

He would suggest one simple, relatively inexpensive security measure to Merry. A steel farm gate with a keypad could easily be swung between those two boulders, and another with a padlock could be hung at the bottom of the old road around the curve.

A human being on foot could still slip past the gates and walk up the hill, but no cars or trucks could enter. No one could leave with anything heavier than a screwdriver. The gates could be opened in the morning for clients and construction crews, then locked at night after everyone left.

He'd talk to Peggy first thing in the morning. He figured Merry would take the suggestion better coming from her. Otherwise, she might decide he was interfering.

Which he was, but he'd be damned if anything was going to happen to either of those women on his watch.

CHAPTER 21

Peggy

In case Merry decided to sneak back to the farm as she'd done the previous night, Peggy parked behind Merry's truck in the driveway. The two women certainly didn't live in one another's pockets, but during the year since Hiram's death, and since Peggy now spent so many hours out at the farm, they'd slid into an easy symbiosis.

Peggy would truly miss Merry's company after she moved to her new house out at Lackland Farm, but they'd still see one another. She felt a kinship with Merry she'd never attained with Marilou, her own daughter.

Normal, probably. Mothers wanted their children to live the lives they hoped to have lived themselves, but perfected in ways that they had not managed. Children wanted to live their *own* lives, however different the drummer they marched to.

Marilou wanted her mother not to make waves, to color within the lines, to be the utterly conventional woman she had never been and could never be. Her husband, Ben, had understood. He'd cheerfully baled her out when she'd been arrested in protest marches back in the sixties. God, she missed him.

Peggy's discovery of horses and her talent for driving had forced Marilou to admit that her mother was out of her control. It drove her nuts, which secretly pleased Peggy immensely.

Peggy saw the answering machine light blinking when she walked into the house, because Sherlock, fascinated by the blinking light, lay with his head on it. Three messages, two of which were from sales people. The third, however, was from her granddaughter Josie. Now, if there were only a way to speak straight to Josie without listening to Marilou.

There wasn't, but eventually, Josie came on the line. "Gram, when can I come out and drive Don Qui?" She sounded wildly enthusiastic.

"Not for a while, baby. He's a handful right now."

"Not with me, he wouldn't be. He loves me and Li."

Actually, he did, but Peggy doubted that would translate into loving being put to a cart. She tried to explain to Josie without success.

"Then, can I come drive Golden? You could ride with me." In the background, Peggy heard Marilou telling the child how busy they were with the end of the school year, etc., etc., etc.

"You'll be coming out to the show on Saturday and we have the clinic on Sunday, but maybe . . ."

Marilou's voice came on the line, "Moooother, we have Sunday school and church and dinner with the Bigelows. I want you to come to dinner too."

"Tell Josie I said if not this weekend then after school next weekend. School's almost out, so she can spend some time with me at the farm this summer."

"It's too dangerous . . ."

Peggy hung up on her, but gently. Peggy had been raised practically guilt free. She still couldn't figure out what she'd done to screw up Marilou.

Peggy poured herself a glass of sherry and settled into her wing chair to watch the news. All four cats draped themselves on and around her, even before she located the remote.

The lead story was the bizarre death of one of Georgia's wealthiest and most socially prominent businessmen. The script the newsman read from made the entire carriage driving weekend sound like a Roman orgy organized by Dionysians with too much money and too little morality. That most of them were old enough to need Viagra and estrogen for an orgy didn't make it into the news.

Someone had leaked the incident with the animal rights banner and the bullhorn. So far, no organized animal rights group had taken credit for it, so it was either a splinter group or an individual.

Peggy closed her eyes and prayed they wouldn't include the story of her dunking the carriage in the lake.

They didn't. Marilou would have pitched a fit over that.

Since the media had been kept off the Tollivers' property, they had to be content with aerial shots from their helicopters. Peggy realized that the thick pine forest grew right up to the edge of the road down to the pond and even closer to the southern and eastern edge of the dressage arena.

In the dense fog, the killer could have dispatched Raleigh, stepped back into the woods a few paces, then slipped around the far end of the arena and emerged among the trailers by the stable, unnoticed and unremarked.

Would a white face show among the pines like the Cheshire cat? Would light hair without a cap?

Both Dawn and Sarah Beth had blonde hair. Dawn was tan, but Sarah Beth's skin was literally milk-white. In either case, simply turning away from the dressage arena to face into the trees would have rendered anyone standing there invisible.

Merry had sworn she'd seen no one. Someone didn't believe that. Maybe they ought to hunt up a hypnotist to regress Merry to see if she could remember someone or something else.

Peggy laughed and scared Marple off her lap. The little cat sat at her feet and glowered before climbing back up and curling into a tight little ball again.

"As if," Peggy said, stroking the soft fur. "I can just see Merry allowing herself to be hypnotized." Something had to give, and quickly. Last night could have been deadly if the cellar hadn't already been half filled with dirt and sand to cushion Merry's fall, or if that snake had been a copperhead or water moccasin.

Come to that, one of Merry's bullets

might have ricocheted off the cellar wall and killed her.

Or the horses could have gotten out and been hurt.

Nope, Geoff was a good man and a great investigator, but he didn't know either the horses or the horse people. Time to insinuate themselves into the investigation. They'd managed to catch Hiram's killer. Granted, they'd almost gotten themselves killed in the process, but this time they'd be smarter.

But how? Peggy eased the newspaper from under Marple's rear end, eliciting a grumble. She read the front page story of the murder. Nothing new. Then she checked the obituary page, which ran eight column inches on Raleigh's accomplishments in business. She put it aside to go over later with Merry and Dick Fitzgibbons, who'd gone to high school with Raleigh.

The viewing was Tuesday evening in St. Andrew's Episcopal Church down the road from Raleigh's farm. The funeral was Wednesday morning at eleven, followed by interment in the adjacent cemetery. Followed, no doubt, by funeral baked meats for the chosen few invited back to Raleigh's mansion afterwards.

Time to drag out the funeral dress she hadn't worn since Hiram's funeral. She doubted neither she nor Merry would receive an invitation to the reception after the funeral, but she doubted anybody would actually kick them out if they attended.

And eavesdropped on every interesting conversation they could.

Geoff would have a cat fit, but there wasn't much he could do except arrest them ahead of time. If he found out they were going.

CHAPTER 22

Geoff

On his way to interview veterinarian Gwen Standish the following morning, Geoff stopped by Merry's farm to make certain nothing new had happened during the night. He found Merry in the arena driving Heinzie, the giant Friesian, in the complicated pattern of an advanced dressage test. Don Qui stood quietly in the pasture, but didn't take his eyes off his friend.

"That's an improvement," Geoff said, waving at Don Qui. "Last year that dumb donkey would have had to be in the arena trotting beside Heinzie or be screaming his lungs out."

"It's taken him a year to trust that Heinzie isn't going to be kidnapped the instant his back is turned. I don't know how I'm going to manage when I take Heinzie to a show."

"You planning to do that any time soon?"

"Maybe next month, but I have to get Don Qui put to first."

"Put to what? A wrecker?"

"You remember the cart for Very Small Equines I borrowed from the Tollivers?"

"The one stashed under the big marathon carriage?"

She nodded. "We're going to haul it out, unfold it and hitch Don Qui up. Maybe this afternoon. Want to watch?"

"Absolutely. You need somebody to call the ambulance to pick up your remains. But I'm afraid I won't get back in time. I've got actual interviewing to do."

"Good luck, and I mean that sincerely. I'll never be totally free of suspicion so long as nobody else has been convicted of the crime. Raleigh may have done with his death what he couldn't do with his computer — compromise my livelihood. Who'll hire a show manager who kills competitors?"

Her tone was light, but Geoff could tell how serious she was.

"Can I come up?" Geoff asked. She looked surprised, but nodded. He climbed up into the carriage. At her command Heinzie walked on.

"I have a suggestion," he said. "You may not like it, but listen first."

"Ooookay."

He told her about the gate locks and Amos's suggestion about the CCTV.

He expected "yes, but." Instead, she thought for a moment, then said, "The guys are coming after lunch to pour the concrete slab for my house. Finally. I'll bet they'd set some heavy posts at the gates in the leftover concrete. I'm not so sure I can afford the CCTV."

"Think about it. Now, how do you stop this thing?"

Gwen Standish ran her equine practice out of a metal office building. Several paddocks separated by white board fences carved the property into small paddocks. Two were occupied by bay horses. In the parking lot stood a white panel van with "Standish D.V.M." on its side plus a couple of pickups.

Inside, Geoff found a small reception area manned by a tubby young woman wearing scrubs printed with pink unicorns. She smiled up at him, revealing perfect teeth that only good orthodonture or good genes could create, and a single dimple on the left side of her mouth. She had a pretty face surrounded by fluffy hair nearly the color of the unicorns. She wore a plain wedding band, so some man appreciated her voluptuous body and good nature.

The nametag on her desk read Meghan Farnham, Veterinary Technician. "Oh, hey," she said, after she read the card he handed her. "Gwen's expecting you. She said to come on back." She pointed to a metal door beside her desk.

Inside he found that the working part of the small clinic looked remarkably well-outfitted with computer terminals and equipment he couldn't identify, but that appeared new — no dings or scratches — and state-of-the-art. Off to one side was a well-equipped dispensary with a row of locked cabinets above. That must be where the legend drugs were kept.

Through a big interior window he saw a full surgical theatre with a tilt table which he guessed had to be large enough to rotate a horse.

In the center of the examining area, a gray mare stood patiently while the woman, who must be Gwen Standish, ran an ultrasound device over the horse's abdomen. She glanced over her shoulder at him and gave him a "one minute" sign.

Raleigh's barn manager Brock hadn't been kidding when he said Gwen Standish wasn't as big as a minute. He guessed she was under five feet tall. Although there wasn't an excess ounce of flesh on her body, ropy muscles stood out in her arms and shoulders.

Most men would consider her cute, with her long chestnut hair in a ponytail tied with a blue scrunchie. Her turned-up nose and wide nostrils, however, gave her a slightly piggy look he had trouble ignoring.

At six feet four, Geoff was seldom attracted to women who came up to his sternum, and Gwen was no exception. He preferred a woman he wasn't afraid he'd break. Plenty of men would take one look at her, however, discount her muscles, and want to protect her.

He suspected she could handle anything less than a Tyrannosaurus Rex all by herself.

She nodded, cut off the machine, and turned to him. "You're fifteen minutes late," she said.

"Sorry. The drive took longer than I thought." He indicated the mare. "Is she pregnant?"

This elicited a smile. Her teeth were small and white, but either she hadn't kept her braces on long enough to rid herself totally of her overbite, or she hadn't worn her retainer religiously. "Sixty-four days from insemination." She slapped the mare on her shoulder. "She's one of Giles Raleigh's

241

Dutch warmblood brood mares."

"What do you think will happen to his place now?"

She shut the mare into one of the stalls. "Give me a sec." She stuck her head through the door to the reception room and said, "Meg, call Brock. Tell him she's still in foal. He can come get her this afternoon." Then she turned back to Geoff and answered his question as though there had been no break in their conversation. "No idea. It's as hard to turn a place like that around as it is an aircraft carrier, so I'd say not much will change for at least six months to a year."

"Do you know who inherits?"

She shook her head. "I know what everybody says, but with Giles Raleigh, that meant squat. He could have gotten mad and left it to a home for aging cats."

"Will you continue to do their vet work?"

"Lord, I hope so. They're my biggest client. Brock trusts me. I think Dawn does too."

"What about Raleigh?"

She wheeled the ultrasound machine into the corner of the room and leaned on the counter beside it. "Raleigh didn't trust his *mother.* He always fussed about my bills, but he paid them on time and in full."

"You ever fight with him?"

She laughed. "Who didn't? He threatened to fire me every couple of months. In this part of north Georgia, unless you want to chance driving a colicky mare all the way down to the University vet school in Augusta, I'm the closest and best equipped clinic." She gave him a glimmer of a smile. "And the best equine surgeon in Georgia, but don't tell my colleagues that."

"You've got an impressive set-up. Are you a sole practitioner or do you have partners? I didn't see any other names on your sign out front."

"Sole practitioner. I like to do things my way, and I try to stay one step above the competition." She waved a hand at the machines. "It amortizes fast. Now, what did you want to talk about? I don't know anything about Raleigh's death."

"You were there, though? That morning?"

"I'd been there all night, as a matter of fact. One of the Hull's Morgan geldings was trying to colic on us. Tully and I worked on him until four or five in the morning before he rewarded us with a steaming pile of beautiful manure."

"Did you see Raleigh harnessing up?"

"The Hulls were stabled on the back side of the stable close to the main house. In other words, as far away from Raleigh's stalls as possible. In all that fog, no way would I have seen his horses unless they stepped on me."

"Or heard them?"

"Stables are never quiet. If I had heard anything, I wouldn't have paid attention. That sort of thing just doesn't register after you've been spent enough time in stables."

"Did you see Raleigh?"

She shook her head.

"Other than the Hulls, did you see anyone at all?"

"Not really. I heard a couple of cars coming up the driveway, but I have no idea whose they were. Grooms would be getting up by that time, but as politically incorrect as it may sound, they're almost all short, grizzled and Latino. I can't tell one from the other." She shrugged. "They're mostly illegal, so they keep changing from show to show."

"You say you've worked for Raleigh for some time. Mostly with Brock, I assume."

She covered her momentary hesitation by stripping off her pair of blue surgical gloves and dropping them into a covered waste disposal can beside the cross-ties. She squirted lotion from a hand cleaner sitting on the shelf over the can and rubbed her hands.

After a moment she looked up and said, "Brock's an excellent stable manager. Very professional. Raleigh's place couldn't function without him. I hope Dawn remembers that."

"I've heard that Brock and Raleigh had a big dustup on Friday afternoon. Any idea what that was about?"

"Why would I?"

"Since you two are friends, I thought he might need a shoulder to cry on."

"Get real. They fought all the time. Meant nothing."

"Your relationship strictly professional?"

"Why the hell is that any of your business?"

"Dr. Standish, this is a murder investigation. Everything is my business. He's a single man, you're a single woman — or I assume you are. You work closely together. Why shouldn't you have a personal relationship?"

"It wouldn't be ethical."

Geoff waited with his arms folded across his chest, his ankles crossed. He'd learned that most people couldn't stand silence. Gwen was no exception.

"Oh, all right. We dated for a while."

"Not lately?"

"We're just friends."

"Big breakup?"

"Neither of us had enough time to maintain a relationship," she said.

"Yeah, been there, done that." The few relationships Geoff had tried to carry on after his divorce had all broken apart on his inability to keep a decent schedule. Women could take being cancelled at the last minute only so often before they moved on. He was facing that and worse with Merry. She did the standing up as often as he did. The result was the same.

He took Gwen through her night with the Hulls' gelding. "After the gelding dropped your manure, what did you do?"

"Stopped by the big house. They'd set up coffee, juice and sweet rolls on the veranda. I needed some in the worst way."

"Anybody else there?"

"Couple of the grooms. I took my stuff to my van and drove back home to bed."

"Who looks after your practice when you're not around?"

"I don't generally work on Sundays except for emergencies. I'd cleared my calendar for that weekend on purpose. I was the official vet for the show, so I hung around most of the weekend."

"When did you hear about Raleigh's death?"

"Brock called me. I can't remember when. He woke me up." She gave a shudder. "That's a truly wacko way to kill somebody."

"How would you have killed him?"

She glanced down at her small body. "With an elephant gun from a long distance. I'd sooner mess with an angry polar bear up close."

"You ever go to bed with him?"

"Not just no, but hell no. Who told you I had?"

"Nobody, but his reputation says that he hit on any attractive woman he met. You are very attractive."

She actually blushed. Merry might have reacted the same way. Women used to adoration, however, like Sarah Beth Raleigh, his own ex-wife Brittany and probably Dawn Raleigh accepted compliments casually as no more than their due.

"Well, *he* didn't think *I* was attractive. Probably Brock warned him that if he hit on me he might lose his veterinary privileges. Nookie he could get anywhere, but a vet of my caliber in the wilds of North Georgia? Nunh-uh."

"Why are you in the wilds of North Georgia and not in a big practice somewhere?"

"You mean like Auburn or Moorpark? I'd rather be captain of a small ship than purser on an ocean liner."

"Got ya."

She showed him around the clinic when he asked. Her pride in the place and what she had built was obvious. She seemed to swell physically when she talked about it.

Ten minutes later he gave her and her secretary Meghan business cards, told both women to report anything they thought might help the investigation, and drove away. Maybe Gwen came from family money. She'd found a big wad of it somewhere to open that clinic.

He stopped in a small mom-and-pop diner between Dr. Gwen's and Raleigh's for a made-from-scratch cheeseburger and real home fries. Afterwards, he felt like putting back his head and taking a nap in his car. Instead he turned toward Raleigh's place. By now the family lawyer should have told the heirs who'd gotten what. Although a will admitted to probate was public property, the lawyer might be waiting until after the funeral to prove it legally. With luck Geoff would be around when the heirs heard what they did or did not get. Might cause some explosions. In a murder investigation, explosions were always happy events.

CHAPTER 23

Tuesday
Merry

Peggy called Dick Fitzgibbons while I was harnessing Golden Boy for Casey Blackshear's ten o'clock lesson. Casey had been quite an athlete before she was paralyzed from the waist down. The moment she'd discovered there was an international Driving for the Disabled program, she decided to learn to drive.

The fun show and clinic, scheduled weekend after next, was actually a benefit to help pay for a para-carriage and horse for her. Her veterinarian husband could afford to pay the expenses for the horse and carriage, but a specially built para-carriage, horse, harness and accessories amounted to a big chunk of change to pay out all at one time. Lackland Farm would keep any profit from the Sunday driving clinic, but the profits from the Saturday show would go to Casey's fund. Casey hoped we could start a para-driving program in the area at some point using her horse and carriage.

In the meantime, her husband Hank, who is our veterinarian, and Dick Fitzgibbons, had removed the seats from an old phaeton Dick picked up for a song at an auction in Pennsylvania, and fitted it so Casey could drive her wheelchair up a ramp into the cart. We had to strap the chair securely in place, and she couldn't let down or raise the ramp herself, but once inside the cart with the reins in her hand, she was good to go. The wheelchair was actually wider than a normal single seat, so I squeezed in beside her when I trained her, but that was a small price to pay for the smile on her face. One lesson had convinced her that she wanted to compete. We expected her to be driving head-to-head with non-disabled drivers before the end of the season.

Now, their adopted daughter Li wanted to drive as well. She was too young, but once Casey was comfortable driving, we figured we could rig a special security seat for Li to ride along with her mother safely. Li wanted to do the driving, of course. She is a very determined and opinionated young lady, but she couldn't be allowed to drive so much as a Very Small Equine like Don Qui for several years, even with an adult riding along.

"How would you feel about driving a Norwegian Fjord?" I asked Casey after her lesson. "Large enough horse to pull the extra weight of your wheelchair, but small enough to manage. They're smart and kind."

"Could Li ride the same one I drive?" Casey asked, as Li flew out of the stable and climbed into the wheelchair and her mother's lap.

"They're larger than Golden and Ned and as broad as a billiard table. But once she's old enough, we can find Li a used saddle and start her on lessons."

"Now!" Li said.

"No way," Casey answered.

They were still squabbling as Casey's van disappeared down the driveway.

After Casey and Li left, and the horse and carriage were tidied away, Peggy found me in the carriage shed tying a small tractor tire to long ropes. "For Don Qui to pull this afternoon."

"So soon?" Peggy asked.

"His meltdown yesterday was actually a big improvement. In the absence of a breaking cart or sledge small enough for him, this is the best we can do, before we put him to the VSE Meadowbrook. What did Dick say?

251

Does he need his marathon cart back right away?"

Peggy lounged against the wall and watched me with narrowed eyes. She'd never seen the drag-the-tire trick, and obviously thought I'd lost my mind. "His new marathon cart is due from Poland this week," she said, "so this one can stay with us."

"Will he sell it?"

Peggy laughed and shoved away from the wall. "Actually, he offered to give it to me, but I refused. Instead, he's giving me a cousin's price. If I can afford it, I intend to buy it. We do need one that will take a pair."

"Great. The farm can probably manage to split the cost with you."

She looked away and said much too casually, "He's going to drive over from Aiken, have dinner and spend the night. He'll drive us to Raleigh's viewing this evening."

I never ask about sleeping arrangements. Peggy has two guest rooms, but whether Dick uses one or not is none of my business. "Great. Geoff wants to talk to Dick about Raleigh. This will save Geoff a trip."

Peggy held the lines as I carried the tire out of the shed and into the arena. "Actually, he wanted to watch you drive Don Qui to this tire, but it looks as though he'll be too late."

"You told him?" I dropped my lines. "Dammit, I don't want half of Mossy Creek looking over my shoulder."

"He does have a vested interest."

"In an emergency clinic?" The best thing to use in breaking a horse to drive is either a sledge — a sliding platform without wheels — or an actual breaking cart. They are usually made of heavy steel, have high dashboards in front to protect the driver in case the horse kicks, a low center of gravity and an easy means of egress — in other words, the driver can bail if the horse runs away.

Hiram had an old breaking cart, but it was much too big for Don Qui, hence we were using the small tractor tire. The little Meadowbrook we'd borrowed was still folded up under the marathon cart in the trailer. It was also too hard to bail out of in an emergency. For the moment it could stay where it was.

"You'll have to hold the release line on the tire," I said. "We can't let Don Qui pull it faster than a walk. If he picks up a trot, the tire could bounce behind him, or God forbid, go airborne and flail from side to side like a Frisbee."

"So if it threatens to take on a life of its

own, I'm supposed to drop the line and let it come loose and fall off?"

"Precisely. Let's hope it doesn't come to that. I'm going to check on the progress of the pour for my house's slab, then we can put Don Qui's harness on and try him out."

The concrete truck had arrived early and was nearly done pouring the slab for my house, while the horse herd kibitzed over the pasture fence. I figured the noise would spook them, but even Don Qui peered up at the gray slurry sliding down the chute with grave interest.

My general contractor agreed to set four heavy fence posts wide apart, two at the bottom of each driveway

"People will be driving big rigs up my driveway," I told him. "With live horses in them. Much wider turning radius — an eighteen-wheeler in some cases. They have to be able to make the turn and get the rig away from the road to shut the gates behind them. Trust me, wider is better."

He'd grumbled, but saw the sense in my argument. "Posts will be in before we leave this afternoon," he said. "I got to go pick up some more stuff at the hardware store, so I can pick up the gates and hardware when I'm in Bigelow. We can set them in and have them up and running before we leave this afternoon. They won't be real secure for a couple of days, but providing nobody runs into them, they should be fine."

"Does that mean you can start laying the logs for my house tomorrow?"

He laughed. "Slab'll harden up over night, but it's got to cure for a week before we set the sills and start laying logs."

Bobby swore he'd be finished in six weeks. Of course he would.

As I led Don Qui out to the arena and prepared to hook him to the tire, I considered postponing the driving clinic scheduled for Sunday because of the stacks of logs and trusses sitting around, but decided against it. Cancelling would be bad for Lackland Farm and for Casey's fund.

I'd gotten a late entry from Dawn Raleigh, who was bringing a pair, not the four-in-hand. No one had cancelled. I had to pay Catherine Harris, who was my judge on Saturday and my clinician on Sunday, whether we cancelled or not. She would stay in Peggy's guest room, but we had to pay her mileage to and from her place in Alpharetta.

The Mossy Creek Garden Club had agreed to handle the drinks and sandwiches, and now that they knew the profit would go to Casey's fund, I figured we'd have a heavy turnout of locals buying spectator tickets. When I looked up, I found that Peggy had finished attaching reins and tire to Don Qui. He stood perfectly still until I asked him to walk on. That was real progress.

I asked him to walk on. When he felt the weight of the tire behind him, I expected another meltdown. Holding the release line far enough behind him to be out of kicking range, Peggy looked terrified.

He stiffened when he felt the weight behind him. I let him stop and stand until he figured out that there was something back there, but that it didn't seem to be attacking him. Then he leaned his sturdy little chest against the horse collar and walked forward as though he'd been pulling all his life. It was almost as though he was thinking, "Well, finally. So this is what all the nonsense has been about."

He cheerfully dragged his tire for twenty minutes in patterns around the arena as though he'd been doing it forever. Both Peggy and I were stunned.

"He's nearly ready to put to the little Meadowbrook," I said and held a carrot for him to nibble, even though he still wore his bridle and harness. Not a good practice to start, but he deserved it. "Good boy, Don Qui."

"You mean I missed it?" Geoff said from the stable.

"You certainly did," Peggy said. She rubbed her back and leaned over with her hands on her knees. "You can do it next time. It's a darned sight more work than I thought it was. I refuse to believe that all this time all he's needed to sweeten his temper was a job."

CHAPTER 24

Tuesday night
Merry

Geoff and I had been exiled from Peggy's kitchen to her library, so that she and Dick could toss the salad and serve the spaghetti. We were having an early dinner since we were all four driving to Raleigh's farm for the "viewing."

In the old days, the custom was to set the coffin up on trestles in the parlor so that friends and neighbors could come and pay their respects, have a drink and a bite to eat. I would have expected Dawn and Sarah Beth to prefer the funeral home, but the two women had opted for the old fashioned model.

No doubt they'd hired a caterer from Atlanta instead of their church's Funeral Ladies, the local group that generally handled the local catering. I'd used our local Funeral Ladies to cater my father's view-

258

ing and reception. The food had been fine. Other things — not so much.

In the old days before embalming, custom demanded that some member of the household — preferably male — sit up all night with the deceased to be certain he didn't come back to life. That's why it's called a wake. God forbid Raleigh should sit up, point his finger at his killer, and howl "j'accuse."

"What do you mean you're having a horse show next weekend?" Geoff slammed his beer down on the side table in Peggy's library. Marple, the little gray female who sat on his shoulder, snapped to attention, and only settled after giving his ear a smack. Geoff sounded personally offended. "Are you asking to get yourself killed?"

"I'm hoping to make enough money to help buy Casey Blackshear a para-carriage and maybe put a down payment on a set of harness as well. I am not going to get killed. The place will be crawling with people."

"So was the Tollivers' place."

"I have low PVC fences around my dressage arena, not steel cable and stakes."

"The stake was a weapon of opportunity. Everywhere I look in that stable of yours I see lethal weapons. Then there's always the usual — guns, knives."

"I have my own guns and knives. I can defend myself from an enemy."

"It's not *your* enemies who concern me," he said.

"Come and get it," Dick called.

I was afraid I wouldn't be welcome at Raleigh's wake. I was wrong. Sarah Beth spied Peggy and me as we entered the enormous foyer of Raleigh's mansion and flew over to embrace us both as though we were long lost sisters.

"I was so afraid you wouldn't come," she whispered. "I'm so sorry about what you had to go through finding — him — and all that questioning. It must have been dreadful."

She looked fabulous. Grief, if that's what it was, certainly agreed with her. For the first time I saw what Peggy had seen — the glow of pregnancy. And since Raleigh's death, she seemed downright happy about it. Maybe now abortion was no longer an option. I wondered whether the baby would carry Raleigh's DNA. Somehow I doubted it. But whose? Could be a business associate or someone from the carriage-driving world. Sarah Beth had plenty of opportunity to hop into bed with other men. Maybe she didn't even know for certain whose child she was carrying.

And what would her pregnancy do to Raleigh's will? In old British law a legitimate child born within nine months of the death of the putative father received a full inheritance. The same in the United States? No idea.

Sarah Beth spotted Geoff behind me and her face fell. "What are you doing here? Can't you leave us alone?"

"Afraid not, Mrs. Raleigh, but I'll try not to bother you tonight." He stepped around us as though we hadn't all driven over in Dick's big Lincoln. She watched his back with narrowed eyes. But not eyes filled with fear. Or at least I didn't think so. She was annoyed, but not scared.

The look on Dawn's face when she spotted him, however, was deer-in-headlights. Or maybe raccoon-scared-spitless-by-rattlesnake. She clung to the arm of just about the best-looking guy I'd seen in twenty years. Obviously Armando Gutierrez, the polo player. No wonder she was willing to risk the wrath of Raleigh to keep him.

Sarah Beth called them over to introduce us. Dawn wasn't precisely chilly, but she showed none of her stepmother's warmth towards us.

261

Armando, however, did. He was not only handsome, with a lean muscular body, he had kind eyes and a brilliant smile in his sun-bronzed face. We shook hands. His was even more callused than mine.

"This is Armando Gutierrez, Merry Abbot, Mrs. Caldwell," Dawn said. "My fiancé." Her chin went up about as far as Peggy's eyebrows, but we both offered best wishes to them.

One is never supposed to offer congratulations to the bride. It implies she has successfully bagged her prey. In this case, I longed to break with tradition since Armando had definitely been bagged and tagged, and damned fast too.

Then Peggy stomped on my instep, and I shut my mouth.

"There's food in the dining room and a bar in the living room," Sarah Beth said.

With a line of mourners — or gloaters, depending on your point of view — stacking up behind us, we moved on while Sarah Beth and Dawn greeted Dick Fitzgibbons and some other people I didn't recognize.

"I need a drink," Peggy whispered. "Fiancé indeed. Talk about your funeral baked meats serving as the marriage feast. I wonder if Sarah Beth is planning to remarry," Peggy said. "And who."

Past the bar, Brock was leaning down talking to Gwen Standish, the vet, in low tones. He looked unhappy. She looked mutinous. I had met her briefly at a couple of shows and knew she was Raleigh's vet, but I didn't know her socially. She had an excellent reputation as to skill. Ethics — not so much.

Brock glanced up and caught my eye. A moment later he half-dragged Gwen out into the hall and toward the door of the conservatory beyond.

"What's that all about?" Peggy asked. "Gin and tonic, please."

The bartender nodded and mixed the drink. "Ma'am?" he asked me.

I shook my head. "Diet Coke, please." I wanted a clear head, and I was still on antibiotics, though I was down from Vetrap to an oversized Band-Aid.

"Let's split up," Peggy said. "You follow Brock. I'll see if the Tollivers are here."

The conservatory was so full of huge plants that you could have hidden a tribe of Jivaros behind the palms. Although the fans moving the warm air were equipped with soft lights, the room was in shadow. I couldn't see Brock and Gwen for a moment, then the door leading to the patio and pool opened and they slipped out. I slunk after them. They stopped in the shadows just outside the door to keep out of sight. I nearly knocked over a twelve foot tall Sega Palm when I backed into it.

"Are you insane?" Gwen said. She was speaking softly, but sounded as though she were speaking through gritted teeth. "You can't walk away. Who'd you think you're playing with?"

"We have to call it off," Brock said. "At least postpone the next trip. The place is crawling with cops. That Wheeler is no dummy."

"All he cares about is the murder. He's not looking at us."

"The hell he's not! If he finds out Raleigh knew . . ."

"He won't. He fired you all the time. This was no different."

"Not like this. He knew the consequences if he got tied into it. The rig's registered to him. He could lose the farm. He swore he'd call the cops. You and I shouldn't even be seen together."

"I beg your pardon?" Her voice rose. "We have every reason to be seen together. What's suspicious would be you getting another vet right now."

"Only if we have some professional connection. We shouldn't be talking now."

She sounded furious. He, on the other

hand, sounded downright whiny. And scared.

"Are you dumping me? Is that what this is all about? Now that he's dead, you think you can climb into that bitch's bed?"

I heard voices and laughter. Someone was coming into the conservatory. Brock and Gwen shut up instantly. If they came back in, they were bound to spot me behind the palm tree.

I am a lousy spy.

Peggy

Juanita Tolliver might look like a field hand most of the time, but when the occasion arose, she cleaned up well. She was middle-aged tubby with the bulge around the gut that comes to most post-menopausal women. Peggy would bet that her little black dress came out of a fancy atelier in New York or Paris, and that the double strand of ping-pong ball black pearls covering her crepey neck came from Mikimoto. Unlike the widow Raleigh, her heels were only a couple of inches tall, but looked like a pair of Bruno Maglis Peggy had seen in *Bizarre* a couple of months earlier. Juanita's hair was streaked with gray, but without a hint of blue and feathered to flatter. As a matter of fact, her hair matched the dark gray pearls. Coincidence?

While everything about Sarah Beth screamed, "Newly acquired for a price," Juanita whispered "Been there, always had that."

She laid her hand on Peggy's arm and gave her an air kiss, then stepped back and said, "You're holding up well. How's Merry?"

"Not in jail."

"Glad to hear it." Without seeming to, she moved the two of them past the dining room and into the butler's pantry beyond. She leaned against the cabinets through whose windows gleamed china, crystal, and a ton of well-polished silver. "Harry is not happy. Sheriff Nordstrom's a nice boy, but he's way out of his depth."

"That's why he turned the case over to the GBI. Has Agent Wheeler come to talk to you and Harry yet?"

"Not so far, although Harry spent some time with him Sunday afternoon after Merry found Giles's body. Seems competent, but Harry and I think he ought to be digging into Giles's finances. I heard rumors he was sailing close to the wind. Not that he didn't as a general rule, of course."

"Anything specific?"

"You know the way Harry and I feel about

Ham Bigelow and his crowd," Juanita wrinkled her nose. "If half of what they get up to ever comes out, the general populace will roll out the tumbrels, and we'll all wind up on the guillotine."

"Not me. I'm a peasant. And I can knit."

She grinned. "I'll remember that, Madame DeFarge." She stopped speaking as a tall man wearing a clerical collar passed through, smiled, but didn't stop. He shoved through the swinging door into the kitchen as though he owned the place.

"Seriously," Juanita said in not quite a whisper, "I suspect not even Dawn knew all the robbing-Peter-to-pay-Paul stuff Giles was into."

"I thought that was called a Ponzi scheme," Peggy answered.

"Near enough." Juanita set her empty highball glass on the glass-topped breakfast table, but immediately picked it up and rubbed the wet circle off with a paper napkin. Then she set the glass down on the napkin with a small nod. Not a woman who left even small messes for others to clean up. "Giles wanted Harry in on a limited liability company with him and Governor Bigelow five or six years ago," she said, "but Harry turned them down. Then came the mortgage collapse."

"I'm sure Agent Wheeler has someone looking into Giles's finances. They even have a name for the people who do that. Forensic Accountants."

"Looking for where all the financial bodies are buried. Anyway, give him a heads-up. Ham Bigelow gets bitchy real quick when anyone looks too closely at his land deals, and the GBI works for the State of Georgia."

"The state of Georgia is just what Ham thinks he is — just like Louis the Fourteenth — *l'etat, c'est moi.*"

The door opened and Harry stuck his head in. "Juanita, I've had it up to here saying nice things about Giles. At the rate I'm lying, my nose is gonna get home before I do. And I want some dinner that doesn't come in bite sizes. Can we go now? Oh, hey, Peggy."

Juanita threw Peggy a look. "Yes, dear. Coming." She patted Peggy's arm and trailed after her husband. "See you at the funeral?" she said over her shoulder.

Peggy nodded. She wondered if Juanita had singled her out simply to pass on information about Giles's financial condition and aim the investigation away from the driving crowd. Everyone kept intimating that Giles Raleigh had crooked deals going, but nobody had as yet mentioned anything specific. Geoff would know more, but he'd never tell her and Merry.

She mentally re-girded her loins and pushed through the swinging doors to the kitchen. Three white-coated servers were shuttling full trays of finger food out and empty trays in to be refilled. A chef wearing a chef's toque and a triple-fronted white chef's jacket was taking a cookie sheet of miniature quiches out of a restaurant-size oven.

Yep. Definitely not the local Funeral Ladies, although the local funeral director would have his own cadre of women who usually handled finger food for the viewing and after-the-funeral buffet. The emblems on the waiters' breast pockets read *The Elegant Gourmet, Dahlonega.* That would come across as arrogant to the locals. Not that Sarah Beth would care, of course, nor even notice. Assuming that Dawn did inherit the farm, Sarah Beth would be moving out soon anyway, probably to the Raleigh condo in Atlanta.

The priest had disappeared through one of the other doors. Although the service was to be held at the local Episcopal Church, Peggy suspected that Giles had never darkened the door of the place. She intended to chat up the good rector to find out.

" 'Ma'am, 'scuse me."

Peggy flattened herself against the wall beside the pantry door to allow a waiter past with a chafing dish of something pinkish and gooey — probably shrimp, although it looked more like molten bubblegum. "Sorry," she whispered and backed out of the room.

She found the priest standing by the dining room table. He wasn't eating greedily, but as steadily as a grazing antelope. She picked up an iced shrimp guaranteed not to burn the inside of her mouth and introduced herself. "You must be the rector from St. Andrews," she said.

He gulped down whatever he'd been eating, leaving a plate still full of goodies — heavy on the caviar. "Yes indeed, Father Clemons. St. Andrews is my baby."

Peggy introduced herself and shook his hand. "Must be nice to have a parishioner like Giles in your congregation." She meant a rich parishioner, of course, although she doubted Mr. Clemons would admit to that.

He nibbled on a quiche. "We didn't see much of Giles, although Sarah Beth is always willing to volunteer. Don't know what we'd do without her. She supplies the energy to keep our needlepoint group in

270

high gear. We're redoing all the kneeling benches."

"I didn't know she did needlepoint."

"Oh, my yes. She gives classes. She did most of the designs." He gave a small smile. "Of course, it takes years to accomplish a project that big. I suspect I'll be long gone before all the benches are finished."

"To a larger parish?"

This time he laughed. A silken orator's laugh from a man who was used to public speaking. "In a manner of speaking. I was thinking more of dead or retired."

"You're a young man — from my perspective, that is. Too young to have grand-children?"

"My wife died several years ago. We were childless."

"You could remarry."

His eyes took on a faraway glint. Peggy followed his glance. He was staring at Sarah Beth in the front hall, with the expression a hound dog gets when he spots a ham biscuit just outside his kennel.

Well, my, my. All those hours working out the details on the kneeling bench project might have brought the reverend a bit closer to Sarah Beth than was good for either of them.

Good grief, he couldn't be the father of

her baby, could he? Episcopal priests were not celibate like their Roman Catholic brethren, but the Episcopal Church still frowned on divorce, particularly among its clergy.

It would, however, be permissible to marry a widow, even a pregnant one. One more motive for Sarah Beth, and, she supposed, for the reverend Mr. Clemons as well.

When Clemons put his empty sherry glass down and excused himself, Peggy picked it up on her linen napkin and surreptitiously stuffed it in her purse. She had no idea whether it was possible to get DNA from an unborn fetus. Geoff already had Raleigh's DNA if he needed to test it, but at some point he might be interested in Clemons's DNA as well. She intended to give the glass to him just in case.

CHAPTER 25

Tuesday night
Merry

"Gwen, the vet, and Brock had a nasty spat on the patio," I said in the car. Dick was driving us home in his big Lincoln. Peggy was sitting beside him, so Geoff and I had the back seat. We might have sat closer in the days before seat belts and this damn case. As it was, we were buckled in at opposite ends.

"What about?" Geoff asked.

"Something that Brock wanted to cancel and Gwen didn't. I think there was a trip mentioned, and a mysterious 'they.' I gather they were not nice people and wouldn't take kindly to any talk of cancellation. Raleigh found out what they were doing and hit the ceiling. Something about the rig belonging to Raleigh. Apparently, he truly intended to fire Brock this time. Doesn't that give Brock a motive to get rid of Raleigh before he could make good on his threat?"

"Depending on what they were into." Geoff tapped Dick on the shoulder. "You know Gwen, right? What sort of people does she come from?"

"No idea. I do know she went to vet school at UGA, but I don't know her family."

"What I'm asking is, does she come from money? New or old?"

"Not to the best of my knowledge."

"Have you seen that clinic of hers?"

Dick stopped at a four way stop and made a left turn toward Mossy Creek. "Never been there, but I have seen the panel van she uses as her mobile station. She can do everything up to and including minor surgery in it."

"Plenty of expensive equipment?"

Dick nodded. "What about you, Merry? You know her family?"

"Nope. I've never been to her clinic either. I use Casey Blackshear's husband in Mossy Creek. It's an excellent clinic and he's a fine vet, but it's not Auburn or UGA vet school." I turned to Geoff. "What are you really asking?"

"Where does the money come from for the building, the equipment, the van — all of it. I doubt she's forty, and she's in practice alone. So, she either has a rich and generous family, inherited it, has backers and silent partners, or . . ."

"She's doing something crooked," I said.

"Not necessarily, but it's a definite possibility. So how does a vet make crooked money?"

"Drugs, obviously," Peggy said. "Even I've heard of Special K." Ketamine. Used by vets to anesthetize.

"Plus PCP and a number of other drugs that are valuable on the street. Take a lot of fake prescriptions to pay for *that* equipment," Geoff said. "And the DEA keeps pretty close tabs on vets to be certain that scheduled drugs are properly accounted for."

"Pardon the interruption, but, Merry, you said you wanted to check the farm before we drove back to town," Dick said.

"Please, if it's not too far out of the way. The contractor hung the new gates and put in one keypad this afternoon. I want to be certain it's functioning."

Dick turned right into the main driveway of the farm and drove up to the new steel gates. They looked secure, but I climbed out to take a closer look. The other three followed me.

"I thought you said they had a keypad,"

Peggy said, pointing at a heavy chain and padlock locking the two gates together.

"It's right there," I said pointing. "Call the padlock my rampant paranoia."

Geoff shook the gates. "Take a tank to drive though those."

"Hey, be careful. The concrete's not totally set yet," I said.

"But, Merry, can't someone park down here off the road and then shimmy around the gateposts and walk up the drive?" Peggy started toward the far end of the gate.

"Don't!"

She stopped.

"The guys strung up two strands of electric fence hidden in the grass and shrubs on both sides of the drive. The fence only goes about six feet in either direction, but you'd have to be a mountain goat to get around it. The fence runs off the same solar panel as the keypad and has battery backup. You'd get zapped before you realized you were in an electronic minefield. It can be circumvented, but only with prior knowledge and a good pair of wire cutters."

"I still say you need CCTV," Geoff said. "Right up there." He pointed to a big oak that overhung the driveway. "Is the other drive set up with a keypad, too?"

"Not yet. The gates are hung, but they're

only closed with a padlock and chain at the moment. No keypad, no electric fence yet. The guys concentrated on the main driveway." I turned to Geoff. "This whole set-up was amazingly inexpensive. How much do CCTVs cost?"

"You can get half a dozen nanny-cams for around a thousand dollars," Geoff said. "If you'd had one the other night, you might know who tossed you on your butt in the cellar and got you snake bit."

"I'll spring for the CCTVs," Dick said. "I'll have someone come out and install them tomorrow."

"Dick, I can't let you . . ." I said.

"Hey, I have a vested interest. I don't want anything to happen to Heinzie." He wrapped an arm around Peggy. "Or my two best girls. Since we're here, let's drive up and check on the horses."

I removed the padlock and chain. When we were all back in the car, I gave Dick the gate code to try. It worked. Peggy already knew it, and I had planned to give it to Dick and Geoff anyway.

After the gates swung open, Dick drove the Lincoln up the winding road with the ease of a long-haul truck driver or a man used to driving horse vans.

In the parking area, Dick pulled up beside

Hiram's white dually. There were dawn-to-dusk floodlights on the peak of the work-shop aimed at the parking lot, and motion sensor lights in front and on the pasture side of the stable behind it. We'd had a terrible time aiming the motion sensors, until we hung them far enough back from the pasture that Heinzie and his buddies couldn't trip them accidentally.

Or I thought we had.

I put my hand on Geoff's arm and pointed toward the stable, "Those lights aren't supposed to be on."

"The horses set them off?" he whispered back.

I shook my head. Motioning for us all to be quiet, he unholstered the small automatic that had fit so smoothly under his navy sports jacket that I hadn't even realized he was armed.

I'm sure agents aren't even supposed to go to the bathroom unarmed, never mind to a wake for a murder victim.

"Get back in the car and wait for me," he whispered. At that moment the stable lights went off, leaving only the light on the workshop shining directly down on the four of us.

"We can't just . . ."

"Dammit, woman, do as you're told for

once in your life." He moved away from me, fading into the darkness.

I opened my mouth, took a look at Peggy as she scuttled around the car in a half crouch, and did the same.

Dick started the car and said, "Get down on the floor, both of you."

"But . . ."

"Merry, shut up," Peggy said. Her voice came from somewhere under the dashboard. I ducked as Dick swung the car and started down the precipitous driveway.

He turned on the headlights after we passed the first turn, effectively shielding us from the parking area. Twenty feet farther, he stopped and shut them off again. "We'll wait for Geoff here." He opened his center console and pulled out a big revolver.

"How come the guys get all the armament?" I asked. "My Glock's in the center console of Hiram's truck. I could have gotten it."

"Unless we're facing an army, which I doubt, this should be enough," Dick said.

We sat. The country is never silent, certainly not at the end of May. Every frog and toad in a ten-mile radius was advertising his reliability as a pollywog progenitor. The evening breeze murmured in the trees and rustled the new leaves. The pine trees answered shuuussshhh. Small limbs on the oak trees crackled and popped.

That was no oak tree!

Real shots don't reverberate like shots on television. They sound thin and unimportant like a balloon popped by a child. Everyone in the car had enough firearms experience to know we'd heard two.

"Stay down," Dick said and shoved my head down when I peered over the back seat.

"We have to help Geoff," I said as I reached for the door handle. "He could be hurt." Or worse. My adrenaline started pumping and my mouth went dry. I did not want anything bad to happen to him. Not until I'd had a chance to scream at him for scaring me to death.

"You move and I'll bash you over your hard head with the butt of this pistol, Meredith," Dick said. When he called me Meredith, I knew he wasn't kidding.

"Flashlight," Dick said. "Coming down the drive."

Peggy made a sound somewhere between a moan and a whimper, but she stayed on the floor.

"Geoff?" Dick called. He used his strong courtroom voice. He'd opened his driver's door and hunkered down behind it in true highway patrol fashion with his gun in his hand. Dick was the gentlest, most courtly man I knew, but he'd been a marine in Korea. That experience doesn't go away.

"Yeah."

"You okay?"

"Yeah. Whoever it was got away." Gun and flashlight in hand, he walked down the hill toward us.

I jumped out of the car and threw myself at him. "You nitwit! You could be dead!"

"Merry, I'm afraid you need a new motion sensor light on the far side of the stable. Whoever was up there shot it out."

He holstered his weapon and tossed his flashlight to Peggy before he wrapped his arms around me. I plastered myself to him like a Nicotine patch. He felt warm and solid. I felt cold and trembly.

"What happened?" Peggy said. She climbed out from under the dashboard.

"When I rounded the corner of the workshop, I saw someone hauling ass down the lane between the pastures, and I mean booking. I ran after him, but he was past the throw distance of my flashlight and on the edge of the light from the stable. After I tripped and damned near fell, he turned and shot out the motion sensor over my head."

"You returned fire?" Dick asked.

281

"Yeah. *I* missed."

"Hell of a shot," Dick said.

"Unless he was aiming for *you,*" I said. I was still clinging to him and tried to step back, but he pulled me tighter. I didn't resist.

"Don't think so, but I hit the dirt just in case. By the time I got up and found my flashlight, he was long gone."

"But where did he go?" Peggy asked. "There's nothing back there but the fence line. It's a cul-de-sac at the edge of the governor's property."

"Beyond the boundary fence, it's all woods and vines and drop offs," I said. "And snakes. I wouldn't go down that hill in broad daylight with a shotgun, much less in the dark with a pistol. Could you tell if it was a man or a woman?"

"Could have been either. The usual bad guy uniform — black jeans, black hoodie, probably ski mask. No face, at any rate."

"Tall or short?" Dick asked. "Fat or thin?"

"Medium. Didn't run like a girl."

"Huh. These days half the women around don't run like girls," Peggy said. "Merry certainly doesn't."

"I'd rather drive a carriage. I only run when I'm chasing horses," I said. "I've seen game trails on the governor's property," I

282

pointed past our fence. "But they're not easy to spot in full daylight, much less in the dark. If somebody escaped that way, wouldn't you have seen a light in the woods?"

Geoff shook his head. "Not in that underbrush, if they aimed the light at the ground in front of them. Barn and stable were both locked."

"We lock the barn when we leave because that's where all Hiram's tools are. My contractor's bonded, of course. He or his foreman is always around when they're working, so they make sure none of Hiram's tools go missing during the day."

"So, the barn is unlocked during the day?" Geoff asked.

"We tried locking it all the time, but we kept having to chase down the key to get something. Waste of time. We store things in there we need during the day."

"Like what?"

"Fence posts, sheets of plywood, wire, extra carriages that we're not using or that need mending . . ."

"So one of the workmen could case the barn during the day and come back after dark to break in," Dick said.

Peggy nodded. "I do hope not. Bobby would be so upset. I've caught a couple of the men peeking in the barn during the day. One guy told me he was just interested in the carriages."

"I found tool marks around the door. *Somebody* tried to get in," Geoff said. "It's a heavy door, but half an hour with a good crowbar would jimmy it open."

"I didn't find any suspicious tool marks before I left."

"Must have scared the bejasus out of whoever it was when we drove into the lot," Dick said. "Want me to come back after I drop you all and keep an eye on the place tonight?"

"If anyone stays, I will," I said.

"No you won't. Not after the last time." He turned to Dick. "Nothing else will happen tonight. Probably long gone across the fence," Geoff said.

"I hope he gets bit by a rattler," I said. Whoever tried to break in had violated my place, and by extension, me. The only good thing was that Geoff seemed to be relaxing his hands-off policy towards me since he'd been shot at.

"I'd like to check the other gate before we drive back to Mossy Creek," I said. "If this is the same person who knocked me into the cellar, that's the way he got in last night. He might have crossed the pasture and left the same way."

We drove around and found the new gate for the second driveway untouched. "He'd need a car to get here," Peggy said. "We didn't hear one drive down this road. So where is it?"

"Maybe he hitchhiked," I said.

"Nobody picks up hitchhikers at night along this road."

"Is there anywhere to park a car on the governor's side?" Geoff asked. "That's where he disappeared."

"I assume so," I said. "I know they have hunting parties over there in the fall, and I see cars and trucks turning in from time to time when I have to go to Bigelow that way. They could be running a meth lab or a casino over there for all I know. I avoid the place. Whoever it was is long gone whichever way they went." I decided to check out the fence line between my place and the governor's land tomorrow morning. Maybe I'd find a marked trail and evidence of a parked car at the bottom of the hill. And I wouldn't tell anyone ahead of time I was doing it. They'd all have a fit.

This time when we drove away, Geoff and I were belted in, but he reached across, took my hand and held it all the way to his hotel.

CHAPTER 26

Late Tuesday night
Geoff

Geoff sat at his laptop in his hotel room and wrote up his notes. Too many people were better off with Raleigh dead. But what pressure had made one of them commit murder at that particular time and place, and in that way?

If Raleigh truly intended to fire Brock, then killing his boss might preserve Brock's job as well as hide the reason behind Raleigh's anger at him. So, what did Raleigh have on Brock? And how dangerous was the knowledge? How deeply involved was Gwen Standish, the veterinarian?

Of course, Geoff couldn't rule out the beautiful widow. If Raleigh had discovered Sarah Beth was pregnant by another man, she'd be better off as a widow before Monday morning when Raleigh could institute divorce proceedings.

Who was the father? Brock? Armando? Mr. Clemons, the priest? Or someone completely out of left field?

And what about Dawn? If Raleigh had given his daughter an ultimatum about dumping the polo player, she'd have motive to kill him before he could disown her. But would he? As an important cog in his business empire and his breeding and training operation, she was not easily replaced. Geoff felt fairly certain Raleigh would have kept threatening, while trying to talk her around.

Or maybe he held a different kind of threat over Dawn's head? Could he actually have the polo player deported? How quickly? So, what did Dawn *believe* her father would do and when?

As for Armando, his alibi checked out. He played two games on Saturday and was on the polo field in Palm Beach as a referee when Dawn called him to tell him about her father. That didn't mean he didn't have some involvement or know Dawn's intentions.

Other possibilities?

Technical delegate Catherine Harris certainly loathed Raleigh, but Geoff couldn't see that she was under any time pressure to get rid of him. He couldn't have her fired. He couldn't even force her to fire Troy, her assistant.

Geoff had been surprised to discover that Troy Wilkinson and Harris slept in separate rooms at the motel. He was even more surprised to find that Morgan, Troy's girlfriend from college, had joined him for the weekend.

Catherine and Troy met at the motel to drive to the show grounds on Sunday morning about the time Raleigh's body was found.

Then there was Gwen, the vet. Geoff wanted to know how she'd managed to equip that clinic and vet van so expensively. He agreed with Peggy that Brock was probably her partner and that they could have something to do with illicit drugs.

Tomorrow he'd call his buddy at the DEA to see if he had any suggestions about what the pair might be up to.

Raleigh had screwed a bunch of people one way or another. Any of them might have killed him or even paid to have him killed.

Harry Tolliver said he'd gotten out of Raleigh's dubious financial schemes while the getting was good, but he could be lying. Others might not have been so astute — or so lucky. For that matter, the governor's cronies could have had Raleigh killed. That crowd did not like to lose.

The forensic accountant in Atlanta had only begun to dig into Raleigh's records. Could it be significant that the person he'd chased at Lackland Farm had disappeared onto the governor's land?

Geoff realized he needed to stop calling it the governor's land. The governor was only one of a consortium of owners. But if they hunted over that land, then the entire consortium would be much more familiar with the pathways than anyone else.

Finally, he needed to ask Dick Fitzgibbons why he and Raleigh hated one another.

Chapter 27

Merry

It was clear and hot for Raleigh's funeral. An amazing number of people had driven up from Atlanta for the services, and all those bodies were taxing the air conditioning. Governor Ham Bigelow and his acolytes stood outside intercepting any previous or possible future contributors to his campaigns. Eventually, he went into the church, made sympathetic noises to Sarah Beth and Dawn, then slid into the pew just behind them as though he were a member of the family.

Sarah Beth was certainly a glamorous widow in a plain black linen sheath that probably cost as much as my pickup truck. She also wore a big black Panama hat, black nylons, and black kid gloves. Even she didn't go so far as to wear a veil. In north Georgia in late May she'd have asphyxiated.

"Everyone knows you don't wear black

kid gloves after Easter," Peggy whispered.

"I don't wear gloves except when I drive," I whispered back. "And they're always brown." I was wearing my good black slacks and a black linen shirt, black flats, and no hat. I had one bad moment when Peggy threatened to wear her teal driving hat, but I talked her out of it.

Dawn was dressed like me. She sat on the front pew with Armando between her and Sarah Beth. They seemed cordial enough for stepdaughter and stepmother. I wondered if that would survive the division of Raleigh's estate.

The Episcopal service for the dead is remarkably impersonal. Everybody gets the same service, because we are all equal in death. Eulogies are a recent addition. I was afraid the governor might give one — he's noted for long speeches — but the only person who spoke about Raleigh was Father Clemons, who piled platitude upon platitude.

The governor did walk along behind the closed coffin with the other pall-bearers including Brock and Harry Tolliver, some of the other driving men and a number of obviously rich businessmen, probably from Atlanta. Neither Dick nor Armando was included.

The interment was in the churchyard itself, so everyone followed as the funeral people wheeled the coffin on a gurney. Most of the honorary pall-bearers were too old, too fat or both to chance actually toting the coffin.

I spotted Catherine Harris with her arm linked through her assistant Troy's. She hadn't come to the viewing while I was there, but that's not unusual in the south. Most people don't bother with both. I wouldn't have if I hadn't been snooping.

The grave was in full sunlight. While the family sat on chairs under a big green tent that covered the open grave, the rest of us had to cluster in the sun. I started sweating immediately. I could feel my shirt sticking to my back.

I was surprised to see Morgan what's-her-name, Troy's girlfriend, standing across from me. I didn't think she knew Raleigh except to speak to. Maybe she came to support Troy. Maybe Troy and Catherine really had never been anything besides employer and employee. Even scandalous gossip can be wrong.

Troy could sure pick 'em. I'd barely glimpsed Morgan at the Tollivers' Saturday night party and thought she was beautiful. In full daylight she was downright gorgeous.

She had long straight mahogany hair, the figure of a Victoria's Secret model — not the anorexic runway kind — and instead of slacks, she wore an actual dress of some sort of floaty black silk. She didn't look like a mourner, but like a woman gloating over her enemy's funeral pyre.

After the service, Peggy and I stayed to speak to Sarah Beth. She was obviously zonked out of her gourd. I hoped all the tranquilizers wouldn't hurt the baby.

"You are coming to the house, aren't you?" she said as she clasped Peggy's hand. "Please — all these people I don't know . . ."

Peggy said that of course we'd come. Nuts. I had horses to work and chores to do and a final meeting with the Mossy Creek Garden Club about volunteers for the weekend's show and clinic. And I intended to put on my heaviest boots and attempt to find a trail through the governor's property.

"Just for that, you can go to the stupid garden club volunteer briefing alone," I whispered. She dug her fingernails into my arm. "Ouch!"

"Serves you right."

We fell into step behind Catherine and Troy, with Morgan coming up the rear a couple of steps behind them.

As we reached the driveway, four patrol cars with blue lights blazing and sirens howling pulled up in front of us.

We all froze. I thought, he's really going to arrest me for murder just because I found the damn body. Feeling my heart speed up and my eyes glaze, I searched for Geoff and saw him talking to Stan Nordstrom. Surely he could have persuaded Nordstrom to do it later, privately and not in front of all these people. I was going to kill him for embarrassing me like this. After I made bail, that is.

"Troy Wilkinson, I have a warrant for your arrest."

"What?" I gasped.

We all stared at Sheriff Nordstrom. He looked like a modern Siegfried in his spit and polish uniform with his shining white gold hair. As I recall, Siegfried wasn't noted for brains. He married his aunt.

"Hey, man, you're crazy. I didn't do anything," Troy snarled.

"Turn around." The sheriff pulled a pair of handcuffs off his belt.

"This is insane." Catherine stepped between them. Not a good move since Stan was armed and about nine-feet three to her five foot eight. "What are the charges?"

"Malicious mischief, criminal assault, and

domestic terrorism for a start. May be upgraded to murder at a later date."

"Murder?" Troy howled. I thought for a moment he was going to turn tail and run, but he glanced over at Morgan and subsided.

"Terrorism?" Catherine shrieked, then dropped her voice to a whisper. "Do you have to do this now?" All the mourners listened avidly. "Whatever this is about, I assure you I'll bring Troy down to your offices tomorrow to straighten out this foolishness."

"Can't take that chance, ma'am," Sheriff Nordstrom said. He turned Troy around and clicked the handcuffs around his wrists. "He could decide to run."

"Ow! Man, that hurts. They're too tight." Troy yanked as one of the deputies clicked handcuffs over his wrists.

"Sheriff, loosen them at once unless you want a lawsuit on your hands," Catherine said. "Troy, do you have any idea what this is about?"

He refused to meet her eyes. The sheriff didn't loosen the cuffs either.

The sheriff sounded downright gleeful. "Son, if you're going to order a banner on line, next time don't use your PayPal account to pay for it."

"Banner?" Catherine asked. "What banner? Troy, what's he talking about?"

Out of the corner of my eye I saw Morgan sidle quietly back into the crowd and off toward the trees.

I headed after her. "Wait up."

She gave me a malevolent glare over her shoulder and quickened her pace. She was fast, but she was wearing five inch spike heels. I was wearing flats. As she reached her red Mini-Cooper, I caught up and leaned my hand on her car door, so she couldn't pull it open without physically dislodging me.

"Deserting the sinking ship?" I asked.

"I don't know what you're talking about. I have to get back to school."

"Did you buy the bullhorn? Or did you con Troy into paying for that as well as the banner?"

"What bullhorn?" she asked. Miss Innocent. As if.

"Honey, you must be right up there with Cleopatra in bed to convince Troy to put his job with Catherine on the line for your stupid animal rights prank."

"Prank?" She shoved me away from the door. She was smaller, but she was younger and probably worked out. I don't. "It wasn't a prank! It's the truth. God, I *hate* you

296

people." She climbed into her car and nearly caught my fingers when she slammed the door, turned on the ignition and yelled through the closed window, "Get out of my way or I'll run over you."

I believed her. I stepped back.

She gunned the little car down the hill and out onto the road. The Mini-Cooper might be small, but it tops out at a hundred and thirty five miles an hour. If Stan Nordstrom and his deputies had been on their toes, they could have given her a gigantic speeding ticket.

As it was, Nordstrom was too busy bundling Troy into the back of a squad car. They really do that hand-on-the-head thing. Catherine wanted to go with him, but Peggy held her back.

"Let me speak to him," Catherine begged. "Troy, surely you didn't have anything to do with that banner. My God, you could have hurt horses!"

He ducked out of her grasp and refused to look at her. As they drove away, thankfully without sirens, Catherine screamed after him, "Don't say a single word until my lawyer gets there."

Some about-face. When she discovered that banner and bullhorn she'd been ready to rip the skin off whoever was responsible.

Now she was going to provide a lawyer? Troy must have *something* going for him.

Was he sleeping with *both* Catherine and Morgan?

When he spotted me, Geoff walked up the hill to intercept me.

"Did you know about this?" I snapped. "*Troy* set up the banner? And just like that, Catherine's ready to forgive him? What was all that about upgrading to murder? Troy couldn't have killed Raleigh. You said he was in bed with Morgan at the time."

"No, *he* said he was in bed with Morgan," Geoff said.

"Could be they killed Raleigh together and alibied each other. That little cobra could probably convince Troy to throw himself into a live volcano so long as she didn't kick him out of her bed."

"Maybe he ordered the banner and they set it up together." Geoff shook his head. "Talk about biting the hand that feeds you."

"I doubt Catherine will be feeding him much longer. I haven't talked to him that much, but he never mentioned animal rights. What is he, some kind of sleeper agent? He knows how Catherine feels about putting horses in danger."

"I'm sure Morgan La Fey told him it was perfectly safe — a way to get some publicity and infuriate Raleigh. Raleigh was supposed to get the full force of the voice and the banner, remember."

"Why? Catherine hated Raleigh all right, but what's he ever done to Morgan or Troy?"

"I intend to find out." Geoff took my arm. "And no, I did not know Stan was going to arrest Troy at the cemetery. Not a bad idea, though."

"How can you say that? Catherine's a basket case and Troy's probably throwing up in the back of the squad car."

We walked up to my truck, and he leaned against the door. "He'd better not. Stan is fastidious about his vehicles."

"Be serious."

"I *am* serious. I hope Troy's switching to damage control mode."

"He should serve Morgan up like a roast pig with an apple in her mouth," I said. "She is not a nice person."

Geoff shook his head sadly. "You really don't understand men, do you? The way he feels about Morgan, he'd go to the firing squad minus blindfold to save her."

That remark about understanding men stung. He was right, of course, but that didn't make it any easier to take. If I'd understood Vic, I wouldn't have married him in the first place.

I remembered Catherine said Troy had been the last person to check the start of the course the night before the marathon. He and Morgan had all the time in the world to set up the prank.

"He did buy the banner and borrow the bullhorn," Geoff said. "And he's studying structural engineering. He could have easily figured out how to trigger and unfurl the thing."

"I still don't believe Troy killed Raleigh," I said.

He put a hand under my arm and guided me to a bench under the shade of a large water oak. A breeze had sprung up, and the shade felt blissfully cool. One good thing about summer in Mossy Creek — it's cooler and shorter than summer in Atlanta and bracketed by a glorious spring and superb fall.

"How did you find out Troy bought the banner?" I asked.

"My office ran a computer check on the sign shops in Atlanta and Augusta looking for a banner ordered with those words," Geoff said. "Nada. Then we tried the Internet. Fourth or fifth try we got a hit on his order. Stan was right. Not a good idea to use his own PayPal account. Like ordering

C-4 on your American Express card."

"Nobody said Troy was a genius. What does Morgan see in him?"

"Access and a faithful minion. Talk about treating *horses* like slaves."

I didn't really care what Morgan had against Raleigh, if anything. I was mad at her for nearly drowning me, Peggy, and the Halflingers. And if Troy's arrest caused Catherine to back out of judging my show this weekend, I intended to use the four oxen dismemberment process on good ole Morgan. "Pretty obvious which portion of his anatomy she's leading him around by."

"Ouch."

I saw the same Dahlonega catering van parked around the side of the Raleigh's mansion by the kitchen door and wondered if we'd be getting leftovers from the viewing.

I needn't have worried. The long dining room table held a carved country ham at one end and a carved roast beef at the other with veggies, condiments, and bread between them. The sideboard was covered with platters of little bitty tarts and brownies, along with soft drinks, coffee and tea. Whichever part of Raleigh's estate was paying for his funeral, the bill would add up to a hefty chunk of change.

"I know Raleigh was a sleaze bucket," I whispered to Peggy as I slathered Dijon mustard on party rye and added a slice of rare roast beef. "As much as I disliked him, I do agree with Mrs. Willy Loman in *Death of a Salesman.* Attention must be paid."

"Yeah, but what *kind* of attention? We both know we wouldn't be here if we weren't snooping," Peggy said.

"There's Armando. I'm going to pay my respects. Geoff says he has a solid alibi."

"Dawn doesn't."

I munched on my sandwich as I threaded my way to the living room. Armando stood with one elbow on the fireplace mantle. He was alone, but completely at ease. He watched the ebb and flow of mourners — or what passed for mourners — with a slight smile. Perfect for an ad in *Town and Country.*

I finished my sandwich and sauntered up to him. "Hey," I said. "I'm Merry Abbott. We met last night."

He gave me full wattage with those black eyes and those white teeth in that tanned face. My knees went weak. The guy radiated pheromones. "Of course I remember. You train driving horses, yes?"

"Right."

"I met your father in Palm Beach several

years ago. Nice man. I'm sorry about what happened to him."

I nodded acknowledgement. "You going back to Wellington to finish the polo season?"

His muscles were lean and long, and he seemed supremely comfortable in his body. "I hope to take Dawn with me. She needs to get away from all this. And my horses are still in Wellington. I have someone I trust looking after them, but . . ."

"Nobody is as trustworthy as you are," I finished.

He gave me that grin again. This time I was prepared. My heart rate only went up ten beats per minute. "Brock can certainly look after *this* place. He's done it for years."

"So Dawn plans to keep him on?" I asked.

"Of course."

"Even when you start training polo ponies here?"

"Come on, you know horse is horse. Riding, driving, polo . . . managing a stable of horses is much the same in any discipline. I will be training and traveling. I hope Dawn will go with me some of the time. And there is Giles's business to run. She has great responsibilities."

"I don't guess Sarah Beth could handle any of it," I said.

303

He snorted with laughter. "Not for a day."

"So she's moving back to Atlanta?"

He looked confused. "I have not heard. This is as much her home as Dawn's. Why would she not stay?"

Because three's a crowd, doofus, I thought.

"In Argentina, families stay together if possible," he said.

But did Dawn consider Sarah Beth family? I wondered if Raleigh had left the women equal shares in his estate. They seemed to get along, but unless they worked out non-conflicting spheres of interest, I didn't think that would last.

"Armando, darling," Dawn was suddenly at his side, "Father Clemons is leaving." She slipped her hand under Armando's arm, smiled at me and moved him away where I couldn't ask him any more questions. Nuts.

Later, I made good on my threat to send Peggy to the Garden Club meeting to go over the final arrangements for Lackland Farm's fun show and clinic. Alone.

CHAPTER 28

Peggy

One of the nice things about being rich was that you get things done quickly. Dick decided over breakfast and before they left for Raleigh's funeral that he would put in CCTV not only at both gates of Hiram's farm, but add one in the parking lot in front of the barn, and another that showed the inside of the stable. He made a few calls and assured Peggy that they'd have CCTV before the day was done.

"Might as well be able to check on the horses at night without getting out of bed," he said. "Who knows, Merry might breed a couple of mares who would need watching when they came close to foaling."

"Wouldn't that be fun?" Peggy said as she poured him another cup of coffee. "Not quite as good as grandchildren, but close."

He wrapped his arm around her waist and pulled her onto his lap. *Shameless behavior for a pair of old fogies like us,* Peggy thought.

"Horses are much better than grand-children," he said. "No diapers, and you can teach them manners and sell them when they're two or three."

"I've never seen a mare foal," Peggy said, and took a bite of his toast.

"You might never see one," he said. "Mares are sneaky. They wait until every-one's back is turned, then pop goes the weasel."

He finished his coffee and took his mug and breakfast plate to the sink, rinsed them and put them into the dishwasher.

Peggy had no idea why she and Dick hit it off. After his wife had died, several years ago, he'd turned into a player, escorting all the beautiful young widows and divorcees in Palm Beach and New York to society balls and gallery openings.

Peggy considered herself neither beautiful nor young, but Dick didn't seem to care. He said he'd gotten tired of having to explain the Second World War to his dates. And despite being waited on hand and foot at his farm, he was comfortable putting his dishes in Peggy's dishwasher. Neither of them was interested in marriage or even liv-ing together, but they did enjoy their oc-casional illicit weekends.

The one who ought to be having illicit weekends, though, was Merry. Apparently she'd have to be a serial killer to get Geoff to visit Mossy Creek on a regular basis.

Peggy loved the garden club ladies, but she wasn't in the mood to handle a committee meeting when she wanted to be doing something with Dick. Still, she'd promised Merry.

Having worked all her life until she retired to Mossy Creek, Peggy had sat through innumerable faculty meetings, which could be more contentious than the Super Bowl. The Mossy Creek Garden Club ladies could handle a dozen jobs at once. Unfortunately, they also liked to talk about them.

If she intended to stay awake for Don Qui's debut as a carriage donkey, she'd have to avoid the Mimosas, which were lethal, as Geoff Wheeler could attest.

The meeting should go fast, a final check of who would do what at the show. Then she could drive out to the farm.

Dick wanted to drive Heinzie, the Friesian he had sold to Merry, and assist her in putting Don Qui to a real Meadowbrook cart instead of a truck tire if Merry decided it was time to try. If all went well, Dick might actually take the reins and sit inside the cart. That might be hair raising, but it would be fun to watch.

Merry

Don Qui sensed my disquiet. Horses —
equines — can always tell. He started danc-
ing on the wash rack. Peggy shoved me out
of the way and took the curry comb away
from me. "Go help Dick drag the Meadowbrook out from under the marathon cart in
the trailer."

Dick and I unfolded it once we'd horsed
it down the ramp and onto the parking lot,
then I pulled it around the stable. I was having second thoughts about putting Don Qui
to today, but I didn't have the nerve to say
anything.

Particularly when Peggy and a
harnessed-up Don Qui walked out the back
of the stable as we pulled the cart around
the corner.

"Shouldn't he pull his tire for a while
first?" Peggy asked. I could tell she was feeling nervous as well.

"Nah," Dick said. He was running on
adrenaline. "I'll take the reins and walk
behind the cart. I won't try to get in unless
he's calm, and Merry will be holding the
long line attached to his halter. We'll tie the
left seat up so I can bail if I have to. What's
the harm? He won't do anything."

"The cowboy's obituary — 'Aw, he ain't gonna do nothin','" I said.

In the end Dick persuaded us.

After he was in draft, Don Qui felt the cart behind him, and as before, he stood considering it for a while. Then he walked forward. I held the long line attached to his halter. Dick held the reins.

It looked like a non-event. Dick inched forward until he could step on the back of the cart and ease into the right seat without halting the cart completely.

Don Qui hesitated when he felt Dick's extra weight and bowed his little back preparing to buck, but Dick clucked and cajoled. A moment later he walked on. I started to relax.

Big mistake.

"Merry!" shouted a female voice. "Where are you? I have to talk to you right now."

Talk about straws breaking donkey's backs. Don Quit had definitely reached the point where one more distraction, no matter how tiny, would tip the balance.

"Whoa!" All three of us, Dick, Peggy and I yelled at the same moment.

Don Qui refused to acknowledge he'd ever heard the word. He kicked back, missed Dick's cheek by an eyelash, and plunged across the arena in a series of bucks that would have done a rodeo proud.

"Oh, my God, Merry!" came the voice. "I'm so sorry!"

As she ran out into the sun I saw it was Catherine Harris. She was grabbing at her broad-brimmed hat, which skittered across the grass away from the arena and not into it. Thank God. A flying saucer in his path was all Don Qui would need to become airborne himself, cart and all.

The mice had been playing hide-and-seek in Catherine's graying hair, and her jeans looked as though she'd slept in them. She was still wearing her driving gloves. She seemed to have forgotten she had them on.

None of us acknowledged her. We were busy. Dick stomped the brake while I hung on to the long line and Peggy wrung her hands.

It seemed to take eons to calm the little devil down. Actually, it probably took less than a minute, and then he did what he'd done before. He seemed to recall himself, stopped bucking and trotted off as though he'd been hauling milk wagons in County Cork all his life.

Dick was happy to let him trot. "He wants to go," Dick said cheerfully. "I'll let him trot until he's sick of it."

I had to run to keep hold of the line, but I

needn't have bothered. Finally, Dick brought him a walk right beside Catherine. I thought she was going to faint.

"I had no idea. I know better, but I'm so . . ." She burst into tears.

I could see Peggy rolling her eyes. Catherine was obviously here to cancel her participation at our weekend show. Where I was going to get another judge or clinician at this late date I had no idea. Maybe Catherine could recommend someone close and not too pricey.

"Dick, can you and Peggy take care of this while I talk to Catherine?"

"Go," Dick said. Peggy nodded.

"Come on," I took Catherine's arm and half dragged her to the clients' lounge. She kept looking back over her shoulder at Don Qui.

"You're not going to show that donkey Saturday, are you?" she asked.

"Good lord, no! This is the first time he's ever been put to. He's a long way from showing." I shoved her down on the leather sofa in the clients' lounge, pulled a pair of diet sodas from the fridge and handed one to her. She looked at it as though she wasn't certain what to do with it, so I took it, popped the top and handed it back to her.

She drank half of it in one long pull. "I

didn't realize I was so thirsty," she said.

"Okay, Catherine. Lay it on me. Are you backing out of this weekend?"

Her eyes widened. "Of course not. That would be unforgiveable."

I let out my breath. She sat staring at me without speaking.

"Did you manage to get Troy out of jail?" I asked.

She leaned back and dragged her hand over her eyes. "Thank heaven, my lawyer called a judge we know. My husband Paul saved his life a few years ago when he ruptured an appendix, so he let Troy out on his own recognizance. That sheriff didn't want to let him go, but he didn't have a choice. There's no real evidence Troy had anything to do with Raleigh's death. And domestic terrorism? Puh-leeze!"

"Where is he?"

"He went on back to school. I'm still afraid that stupid sheriff will try to tie him into Raleigh's death simply because he can't find anybody else to charge."

"What did Troy have to say about the banner?"

She raised both hands against her chest as though she were warding off an expected blow. "It's that damned Morgan. She's bewitched him. He's older than the other

312

freshmen, but he's incredibly naïve. He begged me to forgive him. Of course I did."

I squashed the can the way I would like to have squashed his neck and made another stab at hitting the garbage can. I missed. Again. "No 'of course' about it. In my book he should be fired and left to twist slowly in the wind."

"I can't." She dropped her head in her hands.

"Sure you can."

She whispered through her fingers. "I can't abandon him again." She sucked in a shuddering breath. "He's my son."

I must not have heard her right. "You love him like a son?"

She looked me straight in the eye, and said, "Troy Wilkinson is my *son.* You have to help him, Merry. Talk to Agent Wheeler, talk to that Sheriff person. Tell them he's innocent."

"If he's innocent, he'll be fine." I was reeling. My mouth was operating, but my *brain* was several steps behind.

"He's bewitched by Morgan and acting all stupid and gallant, and he's willing to own up to that banner nonsense. I'll pay whatever fine they want. If you want a settlement . . ."

It hadn't felt like nonsense to me when I

was trying to keep my horses from drowning. "Of course I don't want a settlement. Dick's carriage didn't get a scratch. Nobody was hurt. If he's innocent of Raleigh's death . . ."

She snapped, "Innocent people are convicted all the time." The snap turned into a whine. "I've only just got him back, Merry. I can't lose him again. You *have* to help me."

No, I didn't. "Be sensible, Catherine. Nothing I say cuts any ice with Geoff Wheeler, and Sheriff Nordstrom is still half convinced *I* killed Raleigh. I'm staying under his radar. I don't see what I can do."

She grabbed my free hand and held it hard for an instant before I took it back. "I swore I'd never tell you this, but I'm at my wits end. You have to help him. He's your half-brother."

At first I didn't think I'd heard properly. I backed away from her as though she were contagious. "No way." I felt as though my legs wouldn't hold me.

"It's true, Merry. Hiram Lackland is Troy's father."

"You're maybe two, three years older than I am, and Troy is twenty-five?"

"Twenty-six."

"So you're saying Hiram, my father, got you pregnant when you were how old?"

"Eighteen."

The only way I was going to stop my head from shaking like a metronome was to put my hands on either side of my skull and physically hold my brain in. "Hiram went for married women with experience. He was no pedophile."

"And I was no child. Merry, neither of us intended for it to happen."

"Big whoop."

"Please, let me explain."

"Hey, have at it. I love a good story." My crisis calm set in. Later when and *if* I told Peggy, I'd probably have hysterics.

I edged back to the overstuffed chair in front of the couch and slumped into it.

She wouldn't meet my eyes. "You have to understand how miserable Hiram and I both were that summer. Paul had just left to spend thirteen months finishing his military service in a hospital in Germany. We'd promised my parents we'd put off marrying until he got home, and my mother wouldn't even let me go visit. She was afraid if I went to Germany, we'd elope while I was there, and she wouldn't get to put on her fancy wedding."

That might sound ridiculous to some people, but if Catherine had eloped in Germany, her southern society mother would have considered it treason.

"You'd cut your father out of your life," Catherine continued.

I bristled. No way was this my fault.

"Your mother had remarried. He was still in love with her. He was miserable too and as lonely as I was."

"I'll buy that, but not that he'd drown his sorrows by getting a teenager pregnant. How did you even *know* him?"

"I was a working student that summer where he was training in Virginia. I groomed for him and cooled his horses down in exchange for lessons. He was there for me, and I guess I was there for him. We both needed somebody to talk to. We got to be friends."

"Is that what you call it? A teenager and a forty-something man? An authority figure and his student?" Lord, this was getting worse and worse. As much as I didn't want to believe Hiram could have done something so unethical, so stupid, I didn't really know my father at that point, so I couldn't rule it out.

"Please, Merry." She reached across the coffee table to grasp my hands. I pulled them away before she could. I was afraid of what I'd do if she touched me.

"It wasn't supposed to happen, Merry. You

know how exhibitors' parties are. Open bar. Nobody cared how old I was. I was drinking a lot. So was he. One night after a party, he took me back to his trailer to keep me from driving back to my rooming house, and it . . . happened. Only once. It ruined our friendship. Hiram was horrified, especially when he discovered I was a virgin."

"He didn't use protection?"

"Apparently the condom failed. I didn't think you could get pregnant your first time, so when I missed my period in August, I didn't think anything about it. I went back to William and Mary in September for my sophomore year and didn't get scared until I'd missed my second period. Then I took one of those home pregnancy tests."

"What did he say when you told him?" I could see him arranging an abortion for her, or even offering to marry her. Now that *really* would have infuriated her mother.

"I *didn't* tell him." She sounded appalled at the suggestion. "I *never* told him."

"He never knew he had a son? Catherine . . ."

"At first I decided to get an abortion. But I simply couldn't. I didn't want to tell my parents. I didn't dare tell Paul. I was afraid he'd dump me. He always talked about how I would be his virgin bride." She snorted.

"Not that he was a virgin. Not by a long shot."

"But you couldn't hide it from your folks. What about Thanksgiving? Christmas?"

"I wasn't showing at Thanksgiving. My mother accused me of waiting until my sophomore year to put on my freshman fifteen pounds. I kept hoping I'd miscarry. I tried all the old wives' remedies. None of them worked. Then one of my sorority sisters who realized what was going on gave me the name of a lawyer in Philadelphia who arranged private adoptions. He'd pay my medical expenses, and I'd give up my baby for adoption when it was born.

"I told my parents I was going skiing in Aspen over Christmas. Mother was furious, but Daddy said I was growing up and to leave me be. Mother hates to travel, and Daddy wasn't able to by that time, so they couldn't come up to Williamsburg to visit me. I've always been thin, and until late spring I could wear loose, bulky clothes.

"My sorority sisters knew, of course, and everyone suspected, but nobody said anything. I went to Philadelphia for spring break and they induced labor two weeks early." She covered her face with her hands. "They didn't even let me see him or hold him. They said it was better that way. When

I went home after the semester, I told my parents I'd had a terrible bout of the flu, which is why I was so thin and peaky and cried all the time. By the time Paul came home, I was physically fine. Mother got her twelve bridesmaids, and Paul got his virgin bride. Or so he thought."

"And Hiram never knew he had a son?"

She shook her head. "But I never stopped thinking of my child, wondering who had adopted him, whether he was happy, whether he had a warm coat in the winter or went to the beach in the summer. Then I had Paul, Junior, and Sandra, and Big Paul and I were building his practice. I was working in the office full time and being a wife and mother and life got in the way. I saw Hiram at shows, but neither of us ever mentioned that one night."

"When did Troy find you?"

"He didn't. I found him." She leaned her head back against the couch and closed her eyes as though telling the story had worn her out. I didn't doubt it.

"When Paul died so suddenly, I was devastated. We had a good marriage."

Except for one whopping big secret.

"Then one morning a couple of months after Paul died, I woke up and realized I could finally go find my son."

"So you did? Just like that?"

"Hardly. With computers, it's a lot easier to get information about adoptions now than it used to be, but I had no idea how to go about it, so I hired someone. He found Troy in a little over a month."

"Where?"

"Beckley, West Virginia. His adoptive parents are both high school teachers. Not rich, but he didn't suffer from poverty. He had started college at Blacksburg, but dropped out after one year to take a job in construction when his father had a heart attack. He said he couldn't justify even instate tuition and expenses. He planned to go back, but you know how that is."

I nodded. Once he left, it would be hard for him to go back.

"It took months before he'd agree to meet me. He didn't want to upset his adoptive parents. I respected that, but they finally persuaded him he needed to at least meet me."

"And the rest is history. Happy ending, nice and tidy." I was getting pretty tired of Catherine. I wanted to go hug a horse and get my head around this.

She shook her head violently. "Not at all. He was *so* angry. He accused me of abandoning him. But we talked and talked and emailed and took baby *Facebook* steps to know about each other's lives, and little by little he saw who I was and that I meant it for the best and forgave me." Her nose and eyes were red, and her tears had cut paths through her makeup.

"So how do we get from Beckley to Atlanta?"

"I wanted to do something for him, to get to know him. I offered him full tuition and expenses to Emory. He didn't have any trouble transferring, although his credits were a couple of years old. And I offered him a job working for me at shows on the weekends."

"You know everybody thinks you're sleeping with him?"

She shrugged. "Seemed simplest that way. We both thought it was funny."

I'd bet her mother didn't think it was one bit funny. "So does your family know?"

Her eyes widened. "Oh, no! Not yet. It's just Mother and Sandra and Paul, Junior, now. Paul's at Princeton Law and Sandra's at Randolph Macon. I've worried about the best way to handle introducing Troy. We were thinking maybe Thanksgiving."

Had the woman lost her mind? Then it hit me. Troy was a nice young man, but he had the social polish of a West Virginia trout.

Catherine hadn't only been getting to know her son and introducing him to the driving and social crowd, she'd been grooming him.

"Where does Morgan fit into your plans?"

Catherine snapped to attention. "She doesn't. I know better than to turn her into Juliet to Troy's Romeo by forbidding the relationship, but I've got to make him see that she's destroying his chances for a good life. That banner . . . My God, he could have drowned your horses!"

When a knock sounded on the door of the clients' lounge, we both jumped. Dick stuck his head in and said, "Sorry to interrupt. Just wanted to tell you that Don Qui's back in the pasture and I've locked the Meadowbrook in the barn out of the way. With the show and clinic coming up, I didn't figure you'd have time to drive the little devil before Monday or Tuesday."

"Thanks, Dick. Catherine and I were just going over some final tweaking for the show Saturday." I glanced at her. She gave me a grateful look.

"Yes, I really have to go. Mother's coming to dinner tonight," Catherine said.

I followed her out to her bright red crew cab truck.

"Please tell Agent Wheeler that Troy's innocent," she said. "And whatever you do, don't tell a soul what I told you. Please, I beg you. I wouldn't want my mother and my children to find out before I have a chance to tell them."

I made indeterminate noises. I'd tell Geoff and Peggy and possibly Dick whatever I thought they ought to know.

"Troy plans to apologize to you and Peggy for that awful banner."

"That's not necessary." God, it was the last thing I needed.

"Yes, it is. I haven't told him about your relationship and I won't, not ever, without your permission, but I think if you got to know him you'd like him and want to tell him yourself."

Not damned likely.

She grasped my hand again. Lord, the woman couldn't keep her hands off me or keep herself out of my space. I wanted her gone. I no longer wanted her to judge my show or train on Sunday, but I couldn't cancel without a reason and didn't plan to reveal the one I had. After this weekend I would avoid her and her son — no way would I call him my half-brother. I watched her drive down the hill until the first turn obscured her truck.

Ten minutes later I had Heinzie, the big Friesian, saddled. Since his first excursion riding Peggy and me bareback, I'd ridden him often. Dressage under saddle improved his driving, and vice versa.

Today the riding helped *me.*

Something in my face backed Peggy and Dick off. They went into the clients' lounge and shut the door without asking any questions.

I worked Heinzie in the dressage arena for nearly an hour. By the time I finished cooling him out we were both worn out and sweaty.

Peggy had finished afternoon feed. Everyone except Heinzie was munching happily.

"Don Qui kept an eye on the back door, so he could be certain Heinzie hadn't flown away and left him," Peggy said as she shut Heinzie's stall door so that he could eat his dinner. "He didn't bray. Big step forward."

Bless the woman. She didn't ask a single question. Dick had gone back to her house for a nap before dinner. I hadn't made up my mind what, if anything, to tell them. Dick had been Hiram's friend for twenty years or more. Peggy had been his first and best friend in Mossy Creek.

I hadn't known my father well since I was a child. Peggy and Dick could give me a better take on whether he would or would not deflower an eighteen-year-old virgin and walk away without another thought.

CHAPTER 29

Merry

I finished locking up for the night. Riding Heinzie had helped my mood a bunch. If I had a half brother, I'd have to deal. I was less concerned about the half-brother part than I was about the half-brother as killer possibility.

Peggy was already waiting in my truck, when I heard a car gun up the drive from the road.

"You expecting anyone?" Peggy asked.

I shook my head. The minute I recognized Morgan's red Mini-Cooper, I leaned in, slipped the gun from my center console into the pocket of my jeans jacket and tossed Peggy the truck keys. "Move over and start the engine."

She slid across and started the truck, as Morgan came to a stop a foot from my front bumper. I gripped my Glock and waited while she and Troy got out.

"Mind moving your car?" I asked. "We need to get home."

"Mrs. Abbott?" Troy said. So he hadn't gone back to college as Catherine thought. He'd gone straight to Morgan instead. "Can I talk to you a minute?" He sounded subdued.

Morgan slid out from behind her wheel. "I told you this is stupid. Let's go."

"We came to apologize," Troy said.

"Maybe *you* did. I have nothing to apologize for." She lifted her chin. All that passion, green eyes, red hair, and a body that many men might literally kill for. I wouldn't have liked her *without* the banner and the bullhorn. As it was, I was way past loathing.

"So why did you come with him?" I asked.

"Morgan offered to drive me."

She brushed him off with one peremptory hand. "That harpy he works for told him to apologize or lose his job. He should have told her to shove it, but she's got her hooks into him. I came because I wanted to see the cells where you chain your slaves."

"Sorry, all empty. Move your car or I'll move it for you. This truck can shove your Mini over the cliff." I opened the passenger door.

She said to my back, "We're *right* to do what we do, and if you weren't one of *them,* you'd admit it."

"One of whom?"

"The enslavers of animals. The destroy-
ers."

"Are you one of those people who want
me to turn my horses loose in the Okefeno-
kee Swamp to fend for themselves?"

"They did when they were free."

I turned back to face her. "Some fifteen
thousand years ago, about the time a Mon-
golian shepherd jumped on a pony, or a wolf
ate scraps, curled up warm beside a hunts-
man's fire and got his ears scratched. Your
ancestors might have been able to survive
in the wilderness then too. *You* want to try
it without Bergdorf's and Kroger's?"

"How about the wild mustangs?"

"How about them? They have been on
open range for hundreds of years where
there is at least a modicum of food to eat,
unless they die miserably of drought or
floods or battles for mares or worm infesta-
tions or colic or breach birth or broken legs
or wolves or coyotes or Grizzly bears or
snakebite. Every month I send money to
the human beings who make certain that
they have hay and water, and rabies powder
and a dozen other vaccines, and plenty of
room to roam. And every year human beings adopt some of them and I suspect the

horses are glad of it."

"You can't know that."

"No, I can't. I do see that afterwards they're healthy and relaxed and enjoy being around people. When we domesticated animals we signed a pledge to look after them."

"How paternalistic — you're saying we're better than the animals."

Peggy had climbed out of the truck and come to stand at my shoulder.

"We do have opposable thumbs," she said mildly. "Which makes it easier to serve them by picking up a bale of hay or a hoof pick. Most of us feel a sense of empathy between us and them — herd instinct, if you will. When you put up that stupid banner, you nearly drowned two of your precious animal buddies."

"That wasn't supposed to happen," Troy said. He'd come to apologize, not debate. "No way we thought anybody would get hurt."

"Nobody was, no thanks to you," I snapped. "Troy, I accept that you'd probably have jumped off the Empire State Building to keep getting laid. Morgan used you. She would have been happy to see a couple of horses drown."

"I wanted you *all* to drown, not only the

horses," Morgan snarled.

I saw the astonished look Troy threw her. "You don't mean that."

"Of course I do. We'd have gone viral on the net. I video-taped the whole thing from the woods." She rounded on him. "What did you think would happen? At the very least, that old wrinkly should have drowned." She pointed at Peggy. Uh-oh.

I could see on his face the numb realization that she was dead serious.

"This old wrinkly," Peggy said, "was captain of her swim team at college."

"A million years ago," Morgan sneered.

I put a hand on Peggy's arm. We didn't need to go to jail for assault.

Troy was completely out of his depth. I felt kind of sorry for him, but he should have known better than to let Morgan La Fey drive him out here.

"They'll all *be* better off dead!" Morgan said. 'Kill them all — dogs and cats and sheep and cattle . . .'

"Hey, wait," Troy said. "You never said anything about *killing* them."

"If they're so screwed up they can't live free, then we should kill them. Period," Morgan said. She turned on me. "It's *your* fault. If you hadn't made them dependent, they could survive without you. Since they can't, they should die."

"Human babies are dependent," I said. "Does the same go for them, or is your pogrom just for other species? Just mammals, or do you include birds and reptiles and fish?"

"Man," Troy said. He was staring at Morgan as though he'd never seen her before. "Like I don't believe in testing on animals, or dog fighting and puppy mills and stuff, but *nobody's* killing my dog."

I had a sudden vision of Peggy armed with an AR-15 ready to fend off anyone who tried to hurt her four cats. I'd be standing down at the end of my road with a bazooka or a hand-held missile launcher if I could get my hands on one, ready to protect even Don Qui with my life.

"Grow a pair, why don't you?" Morgan sneered at Troy. "What good are animals? They're already victims, having chemicals poured into their eyes so the rich can have a new moisturizer, or slaughtered so the rich can eat sirloin, or tearing each other apart so the rich can bet on them, or pulling wagons or letting people sit on top of them so the rich can bet on races." World class sneer.

My God, this wasn't about animals. It was about Morgan versus the rich, which, according to Dick, she was part of. She'd even been a debutante. Maybe that was what caused the disconnect.

Peggy had spoken of herd instincts — pity, compassion, love, grief, loyalty — the ineffable connection between human beings and The Other. How could Morgan possibly feel the awe of gazing down at a cat asleep on her lap? Or a horse nuzzling her cheek? For that matter, watching a whale spout or a tiger pad through his jungle. She wasn't doing this because she felt a part of the animal kingdom. She was doing this because she *didn't*.

Morgan was running on hatred and envy. No empathy for animals or human beings either.

I am so grateful and in awe of people who fight to save the mustangs or rescue fighting dogs or stop testing of cosmetics on rats and rabbits or scrub excrement off kennel floors, or protect manatees or break up puppy mills or battle for humane treatment of chickens . . . the list is endless. I may not always agree with them or their methods, but I know they care. Animals are real to them.

"I have a suggestion for you, Morgan," I said. "Go herd sheep in Montana or drive cattle in Texas or volunteer at a veterinarian's office. Go watch what happens when a dog visits an old people's home or opens a door for a kid with MS. See if you get it. I don't think you will, but if you don't give it a try, your soul is going to shrivel up and die on you."

"You self-righteous bitch," she whispered. "I hope one of your precious horses kicks your brains out. Come on, Troy."

"Nunh-uh," he said. "Mrs. Abbott, can I have a ride back to Mossy Creek? My — Catherine can pick me up there." He didn't sound angry so much as stunned.

Morgan threw him a venomous look, dove into the Mini, whipped it around, barely missing the fender of my truck, and spurted gravel all over us.

"Slow down," I shouted. I didn't want her to fly over the edge on her way down. Or did I?

"I'll phone you," Troy called after her, his voice full of hope even now. "We have to talk."

"Don't bother," she shouted over her shoulder.

"I think you just lost a girlfriend," I said.

He watched until the Mini drove out of sight. "She didn't mean all that stuff. She's really a nice person underneath. She's just upset."

"Gee, ya think?"

His shoulders hunched. He was trying to convince himself, not me. And not doing a very good job of it.

In my book she was a dangerous harpy. If anybody I'd met lately seemed capable of murder, she did. But why would she target Raleigh? Did she even know the man?

After a moment, Troy looked up at me. His eyes belonged on a Cocker Spaniel that had just been kicked. "Man, I thought I knew her. I believed in what she said we were doing. Get a little publicity, you know? No harm, no foul. How come I still love her?"

"You'll get over it."

He called Catherine, who promised to pick him up at the Hamilton Inn.

On our drive into Mossy Creek, he sat in the back seat of the truck and never said a word. Neither did Peggy, although I could tell she was itching to discuss what had just happened.

Maybe Raleigh had an actual reason to think that banner was aimed at him. Maybe he even guessed Morgan was behind it and knew why. Had he done one of his seduce-and-run numbers on her? She wouldn't take being dumped by a rich and powerful man well. If she threatened to cause a scandal, he'd fight back hard and dirty.

If he decided to get Troy and Morgan kicked out of school, he'd find a way. A previous animal rights stunt might lead to expulsion. Then there was the perennial favorite of campus cops — smoking dope in the dorm. Everybody did it. The cops usually turned a blind eye.

But they could be convinced or bribed *not* to look the other way.

Had he threatened Morgan after the banner incident?

Maybe she agreed to meet him at the dressage arena Saturday morning to talk him out of it. He'd think she was capitulating. Did she have the strength to knock Giles off his driving seat? Did Troy?

She might step out of the trees and sweet talk him into getting down on his own. Then a tap on the head to drop him, and zap, in goes the spike.

Theoretically, she and Troy had been together in bed at the motel. But he'd have lied for her in a heartbeat. Or he might have been so zonked out from marathon sex that she could have driven an ATV out of the motel room without disturbing him. Or she could have drugged him. Or they were together killing Raleigh.

As Morgan had said, he needed to grow a

pair. She conned him into raising that banner, but after his reaction to her "kill them all" speech, I couldn't see him murdering Raleigh. I needed to report to Geoff, and incidentally ask him if the medical examiner had found any bruises on Raleigh's skull.

CHAPTER 30

Thursday morning
Merry

We needed horse feed, so I ran by our local feed store on my way out to Lackland Farm to pick up a dozen fifty-pound sacks of rolled oats. As I backed out, Brock pulled into the café next door. What was he doing in my neck of the woods? Meeting somebody? It wasn't early for someone like us, but it was early for normal businessmen.

As I pulled out, I saw a black BMW pull into the parking lot and park beside Brock's truck. A moment later Whitehead, the governor's pit bull, climbed out and went inside. Coincidence? Was Brock meeting Whitehead? How could the two men possibly know one another?

Only through Raleigh.

I pulled my hat down low and slunk into the café. Thank God Whitehead and Brock were sitting in a back booth. Neither looked up when I sat down behind them and buried my face in my menu.

"There's a vacancy on your damn board right now," Brock said. He kept his voice low, but I could understand him.

"So?" Whitehead said.

"Put me on it."

Whitehead laughed. "For God's sake, why would we do that?"

"Because the minute I marry Sarah Beth I'll be able to vote her shares."

"You so sure she'll marry you?"

"Hell, man," Brock said, "the woman's carrying my baby."

Whitehead hesitated. "Once you're legally married, then, we'll consider it."

"Then give me an advance on the salary I'd make."

This time Whitehead laughed out loud. "A salary for a job you don't have? I don't think so."

"I need that money. I owe some people."

"Go to a loan shark." Whitehead slipped out of the booth. I turned away and practically memorized my menu.

Brock followed, "Hey, don't walk out on me."

Whitehead didn't answer him. He tossed a bill beside the cash register and let the door close in Brock's face. Brock followed him, protesting all the way.

"You want some coffee, hon?" The waitress asked.

"Uh, I've got an emergency," I said. I gave her a couple of dollars and left. Neither Brock's truck nor the BMW were in the lot, so I drove to the farm and unloaded the feed.

Peggy had errands to run Thursday morning, so I was alone. As soon as I fed and watered the horses, I organized my incursion into the governor's land. I had to know whether it was possible to reach the highway from my pasture through the governor's land.

I put on my snake proof Wellington boots with heavy socks under them, and an old pair of heavy canvas pants I used in the wintertime. I'd be hot, but that was better than being bit by a copperhead. These clothes would protect me from poison ivy and oak as well. I put on my thickest leather driving gloves, my hard hat, and a pair of wraparound sunglasses, holstered my pistol, and grabbed the machete I used for clearing brush. I also made certain my cell phone was charged and getting a signal. Sometimes when the weather's bad, cell phone reception to and from Hiram's mountain disappears only to reappear with the sun.

"Okay, George of the Jungle, let's see where the sniper went."

Not for the first time I wished I had a dog. Not necessarily a big dog. A yappy Jack Russell terrier would do to alert me to danger. Maybe I should check out the Bigelow animal shelter.

Nah, not until my house was finished and I moved away from Peggy's. It would be lonely enough without her and the cats. I needed a few barn cats to keep the rats in check, although after Morgan's ranting I was no longer sure if letting cats kill rats in my barn was enslaving them or setting them free to fend for themselves.

My musings had taken me to the far end of the lane between the mare and gelding pastures. It was a cul-de-sac with my fence at the property line. No gate. On purpose.

I hadn't given much thought as to how I intended to get past the fence. It was heavy thoroughbred diamond wire mesh with white electrified tape along the top. At the moment, the tape was not live. Generally, horses get one shock and never go near it again. However, I had a stallion once that tested it every morning, just to make certain nobody had screwed up and left it off, so he could go hunting for a mare to breed.

In the north corner, I found someone had

carefully clipped the wire mesh to make a hole large enough for a human being. I crawled through and reached back for my machete. I could see the grass was flattened, and the vines pulled aside, but the ground was too hard to take foot or hand prints.

I scrambled to my feet and bonked my hard hat on a low-hanging branch. The men who owned this land theoretically used it as a hunting preserve, but I doubted they bagged many deer on it. There was more to eat on my side of the fence.

The trail I found was narrow and ill-defined, but passable on foot. It led along the fence for ten yards or so, then veered off down the side of the mountain in a switch-back. I swung the machete to clear the way, even though that meant leaving evidence that someone had been there.

The woods were too still. This early in the year there should be several species of birds calling for mates. Even the breeze couldn't make it through all the underbrush. I had grown up on manicured training facilities. This was alien. I was not welcome.

Something stirred under the carpet of dead leaves. I froze. I couldn't see a snake, but it was there. Since it was slithering away from me, I let it go in peace, but after that I was even more careful where I put my feet.

I was concentrating on the path so hard I nearly cracked my hard hat on the upright of a fancy aluminum deer stand nailed against the thick trunk of a tall oak. I traced the ladder up to the platform and realized that it was aimed directly at my stable. Whoever sat up there had a perfect view of everything that went on at my place.

I wasn't about to climb the thing. I don't do heights. I'd have to tell Geoff about it.

Which would mean I'd have to tell him about my trespassing as well.

In the nineteenth century there was a minor gold rush among these rocks. The miners were responsible for the arsenic that seeped into the ground water and kept the governor and his cronies from securing permits to sink wells in these woods. Getting off the path was foolhardy. I could fall down a mineshaft.

The deer got down the hill. Surely I could.

Then ahead I saw light. Ten feet farther I came to the edge of a raw, twenty-foot cliff of scree and dirt with a rough trail down. Below me lay a parking area, and a gravel driveway that disappeared back into the trees. I could just glimpse the highway beyond.

I'd proved my point. It *was* possible to get from my pasture all the way down here to a parked car. *I* wouldn't want to do it at night, but if I were one of the people who hunted over this land regularly and had a good flashlight, I'd feel fairly comfortable.

By the time I struggled back up the hill and climbed through the wire, I was filthy and sweating like a hog in August, but the trip was worth it.

CHAPTER 31

Thursday morning
Geoff

Geoff started to drive to Stan Nordstrom's office to see whether Troy had said anything substantive before he was released. As Stan said, they could always get him back if they needed him — lawyer and all.

His cell phone rang before he'd been on the road ten minutes.

"Hey, Geoff, it's Artie."

As though Geoff wouldn't recognize the Atlanta medical examiner's high tenor. Not only were they colleagues, but he and Artie ran together as often as they could. Geoff ran for exercise. Artie ran marathons, including both the Boston and New York. He always finished in a respectable time. Keeping up with Artie kept Geoff on the edge of a heart attack, but he always felt virtuous afterwards. Artie was as lean as a whippet. Geoff figured he had a BMI somewhere around minus a hundred.

"I hope you're calling because you've finished Raleigh's autopsy," Geoff said.

"Why else? I cut thirty minutes off my run this morning, since I didn't have to slow down for you."

"I have a life."

"Of *course* you do." Archie snorted. "Unlike a beautiful wife and two excruciatingly intelligent children, which is what I have in place of a life. Who do you go home to, sport?"

"Just tell me what you found, smart ass. Any surprises?"

"You might say that. When we opened him up, we found evidence of two wounds, not one."

"Two wounds?" Geoff said. "Someone staked him, pulled out the stake and staked him again?"

"Not exactly," the ME said. "He was already dead when the stake went into his brain."

"I don't understand."

"See, thing is, we almost missed the second wound track. The two wounds were struck so close together that unless you looked carefully, you'd think the stake killed him."

"But your staff looks carefully," Geoff said.

"You bet we do. We are the greatest and don't you forget it."

"Okay, my diffident friend."

"The two wounds started off at the same place, the same hole, so on the surface they looked like a single wound. It's impossible, however, to see the track of a wound inside the body from outside. A tiny variation in direction or force, and bingo, two wound tracks."

"That's what you found."

"Right. We noticed that the first wound — the one that actually killed him, instantly, as a matter of fact — was half an inch longer than the steel stake and much, much thinner. Also, the stake carried dirt and debris into the wound. The longer wound was free of debris. Clean as the proverbial whistle."

"What was it?"

"Got me. Ice pick, maybe, but even that might be too thick. You know those things they stick into a cow's stomach when it blows up with gas?"

"No, Artie," Geoff said patiently. "Actually, my experience with gassy cows is limited."

"Mine's not. My granddad kept a dairy herd when I was a kid. See, a cow has more than one stomach . . ."

"Artie."

"Oh, sorry. When one of Granddad's cows got bloated, the vet would come over, take this long skinny needle in a plastic plunger. It's called a trocar, my non-medical friend. He'd feel where to shove it and *blam* he'd stab the cow in the stomach. There'd be this big whoosh and the cow's belly would go down five or six inches. Amazing."

"So Raleigh might have been killed by an instrument that deflates a cow's stomach?" Geoff thought of Dr. Gwen. She might practice exclusively on horses now, but she'd no doubt used a trocar in vet school. Time for another chat with the good doc. Troy could wait. Do him good to sweat a trifle.

Artie continued. "Trocars are used in laparoscopic surgery and drainage in human beings as well. You can use it to insert ports in an abdomen. Sometimes it's got three sides. This one didn't, if that's what it was. I didn't say it was definitely a trocar," Artie said. "But something like that. If it was inside its plunger, the killer would press it against the base of the skull then drive the plunger home. Very neat. But it could also be some kind of thin knitting needle, or a special knife. Even a thin crochet hook with the hook cut off and the end sharpened. Tell you this, though. Whoever did it was either darned lucky or had at least a little medical knowledge. It went right into the brain."

Gwen again.

"Why use the steel stake?"

"Hey, that's your job, not mine. I'd guess the killer wanted to cover up the original wound and never thought we'd find it."

"How much force would have been required?"

"Not much if you knew what you were doing and the victim was either unconscious or unsuspecting."

"Any sign he was unconscious?"

"Small amount of bruising on the skull. Could have been from falling off the carriage, although it might have been enough to stun him. We did find Viagra and anticholesterol drugs, but no barbiturates."

"Paralytics?"

"Ah, good old succinylcholine. Seems to be the serial killer's drug of choice these days. Nope. No curare either. Some alcohol, but he wasn't drunk. Far as we can tell, he was conscious. Wasn't tied up. He was a healthy middle-aged man with a fattish heart."

"Could you give some thought to the murder weapon, Artie? Check your medical equipment. See if something looks right, then call me back."

"You think all I got to do is play Colonel Mustard with the Candlestick with you? I got five DBs in the morgue that need my special touch."

"Thanks, Artie." He hung up and dropped his head onto the back of his seat. Two wounds, two weapons. A doctor? Nurse? Vet? Knitter? He'd recheck his list of drivers at the Tollivers' show.

Did two wounds mean two killers? Morgan and Troy, say, or Brock and Sarah Beth, or Gwen and Brock, or Dawn and Armando. No, not Armando unless he had discovered time travel. Dawn and Sarah Beth? They both had a motive to get rid of the man quickly. Maybe it was some doctor he'd totally overlooked who'd killed Raleigh for pawing his fifteen-year-old daughter or costing him a bundle in a sour deal.

He sighed and started the car. Troy could wait. At this point he needed to talk to Dr. Gwen. She hadn't attended the funeral, but she had been at the viewing and probably considered that sufficient.

He considered calling ahead to make certain she wasn't out on a case, then decided he'd drop in and take his chances. He wanted to see her face when he asked to check her trocars.

He was in luck. The vet's big mobile clinic was parked beside a red Mazda sports car and a beige Honda. He'd bet Gwen drove the Mazda. Not exactly a Lamborghini, but not cheap either. If the Honda belonged to the receptionist, then there weren't any patients waiting. He didn't know how many patients actually drove their horse vans over to see the doctor, but some surely must.

The bell over the door sounded when he walked in. The receptionist looked up from her desk. "Oh — Agent Wheeler, isn't it?" She smiled that lovely smile. "Doctor's not here."

"Her car's outside," Geoff said. "So's the van."

"I know, but I hollered for her to say good morning when I came in and checked her office. She didn't have any appointments scheduled for this morning. Her phone's going straight to voice mail, but that's what she does while she's working somewhere. Probably an emergency. Somebody drove by and picked her up."

"Could she be out in your paddocks?"

"I didn't see her when I looked, but I guess so. I've got plenty to do getting this month's bills out. She's such a little bitty thing, she can hide behind a big ole draft horse and you'd never see her." She glanced at her watch. "Lordy! I didn't realize it's been so long. It must really be a bad one if she hasn't called."

"Mind if I check?" Geoff asked.

"Sure, go on through and out the back door. I guess she could be in the hay shed. I didn't go out there, but I called."

There were no patients in the post-op stalls. No Gwen anywhere.

He had no reason to feel uncomfortable, but he did. His gut was nearly infallible when it came to trouble. This, he felt certain, was trouble.

He walked out into the pasture. Two horses grazed in separate paddocks. They barely lifted their heads when they saw him. Neither was large enough to hide Gwen. He walked on toward the hay shed.

The hay shed was three-sided with the open side facing east, away from the usual direction of the wind. He called for Gwen but got no reply.

He caught the first scent when he was ten feet from the shed. If the receptionist had come out to search for Gwen, she'd have smelled it too.

The odor of death was unmistakable. He

351

told himself it was most likely a possum or even a wounded deer that had crawled into the hay shed to die.

Nonetheless, he stopped to pull on a pair of Latex gloves and set up his cell phone to take photos.

He took several shots as he moved closer to the shed. When he rounded the end, he could see that most of the winter's hay had already been fed. All that remained were two piles of ten to twenty bales, each stacked three deep at either end of the shed. The center portion was empty.

No matter how many times he smelled death, he never got used to it and hoped he never would. He pulled out his handkerchief and covered his mouth and nose as he checked the bales at the north end of the shed — the end closest to the back door of the clinic.

They were bales of grass hay, each bale cinched neatly with two strands of orange twine.

He turned toward the stack at the far end. This was a different sort of hay — greener, made up of thicker stalks. That's why the two piles had been separated. He thought it was alfalfa. Each bale was cinched not by twine, but by two strands of wire.

One of the wires holding the top bale

together was in place. He didn't see the other. A couple of flakes had popped loose, but not fallen totally away from the bale. As he bent over the broken bale, he caught a glimpse of blue peeking out from between the alfalfa and the south wall.

He leaned over the bale and found himself staring down into Gwen Standish's eyes, already milky in death. He slid to his knees in front of the bale. Checking for a pulse would be useless, but he tried anyway, searching for a carotid pulse just above the angry red line that ran around her neck.

Whatever had strangled her was still embedded so deeply in her neck he couldn't see what it was from the front, so he turned her head. It moved easily.

"Damn," he whispered. At the nape of her neck he saw that two ends of steel wire had been crossed like a garrote, pulled tight, then twisted together. He'd be willing to bet it was the missing wire from the alfalfa bale.

He caught the glint of metal and saw a pair of wire cutters on the ground where Gwen might have dropped them. He laid her head down gently in the same position he'd found it. Let the crime scene techs take it from there.

He hated strangulation cases. Gwen had

been an attractive woman. Strangulation destroyed all beauty and replaced it with purple skin, bulging eyes traced with broken veins and the tiny red dots, and a protruding tongue.

He flashed his penlight on her neck and saw deep scratches where she'd fought to pull the wire away. Her nails were torn and bloody, but he suspected the only DNA under them would be hers. Still, they'd check. Maybe they'd get lucky.

She was still warm. Since rigor mortis started at the extremities and worked up and in, and since her head had turned easily, she hadn't been dead long. No ligature marks around her wrists, so she hadn't been restrained.

He backed away before he could contaminate the scene and got as far as the bales of grass hay across the shed before he had to sit down. He knew cops who could look at a double axe murder without turning a hair. He couldn't.

No matter what good shape Gwen was in, she maybe weighed ninety pounds. An easy target for male or female of significant size and strength.

He knew better than to argue ahead of his data, but he could visualize the scene. Gwen would have come out to feed the horses in pasture as soon as she came in this morning — probably at dawn. She'd have used wire cutters to clip one of the two wires on the alfalfa and pull it loose. That's when the killer must have interrupted her.

She turned her back on her killer, someone she knew. If she'd been afraid, she'd have used the wire cutters as a weapon. Instead, she bent down to cut the second wire. The killer grabbed the loose wire, dropped it over her head, and pulled her back across the hay or over his knee — maybe off her feet. Strangulation took several minutes. Once she was unconscious, however, the killer could have simply twisted the ends of the wire together and left. The twist in the wire around her throat was too tight to have been done solely by hand. Her killer took time to be neat. That made his flesh crawl.

Whoever had killed her had not brought a weapon along, or had chosen not to use it. Did that mean the killer had not come to kill?

Geoff turned and walked carefully back to the clinic. The path and the floor of the hay shed were raked gravel. No footprints.

He dialed Stan Nordstrom's direct line, told him what had happened, then went back inside to tell Gwen's receptionist she'd have to look for a new job.

"What is it with you?" Stan Nordstrom said. "We get our share of vehicular homicides and drug killings, but nothing like this."

"Sure, you do. Raleigh was all yours until you called me in."

"Well, this has got to be related. We know Dr. Gwen spent the night before Raleigh died at the Tollivers' place working on a colic case. She must have seen something as she was leaving — maybe your girlfriend playing pin the tail on the donkey with Giles Raleigh. And tried a little blackmail. People always think they're too smart for a black-mailer to turn the tables."

"Merry's not my girlfriend, and she doesn't have enough money to pay black-mail."

"She have an alibi for this morning? You, maybe?" Stan raised his colorless eyebrow.

"How many times do I have to tell you, I am not sleeping with her."

"Why not? I would, if I didn't know my wife would kill my ass."

"Merry wouldn't have you."

Now both eyebrows went up. "Turned you down? The great Geoff Wheeler?"

"Moving right along," Geoff said, "what about Troy? Is he in jail?"

"Mrs. Harris's lawyer already arranged bail for him." He shook his head. "That Harris woman's lawyer wouldn't let him say so much as his name. She musta' pulled strings, because we barely had time to fingerprint him before here comes some hotshot attorney from Dahlonega with a bail slip from some tame judge. That lawyer drove Troy over to the church to pick up his truck."

Geoff looked down at Gwen's body. It seemed even smaller in death. "How long would you guess she's been dead?"

"Not long. Early this morning or late last night. It was chilly last night, which would have speeded up rigor, but not by much."

Geoff followed him over to one of the horse paddocks and leaned on the fence.

"Whew. Better," Stan said. "I guess you're used to the smell. I'm not."

"You don't ever get used to it," Geoff said.

"Who's got enough money to make black-mail worth Gwen's while?"

"I've had one of our people in Atlanta checking on finances. Catherine Harris is comfortable, but not rich, and Troy doesn't have any money to amount to anything. Morgan's family is loaded. To say they don't get along is like saying Al Qaida doesn't get along with the CIA, but in a pinch, she's still their baby girl. She's definitely still Troy's."

"Yeah. He'd kill for her, I guess. Dumb-ass," Stan said. "Need to check on his whereabouts. Brock's too, I guess. He's probably still at the Raleighs', but it would be nice to know he's been there all night."

"Check on Morgan and Catherine Harris too," Geoff said.

"What are you going to do?" Stan asked.

"After I leave here, I'm going to check on Merry Abbott. I'm hoping this time she has an air-tight alibi."

Half an hour later, Geoff and Stan watched the EMTs load Gwen's body into their van and drive off. No sirens. No urgency.

Stan had sent the receptionist home in a squad car with a policewoman. Geoff had expected hysterics, but she was one stop short of catatonic. The woman could barely put one foot in front of the other. Stan wouldn't get anything out of her for hours, maybe for days.

The office itself wasn't precisely the crime scene, but Stan and Geoff agreed that until they knew for certain Gwen hadn't been killed inside the clinic, they could consider the whole place a crime scene, and thus, they didn't need a warrant. The minute he'd gotten the receptionist out, Stan sent a couple of officers in to search the office, and another officer to secure Gwen's house. She lived in a fifties bungalow less than a mile from the clinic.

"We'll need a search warrant for the house," Stan said. "It would help to be able to specify what we're looking for."

"Money," Geoff said. "Evidence of where she got it."

Inside the office, two officers were carefully going over the storeroom.

"There's Ketamine out the wazoo," a young officer who might have been Stan's younger clone said. "Lot of stuff would sell well on the street in Atlanta."

"If it's still here, she probably wasn't killed in a theft," Stan said. "I'll get one of my people over here with the receptionist after she comes out of her shock. They can match inventory to prescriptions and suppliers."

Geoff wasn't needed inside, so he went back to the hay shed. The center portion of the shed between the alfalfa and grass hay had been empty until the techs tossed the bales of alfalfa away from Gwen's body. Stan's officers hadn't moved the bales of grass hay at the other end of the shed.

He didn't know much about horses, but he knew Merry seldom fed her horses alfalfa. She said it was too rich, and could cause digestive problems. It was also much more expensive than grass hay.

Maybe Gwen felt it was worth taking the chance to put weight on an underweight animal.

In moving the alfalfa into the center of the shed, the techs had upended several of the bales so that the bottom bales were now on top of the pile. "Man, these things are heavy," one young officer said as he dug his fingers under the baling wire and hefted.

A puff of dust arose from beneath his fingers. He began to cough.

Geoff took a look at the cloud, grabbed the young man and dragged him into the air. "Get out of there, all of you," he called.

Still coughing, the man said, "I'm allergic to dust. I'm okay."

"Maybe, maybe not. Whatever that is, it's not dust." He could think of a dozen powders from plain old baking powder to anthrax that might be in that bale. "I need a respirator and a bunny suit," Geoff said.

Five minutes later, wearing a fresh bunny suit and a respirator, Geoff dug his pocket-knife into the bale of alfalfa, dropped a dab of white powder into one of the test tubes from Stan's squad car and handed it over to the officer. He added the test agent, shook the tube, watched it turn indigo and whispered, "Oh, man."

"Get Stan," Geoff said.

An hour later the dismembered bales of alfalfa lay strewn around the shed. Of the twenty-two bales, thirteen contained neatly wrapped kilos of cocaine that now sat on a blue tarpaulin. "Well, now we know how she paid for that fancy equipment," Stan said. "Not easy carving hidey-holes in alfalfa, then resealing them so they don't look like anybody's tampered with 'em."

"Wouldn't work with grass hay," Stan said. "The bales are too loose. Alfalfa has tough stems, but it packs solid."

"I wonder where she buys her alfalfa," the cop said.

"I can make a guess," Geoff said. "She wouldn't need a whole load. If Giles Raleigh fed alfalfa, she could have bought bales from him."

"And Brock," Stan said with satisfaction.

Geoff called Merry on his cell. "Where do you buy alfalfa?"

"I don't. Why?"

"Where would you if you did?"

"Probably Texas or Oklahoma. Maybe Florida. It's cheaper if you bring back a big trailer load and sell parts of it to other people, but you have to watch for blister beetles. One beetle can kill a horse. Why?"

"Tell you later. Where are you?"

"Where would I be? At the farm, of course."

Did she sound defensive? That usually meant she'd been up to something he didn't want to know about.

"How long have you been there? What are you doing?"

"I've been here all morning, and now I'm putting Heinzie to. What is this?"

"Peggy with you?"

"She and Dick just got here. They brought lunch."

"Don't go anywhere. I'll be there in an hour." He hung up on her protestations.

"Alibi?" Stan asked.

"Probably not."

"Can I trust you to find out, or do I have come over there myself to question her?"

"You don't honestly think Merry had anything to do with this, do you?" Geoff asked. "Looks pretty straightforward to me. Brock and Gwen had a falling out at the viewing. I'd guess it had something to do with the coke."

"So why didn't he take his merchandise when he happened to drop by to kill her?"

"He'd need time to cut it out of the hay. He wouldn't want the receptionist catching him," Geoff said. "He probably plans to come back tonight after everyone's gone. Normally we'd have released the crime scene by then. It's sheer dumb luck the tech discovered the cocaine."

"Yeah. I'd like to keep a lid on this until I get my hands on him," Stan said. "You want to talk to the DEA?"

"No way. You take the credit," Geoff said.

"How sure are we it's Brock? Say sixty per cent?"

"My gut says Brock will turn up. If by any chance she wasn't in business with Brock, then whoever her partner is should come to take back his dope the minute he finds out she's dead and we've left the scene. He can't take a chance we'll find his stash."

Stan's elation was catching. His whole team was walking around wearing happy grins and giving one another fist bumps.

Giving Stan the drug bust glory would make him Geoff's friend for life. And keep him off Merry's back.

CHAPTER 32

Merry

Peggy and Dick had brought plenty of food to feed Geoff too. While Peggy and Dick were at the table in the clients' lounge with us, we made small talk. The minute they left to put the Halflingers to, I asked him, "Why on earth do you want to know about alfalfa?"

"None of your business."

"What's going on? I'll find out, you know."

"Eventually," he said as he crumpled his paper napkin and lobbed it accurately into the waste paper basket in the corner. "So, you were here alone this morning?"

"Uh-huh." I hadn't told him yet about my foray into the jungle next door. I wasn't looking forward to his reaction.

"I know that look. Everywhere but at me."

I lobbed my napkin at the waste basket and missed. That's why I never played basketball.

"You're up to something."

"If you say, 'Lucy, you got some s'plainin' to do,' I swear I'll deck you."

"Give it your best shot." He opened his arms wide.

"Oh, heck. I did pick up feed this morning, and I saw Brock meet the governor's man Whitehead for breakfast at the diner next to the feed store."

"What time?"

"Six-thirty, seven."

"Then you came back here and didn't leave again."

"Well, not precisely. I listened in on their conversation."

"Merry, for the love of God . . ."

"Don't you want to hear what they said?" I reported almost word for word.

"Tell me you drove straight home after that and didn't leave," he said.

"Almost."

"What the hell does that mean?"

So I told him about my trek onto the governor's property. He was not happy about it.

"Damn." He flipped open his cell phone, held up a hand to shut me up and said, "Hey, Stan, Brock's got an alibi of sorts. If TOD is early enough, he might have done it." He listened, lowered the phone and said to me, "Go *away.*"

I slammed the door after me and went to find Peggy and Dick.

We had the Halflingers washed down and back in the pasture before Geoff came out.

"I have to go," he said.

"What is going on?" Peggy asked.

"Tell you tonight. How about I buy you all dinner?"

"You don't . . ."

"Yeah, I do." He took my hand and pulled me out to the parking lot, at which point he leaned across and kissed me, hard. "You could have gotten shot as a trespasser. That would have pissed me off."

"Thanks for your concern."

"You saved us a lot of trouble. Try to stay out of it yourself."

He left me staring after him as he drove off much too fast down the driveway. He'd be lucky if he didn't go over the cliff. I wandered back into the stable in a funk. Just when I was sure the man was as cold as a flounder, he did something that — I mean, that was not a *friendly* kiss. He must be relaxing his rules about messing with anybody involved in one of his cases. Good. I could build on that.

CHAPTER 33

Geoff

By the time Geoff got to Stan's interrogation room, Stan had brought in Brock. He acted enraged, but Geoff saw fear in his eyes. He'd been properly Mirandized, and so far hadn't asked for a lawyer. Amazing the number of otherwise intelligent people who thought they could handle the police on their own. The police fostered that view for as long as possible.

"I got a barn to run," Brock said. "Y'all drag me down here and treat me like I'm the one did something wrong. I told you already, I didn't kill Mr. Raleigh."

"Uh-huh," Stan said. He looked down at the yellow legal pad in front of him as though referring to notes. Geoff could see over his shoulder that they looked like Stan's grocery list.

After a moment, in which Brock slid around on his chair, Stan looked up and smiled. "Got to give y'all credit. Slick trick, doctoring those bales of alfalfa so nobody could tell they were stuffed with coke."

Brock jumped a foot. "What in hell you talking about?" He started to stand, but Stan waved him back to his chair.

"Probably wouldn't fool a sniffer dog, but then they don't normally sniff hay haulers, do they?"

Geoff watched Brock's pupils dilate. A thin film of sweat had broken out above his eyebrows.

Stan looked down at his pad and asked, "Just so we're clear, where were you this morning?"

Brock caught his breath. "What time this morning?"

"Oh, say, between midnight and now."

For a moment Brock looked confused. Then he looked even more frightened. Geoff wondered whether he'd spent the night in Sarah Beth's bed, and if so, what time he got up to tend to the horses.

"I got to bed early."

"Where?"

"At home."

"Whose home?"

"I live in the guest cottage behind Raleigh's stable," Brock sounded annoyed, but he'd relaxed. This wasn't the scary question.

"Alone?"

"Yes, alone."

"Mrs. Raleigh didn't join you?"

"What the hell kind of question is that? The woman just lost her husband."

"The woman's also carrying your baby," Stan said quietly. "I don't imagine your girlfriend Gwen was happy about that, Mrs. Raleigh being a rich woman and suddenly available and all."

"I didn't even know Mrs. Raleigh was pregnant." Brock's pupils had gone back to nearly normal size. The pulse at his neck still thrummed, but not as fast as it had.

"Then why'd you tell Whitehead she was?"

Stan's Berserker forebears showed in his smile. Brock must have caught a whiff of Norse Warrior too, because he seemed to diminish in his chair right before their eyes. Whitehead?"

"You mentioned it at breakfast this morning, right?"

He gaped. "Who? Wha . . ."

"You ought to know by now you can't stir your coffee in public without somebody noticing," Stan said. "Why'd you need money so bad? Deal for the coke fell through?"

"What coke? Who says I need money? You keep talking about coke like I'm supposed to know about it."

Stan gave him a sad "more in sorrow than anger" look. "Thirteen kilos on their way to Atlanta to a secure evidence locker. Amazing the number of prints Saran Wrap preserves. Since we took yours on Sunday after Raleigh's death, we had them on file all ready to check."

Brock looked as though he might throw up. Stan was as fastidious about his interview rooms as about his squad car, so Geoff hoped Brock would not toss his cookies.

"Guess whose prints we found all over all the packages? Yours, my friend."

Brock went very still. "Do I need a lawyer?"

"You can have one if you want one." Stan sat across from him totally relaxed. " 'Course, we'll stop the interview and put you in a cell 'til he gets here. 'Course, I won't be able to help you then."

Geoff could see the wheels turning in Brock's brain.

"Help me how?"

"You've got thirty seconds to get in front of this," Stan said. "First rat gets the cheese. Maybe we can cut a deal if you give us some names. People higher up the food chain."

Geoff could almost read the sign on Brock's forehead: *abandon ship, every man for himself.* "I can't go to jail. If I talk, can I get probation?"

Stan cut his eyes at Geoff and said, "Lord knows. The judge might give you probation, depending on how good your information is."

On a cold day in hell Brock would get probation.

"All I ever did was help pack and drive the hay up from Florida," Brock sounded close to hysteria. "If you want to know who it belongs to, ask Gwen. I don't even know who picks it up. It was her gig from the get go."

"Where from? How often?"

"Look, you sure I can get probation?"

"You got to give me more than that," Stan said. "How'd you get into this?"

According to Brock, Gwen worked in a big south Florida practice after she qualified as a vet. "They handled a bunch of high-dollar racehorses for some of the drug kingpins. Gwen got to know them. They were her ticket to her own practice."

"How'd you two hook up?"

"Raleigh goes down to Wellington and Ocala to drive every winter for a couple of months. We used Gwen for our vet down

371

there, and she and I hit it off."

"Who worked out the way to hollow out the alfalfa and fit the coke inside?"

"I guess it was a joint effort."

"How long have you two been doing this?"

"Gwen had something going before with prescription drugs. She said it was easier to conceal in a large practice, but it's chancy and doesn't pay all that well. She'd made enough to set up her clinic, but not to pay for the equipment she wanted."

"Why pick north Georgia?"

"Lot of horse people up here go down to Florida. They agreed to use her if she settled here. She really is a great vet."

"How long you been working together?"

"I told you, I'm just the driver! I just started!"

They waited. Geoff watched Brock calculating how much he could lie, then give it up. "Three years."

"How many loads a year?"

"Three or four, if the price of alfalfa was cheap enough in Florida to make it worth Raleigh's time to bring up extra loads."

"Who else was in on it?"

"Nobody up here. Gwen made the arrangements. I don't know any names. I'd pick up the alfalfa, meet a couple of guys to help me stow it inside the bales, then I'd drop off the bales with the coke in Gwen's shed, and take the clean stuff on to Raleigh."

"Then what?"

Brock shook his head. "I don't know who picked it up from her. She'd pay me, and that would be the end of it until the next time."

"When was your last load?"

"First week in April."

"That's over a month ago. Why was it still at Gwen's?"

"She said the guys who were supposed to pick it up had been busted up north somewhere. Her Florida connection figured it was safe where it was, until they could get another crew together."

"Where were they moving it?"

Again Brock shook his head. "I told you, I don't know anything about that end of it. All I did was help pack it and drive it to Gwen."

"How did Raleigh find out?" Geoff asked. They were moving into murder territory now, so he took over.

"Who says he knew?" Brock's eyes swiveled to look at Geoff, all his belligerence back in place.

"You did. You told Gwen he intended to fire you and turn you over to the cops."

"How did you . . . ?"

"Is that why you killed him?" Geoff asked.

Brock came up out of his chair. "You can't pin that on me!"

"So how'd he find out?" Stand asked.

Brock's head swiveled back to Stan. "I accidentally brought one of the stuffed bales to Raleigh's. He caught me taking out the coke, so I could get it back to Gwen. I swore it was a one-shot deal." Brock spread his hands. "He believed me, but he was madder'n I ever saw him. I could'a talked him around. He wouldn't'a fired me."

"Would he have, if he discovered you'd knocked up his wife?" Stan asked.

"He didn't know, my hand to God." Brock subsided.

"So how come you were so desperate for money? You must have accumulated quite a stash in three years," Geoff said.

"I wish."

"Been sampling your own wares?"

"No way, man. That junk's for losers. I spend my life around horses. Where there's horses, there's big money gambling. I'm into some very unhappy people for thirty large. I can't ask Sarah Beth. The will's not even probated yet. After I told Gwen I wasn't going to bring in any more loads, she refused to give me a dime." He narrowed his eyes at us both. "Why am I the

374

one sitting here? You got Gwen in another room? All you got me on is transporting."

"And murder," Stan said.

"I told you, I didn't kill Raleigh."

"But you killed Gwen."

He didn't react for a moment. "Say what?"

"I said," Stan said, "you killed Gwen."

"Gwen's dead?" He jumped up so quickly he knocked his chair over and came close to following it all the way to the floor. "Oh, lord, they killed her." He yanked the chair and himself up, but made no attempt to sit down again. "You gotta protect me, man. They find out I told you anything, they'll kill me too."

"Thought you said you didn't know who they were," Geoff said.

"I don't. My hand to God."

"Where were you this morning?"

Brock stared at *him* now. He was like a bull that didn't know which side the dogs were going to attack. "Hell, you know where I was. I guess Whitehead called y'all right after we split, didn't he?"

They didn't answer him. Stan called for a deputy to lock Brock up as a material witness until the various agencies could untangle the jurisdictional mess and decide who to charge with what.

After Brock was taken away, loudly protesting that he'd never killed anyone, Geoff said, "Hard to believe in two separate killers for two separate killings so close together."

"Yeah. If Brock is out on Gwen's death, chances are he's out on Raleigh's too."

"Too many suspects," Geoff said.

"Including your girlfriend."

"She gave us Brock's alibi, remember? And incidentally, her own as well. If she was listening to Brock and Whitehead, she wasn't strangling Gwen forty miles away."

"She could have killed Gwen early same as Brock." He waved a hand at Geoff. "I guess she didn't," Stan said. "I released the news of Gwen's death, but not that we'd found the drugs. Once they know those bales of alfalfa are still sitting in Gwen's shed, they'll have to take a chance on getting them. We may not solve the murders, but we should be able to take some poison off the streets."

"And maybe get a lead to Gwen's contact in Miami."

CHAPTER 34

Merry

I was getting used to Geoff's begging off dinner invitations, even ones he'd tendered himself. Dick and Peggy and I didn't wait for him. Friday we were setting up for the show. A million things could go wrong and probably would. At least Catherine hadn't bailed on me.

Geoff showed up as our waitress served our hot brownies. He plopped down, ordered coffee and two brownies a la mode with extra whipped cream. He caught my expression and raised his eyebrows. "This is lunch *and* dinner."

I raised my hands. The man could probably eat a dozen of those things and stay as thin as he was.

"Sorry I'm late," he said a couple of minutes later as he dug into his mountain of calories. "I was helping Stan with a . . . a situation." He told us about Gwen's death and the cocaine. I didn't know about Peggy and Dick, but I was furious at Geoff. "A woman gets strangled, and you don't think to mention it?"

"I'm mentioning it now. Her murder was on the afternoon news."

"Who has time to listen?" Peggy asked.

"Stan released the announcement about Gwen's death to the media after the still watch on the cocaine was in place. We're hoping someone will try to pick it up tonight."

I tried to keep the fear out of my voice. I didn't want Geoff in the middle of a gun battle. "You going back to Gwen's?" I asked. Casually, I hoped.

He shook his head. "This is Stan's show. With a little help from the feds. "Me? I'm going to try to get some sleep."

"Me, too," Peggy said. "I thought an itty-bitty horse show would be a piece of cake. The first person who pulls up to our gates tonight with a horse trailer is going to get punched in the face."

"I thought you wanted a bunch of people," Geoff said.

"We specifically said no one would be allowed in until tomorrow. It's like those people who show up for Saturday morning yard sales at six *Friday* morning," Peggy said.

"Where do you expect them to park tonight?" Geoff asked.

"Ask me do I care."

He cut his eyes at me. "What about the horses?"

"They'll be fine until morning. People travel with hay and feed and water. Some drive eighteen hours at a stretch to get to a show in upstate New York or Florida. The horses will go to sleep." I glanced at Peggy. "We're not leaving them completely high and dry. I expect my cell phone to start ringing any minute now."

It did, right on schedule. I put it on speaker.

"Hey, is this Meredith Abbot? This is Marvin Cudlow. We're registered for the show and the clinic."

"Yes, Mr. Cudlow?"

"I know you said you wouldn't be open until tomorrow, but we figured we'd drive on over tonight, get a good place to park, you know? Anyway, your gates are locked. There's some kind of keypad. Could you give me the code? It'll save y'all a trip out here to let us in."

Peggy grabbed the phone. I expected her to bark, but she said in her syrupy sweet southern put-on voice, "Marvin, honey? The reason we can't let y'all in tonight is that

379

our insurance policy doesn't kick in 'til tomorrow." She rolled her eyes. "And my lawyer would simply *kill* me if I gave you the key code."

"But Becca and me, we drove all the way from Chattanooga." Three hours, max. I'd expected anger. Instead, his voice came out a whine. "Can't y'all make one tiny exception? We sleep in the trailer on the road, so we don't have to leave the horses in some strange place all alone."

This time I managed to snag the phone. "Marvin? About five miles straight ahead of you is a big Baptist church with a giant parking lot. I've made arrangements for camper trailers and folks who show up early to park there. You should have gotten information on that when we sent you your confirmation. Did you?"

"Well, yeah, we did, but I figured since we were so early . . ."

" 'Fraid we can't break the rules, but y'all should be fine tonight. The congregation's leaving all the lights on in the parking lot, and there's an outdoor spigot if you need water. There's a big grassy area too. Perfect for you to walk your horses. What do y'all drive?"

"We brought our pair of Welsh ponies and a pony phaeton."

I rolled my eyes. Two small ponies and one relatively small carriage. Probably more space in the camper portion than in the trailer itself. "See you after lunch tomorrow." After a few more attempts to change my mind, good ole Marvin gave in and hung up.

Geoff was watching me in fascination. Dick was grinning.

"The first thing I learned about managing a show," I said, "is that nobody reads directions, or if they do, they figure directions don't apply to them. They also don't read signs. They'll stare right at a sign that says 'restrooms' with an arrow pointing left, and ask the first person they see if the restrooms are to the right."

"Tell me again why we're doing this," Peggy said.

"Publicity for the farm and a carriage for Casey."

"Oh. Yeah. Remind me often. Geoff, you don't happen to have any illegal Ecstasy on you, do you? I've heard it mellows you out."

"Sorry, Peggy. Not even an aspirin." He spooned up the last bit of ice cream and shoved his chair back. "Bill's already taken care of."

Dick started to protest, but Geoff waved him away. "Turn about."

Outside, I started to follow Peggy and Dick to his van, but Geoff took my arm and led me to his. He shoved me into the passenger seat and drove us off without a word.

"Okay, hotshot," I said. "Where we going?"

"Amos Royden is meeting us at the hotel."

"Why?"

"Two murders aren't enough of a reason?"

"They weren't in Mossy Creek."

"Close enough, and with a singular attachment to you and Peggy. Amos wants to talk about your security arrangements. I figured you'd be itching to hear about the drug bust."

"Is that a sop to my curiosity?"

"Actually, it's to head off your imagination."

"I don't make things up." Well, not usually. I did, however, omit certain things. "How fast can you get DNA test results?"

"Privately? Twenty-four hours, but it costs. Why?"

"I need a test done pronto. Can you handle it?"

"Whose?"

"Mine."

That shut him up. I also wanted Troy Wilkinson's DNA, and Geoff might be able to get those results without too much rigmarole. If I had a half brother, I wanted to know. My family had a right to know. And I'd have to revise my opinion of Hiram, my father.

Amos wanted a complete briefing about the incursions at the farm. He was pretty PO'd at both Geoff and me for not calling him out, especially after shots were fired. He had a point.

"The farm isn't technically in Mossy Creek," I said, "even if we did fudge a little when Hiram was killed."

"Don't quibble. Whether your farm is in Mossy Creek or not, you and Peggy *are*. Now, about this weekend . . ."

We spent half an hour going over security arrangements and handling of the money. Sandi, his dispatcher, would handle ticket sales and contributions from spectators, while the garden club ladies would deal with the money from food and drinks. The people who were driving had to send in their money when they registered, so Sandi would hand out driving packets and check off names as well.

"She has a stall plan for the people who are stabling their horses," I said, "and a parking plan for trailers and cars. Louise's grandson Pete is coming home from summer school for the weekend to run a golf cart shuttle for spectators from the road up the hill for when we run out of places at the farm parking lot. I hope we'll need the space, but you never know. We may have no spectators at all."

"You'll have spectators," Amos said. "Everybody wants to help Casey. Is she actually driving tomorrow?"

"You bet. Dressage, cones, and hazards. I'll be in the carriage with her, of course, but she'll actually do the driving. Golden will look after her."

"I'll station my deputy down at the road," Amos said. "But if anything happens in Mossy Creek that needs him, I'll have to pull him off."

I nodded my understanding. "Our parking area is big, but we're going to park the smaller trailers along the far side of the stable where the manure pile used to be. That's where the portable johns will be set up. There aren't supposed to be more than three or four big rigs. Plenty of space for them to the right of the barn on the grass verge. Some cars can park back of my new slab close to the pasture fence. It's not supposed to rain, so the ground should hold firm."

"Supposed to be low eighties and partly

cloudy," Amos said. "I checked."

I laughed. "So did I. And prayed."

Amos offered to drive me home since Geoff was already at his hotel.

As I got out of the squad car in Peggy's driveway, he leaned across the seat and said, "This is a nice thing you're doing for Casey."

"It's good publicity for the farm, and my own horses are going to have lessons at the driving clinic on Sunday. Thanks for the lift, Amos. Love to Ida."

The lights were out in Peggy's house. Very shortly they were off in mine as well. Could I sleep? Get real. Not only was I managing this show, it was on my property. I prayed everyone would have a good time. Including me.

I stopped by the Baptist church parking lot early Friday morning on my way to the farm to check on Marvin Cudlow. I expected him to be tetchy, but both he and his wife Becca were charming. They invited me in to their trailer for coffee.

"Horses okay?" I asked. The coffee was good, but then they were using a top of the line coffee maker and fancy just-ground beans.

"Oh, sure," Marvin said. "We take 'em to

Walnut Hill in New York and the national drive every year. They're used to long trips. We hand-walked 'em already this morning."

"And picked up the manure," Marvin's wife, Becca, said. "Don't want the Baptists to find road apples all over when they come to church on Sunday."

"Thanks. I wish everyone were as considerate," I said. "Since I'm on my way down to the farm right now to unlock the gates, you all can come ahead as soon as you like."

"Will that get you in trouble with the dragon lady?" Marvin asked. When he saw my face, he said, "I wouldn't like to try to put anything past her."

"I'll tell her you said so."

I was keeping all my guys out in the pasture overnight the next three days to free up the stalls for people coming to the show and the clinic. I fed the horses and Don Qui in buckets on the fence line. That generally worked fairly well with a minimum of bucket poaching, except for Don Qui, who raced from bucket to bucket cadging a mouthful from everyone else's breakfast when he could sneak in under their necks.

With the exception of Heinzie, his erstwhile brother, nobody let him get away with it, but he didn't end up getting his head kicked off either.

My crew of garden club ladies brought Louise's grandson Pete to do the heavy lifting such as putting up the tent for Sandi on my new concrete slab. They were so used to putting together events for Mossy Creek, they needed almost no supervision. What little they needed, Peggy provided.

I spent the morning checking paperwork, setting up office equipment in the clients' lounge, scrubbing the clients' bathroom, putting plenty of toilet paper and paper towels in the porta-johns, setting out mega-garbage cans in strategic locations, setting up sign stanchions for the signs Sandi was bringing, checking off the list I carried in my pocket and praying to avoid rainstorms and disasters of every shape and form. Even this small of a show was a heap of work.

The bulk of the drivers didn't plan to show up until Saturday morning in time to drive their dressage tests, but a few arrived early Friday afternoon. I had limited stall space for visitors and carriages, so in order to free up space for other people's carriages, I locked all my own carriages in Hiram's workshop. I planned to drive on Sunday in the clinic, but not during the show. Dick had already volunteered to set up Casey's carriage and drive with her if I got caught with an emergency.

After lunch, young Pete and I set up the cones course and the hazards in the mare's pasture. I noticed that the slash in the fence between the governor's land and us was untouched, so if anyone had prowled around in our absence, they hadn't come that way.

Louise's husband Charlie dragged the dressage arena with the tractor while Peggy and I set up the judge's table and chairs at C, the end of the arena nearest the stable.

There are a million theories why the letters spaced evenly around a dressage arena start facing C in the middle at one end, then heading right around the arena letters M, R, B, P, and F. A is at the end opposite C. Then the letters down the other side from A are K, V, E, S, and H. Nobody really knows why, but they are standard around the world.

We were as ready as we would be before four. I planned to spend the night in the clients' lounge in my clothes. I'd shower and change in time to feed the horses in the morning.

At the last minute, Catherine decided she really would prefer to arrive Saturday morning and spend Saturday night after the exhibitors' party in the Hamilton Inn. She agreed to pay for her and Troy's rooms. Originally, he hadn't been slated to come with her, but apparently she didn't want him out of her sight or where Morgan could get ahold of him again. Since Dick was still in residence at Peggy's, having Catherine in a motel would lower the scandal quotient. Not that either Peggy or Dick cared.

Catherine had said Troy didn't know he was my half-brother, and I wasn't certain I wanted him told. I definitely didn't want him to complicate this weekend. Time enough to confront that problem when my DNA results came back. Catherine would be duty bound to furnish Troy's. We could check them against mine, and know for certain whether or not he and I were siblings.

Saturday morning

I schooled myself not to react when Troy climbed out of Catherine's truck, but I found myself staring at him while I talked to Catherine. How alike were we physically? We were both tall. My hair (without cosmetic assistance) is basically dark blonde tending to dishwater. His hair was light brown. Mine is straight. So was his. I have enormous hands for a woman. He had enormous hands, period. I couldn't tell about bone structure. He didn't look much like Hiram to me, but he didn't look much like Catherine either.

The garden club set up their mega-coffee-pot and handed out cinnamon rolls to the drivers and apples for the horses. Volunteers manned the driving venues, trailers arrived, cars arrived, Sandi arrived with signs, and before eight o'clock the place was settling for the first dressage test.

I turned over the office to Peggy and Dick, and got ready to head off trouble before it started.

There's seldom an early morning on top of Hiram's hill without at least a hint of breeze and some fog. This morning was no different. Although we'd all be in shirtsleeves before noon, this morning the lady drivers were already wearing their driving jackets and aprons. I had hung a couple of mirrors outside the front door of the stable, and two women were already jockeying for position to settle their elaborate hats.

As I walked by, a gust of wind caught one big feathered creation and lofted it clear off Juanita Tolliver's head.

"Botheration!" she yelled and dove after it. I caught it just before it hit the ground.

"Thanks, sweetie," she said. "I dropped my dadgum hat pin before I could stick it in." She bent over to search for it. I could see the tight pin curl on the top of her head crisscrossed with bobby pins. "Gotcha!" she said triumphantly as she came up with a hatpin dangling from her fingers. The end of it was crowned with a series of bright red beads the color of pigeon-blood rubies. At least I assumed they were beads. Some of the antique pins the ladies had inherited from their great-great grandmothers sported actual gems. The more unusual the pin, the more cachet to the wearer.

Juanita set her hat on her head and jabbed the pin through the felt. "There. See if you can fly off now, doggone you," she said. She tossed me a wave and walked off to warm up for her dressage test.

A lady I did not recognize took her place at the mirror, sat a bright yellow straw hat surrounded with yellow silk peonies on her head and repeated the pin curl and hatpin jab. Her jacket was the same jonquil yellow, which went beautifully with her red hair. She looked from the waist up as though she were ready for a drive through Central Park in eighteen eighty, but her black slacks and dusty paddock boots kind of ruined the ensemble.

"Are they supposed to look like that?"

I jumped and turned to find Geoff behind me holding out a cup of coffee.

"Two artificial sugars, one milk," he said.

The man knew how I liked my coffee. "Thanks," I said and cupped it in my palms to warm my hands before I took a swig. "What happened at Gwen's last night?"

"I love it when a plan comes together," he said with a broad grin. "Four big men. No gunfire. They came like little lambs. The DEA thinks they're probably Russian Mafia, but of course they're not talking." He shrugged. "At least we know who we're dealing with."

"*Will* they talk?"

He shook his head. "Doubt it, but you never know. Thank God, it's not my problem. Not this time, at any rate."

I took a deep breath. He was safe and here with me. "So, want to watch a dressage test?"

"Sure."

We were halfway around the stable when I stopped as though I'd run into a steel girder.

"Hey, you okay?" he said. "Coffee too hot?"

I grabbed his arm and turned him around. Dawn Raleigh was standing at the mirror settling a black Fedora onto her blond hair. Armando stood behind her.

"Mourning hat, I assume," Geoff whispered. "Where we going?"

"Just come. I need to ask you something."

We walked around to the far side of the parking lot where we were alone before I stopped him. "Tell me again about Raleigh's wound."

"Wounds, plural."

"I got that. Tell me."

He described the wounds in detail.

"He was killed by a hat pin," I said.

Geoff didn't say anything for half a minute. I thought he'd laugh, but instead he shook his head. "Had to be sharper than a hat pin."

"Come with me." I opened the door of Hiram's truck and the glove compartment. Still wrapped in tissue paper, nestled Peggy's new hat pin for her blue hat. The one she'd bought at the Tollivers' show. I unwrapped it, took the little protector off the business end and poked it into Geoff's hand.

"Hey!" He jerked his hand away.

"I didn't even draw blood. But I could have." I handed it to him.

He tested the tip. "Damn. I had no idea those things were so sharp."

"Have to be to go through all those layers of tulle and silk and felt and feathers and still hold."

"Would a woman be strong enough to shove it into Raleigh's spine?"

"Would *I*?"

"Yeah, you would."

"So would most of the women here, not that it was necessarily wielded by a woman. A man could have pinched his wife's hat pin, climbed up on the box with Raleigh, laid his arm along the back of Raleigh's seat, then *wham*."

I slid into the truck and across the center console. Geoff slid in behind me and slammed the passenger side door. Anyone who wanted me desperately could call me, but they might have to wait long enough to let us finish our talk. I casually laid my right arm along the back of his seat and turned halfway toward him.

"We've been thinking of all the ways the killer could have conned or forced Raleigh onto the ground to stab him with the stake," I said. "Not just off the box, but on his face in the dirt. None of the explanations ever made sense. But if he was struck while he was still sitting in the carriage . . ." I jabbed my index finger into the base of Geoff's skull.

"Hey! That hurt." He twisted away.

"Then he fell off face down . . ."

"Raleigh falls off the carriage, already dead," Geoff said. "The killer climbs down, pulls the hatpin out, shoves the stake in fast, and slips back into the woods." Geoff ran his hand down his face. "Simple when you know how."

"So long as the hat pin was inside the wound, the only blood would be on the weapon itself, wouldn't it?" I asked.

He nodded. "He died instantly. Dead bodies don't bleed, they seep. So why use the stake at all?"

"You said it yourself, Geoff. To obscure the original wound."

"Yeah." He leaned back against the seat and closed his eyes. "Stick the pin back in your hat, and go back to the show. We weren't searching for another weapon at that point. We thought we *had* the weapon."

"Could the killer count on that?" I asked. "Or would he or she want to dispose of it?"

He ran his hand down his face. "It could be anywhere. I hate like hell to ask the forensic boys to go back to Harry Tolliver's place to search the woods again."

"Maybe it's not *in* the woods," I said quietly. "We've been trying to figure out why someone has been breaking into this place and knocking me into cellars. As improbable as it is, maybe they are looking for something. Something like a discarded hat pin?"

"Why bother? You people wear gloves all the time, so no fingerprints, probably. A hat pin is a hat pin." He turned in his seat to look at me. "Isn't it?"

"Not always." I shook my head. I could feel my excitement building. I told him about inherited hat pins, valuable hat pins, memorable hat pins, identifiable hat pins. "Somebody killed Raleigh using a hat pin that might be traceable. I don't know how, but what if *somehow* I wound up with the thing. The killer has been searching for it ever since. Is that crazy?"

He nodded. "Yeah. It may be, but just let's entertain that thought for a minute. Where could it be?" He felt around the inside of the truck. "Anything else in the glove compartment?"

"My truck was locked and my trailer was down at the opposite end of the parking area from the space where the body was found. If it were me, I'd get rid of the thing close to where I used it. But I couldn't toss it into the trees. Your techies would undoubtedly have found it. I'd want it off my person. I couldn't be certain no one would search for another weapon."

"Where would you hide it?"

"I'd bury it in a bale of hay," I said.

"No good. It would be found the minute the bale was used."

"What if it was my *own* bale of hay?"

"Then why come after *you?* If that is indeed what the killer is looking for."

"Okay. Then *you* come up with an idea."

"Let me have a minute to think," he said and put his left knee on the seat so he could twist to look directly at me. "What did the killer have access to at the Tollivers' that he hasn't been able to access since?"

"That's why they ran us off the road," I said, warming to his line of reasoning. "If we'd crashed, if we'd been unconscious or dead, whoever ran us off could have searched at leisure." I shook my head. "But how does that help? We still don't know who owns the killer SUV."

"How many dark vans would you say were parked at the Tollivers'?"

I shrugged. "Fifteen, maybe."

"Locked?"

"Probably not. At a private show, most people leave their keys on the front seat or the dashboard in case the vehicle has to be moved to let a trailer go past."

"So anyone could climb into an SUV, drive it for thirty minutes or so, drive it back, park it in the same spot, and walk off."

"What if the owner wanted his van while it was gone?"

"Make up an excuse. *I'm so sorry, my truck was blocked in, and I had to pick up a pre-*

scription for my sick horse."

"Lame."

"Would you question one of your friends?" Geoff asked.

"Probably not," I said.

"What did you bring home from the Tollivers'?"

"The things we took with us in the first place," I said. "Tack, horses, stable stuff, carriages, feed, hay. We've fed the hay. No hat pin." I hesitated.

"What?" He must have seen something in my face.

"We brought home one thing we didn't take with us. We borrowed the Tollivers' little Meadowbrook to drive Don Qui."

"Where had it been parked?"

"Harry Tolliver moved it out of the way to leave room for the other carriages and trailers. It had been sitting in the back end of his stable by the woods." I gasped.

"Right. Out the way but close at hand for anyone walking out of the woods."

"I pulled it to our trailer by the shafts, then collapsed it and slid it under Dick's big marathon carriage. I didn't see any hat pins."

He nodded. "Presumably it was hidden somehow. What did you do with it when you got it home?"

"We left it locked in the trailer. It fit perfectly between the wheels of Dick's marathon carriage. We didn't need either carriage right away, so we left them both where they were under Dick's dust cover in the trailer." I stared at Geoff. "That cover comes all the way to the ground. Somebody looking in the back window of our trailer wouldn't have seen the VSE carriage folded up under the big one."

He began to laugh. "Talk about frustrating. Your killer tries to run you off the road. Doesn't work. He hunts for your little Meadowbrook here and can't find it. You almost catch him, so he knocks you into the cellar. Then he comes back, still can't find the carriage, and we almost catch *him*. Poor guy must be half crazy with frustration."

"The next time he tries to get in, he finds locked gates, cameras, more lights, deadbolts on every door. I almost feel sorry for him."

"Don't."

"But did the same person kill Gwen or was it the drug dealers?" I asked. "Two separate killers seems pretty far-fetched. Unless it was two people working together."

"Try this on for size," Geoff said. "Gwen was up all night at the Tollivers' before Raleigh was killed. After she finally cleared her colic, she'd want a few hours of sleep back home. Everyone else would hole up to catch a little sleep in their trailers or inside the stable.

"She swore she didn't see Raleigh putting to, but maybe she saw his killer. Someone who shouldn't have been there that early, or later said they weren't. Eventually she realized what she'd seen and tried her hand at blackmail. She still hadn't been paid for the coke shipment, remember, because it hadn't yet been picked up. She could have seen blackmail as a stopgap measure."

"Or maybe a little windfall she wouldn't have to share with Brock."

"She was one greedy woman. As small as she was, she wouldn't have stood a chance against a surprise attack from someone holding a wire garrote."

I shivered. "We've been calling the killer he, but it doesn't have to be, does it? I mean, if it really was a hatpin . . ."

"If somebody walked up to Raleigh that morning brandishing a revolver or a kitchen knife, he'd have reacted differently. He wouldn't consider a hatpin as a weapon, nor a woman as a threat."

"Why not just abandon the hatpin in the wound?" I asked. But I already knew the answer. "Wait —"

"You said it yourself. Somehow it's recognizable."

"So where is it?"

"Where's the little Meadowbrook?" he asked.

"We set it up to drive Don Qui. Then Dick locked it in Hiram's barn out of the way."

"Murderous bastard still can't get to it."

"I have the key." We climbed out of the truck. I pointed three people with questions to Sandi, unlocked the barn, slipped inside with Geoff and twisted the deadbolt behind us. The little Meadowbrook stood like an altar boy beside Dick's marathon carriage.

Hiram installed lots of work lights when he used this barn as his workshop, so we had plenty of light even with the doors closed. At first glance I couldn't see where to hide anything like a hatpin around the Meadowbrook. The carriage was all wood except for the two leather seats. I propped the folding left seat up against the fender, used Geoff's penlight and searched for pin pricks in the upholstery. Nothing.

The right-hand seat was screwed down and couldn't be lifted. In order to check it out, I had to lie down on my back and look up. I was about ready to give up and let Geoff try, when I saw that there were a couple of loose stitches along the bottom seam of the seat. No stuffing poked through, but there seemed to be a lump under the leather.

"Give me your pocketknife," I said.

"How do you know I carry one?"

"Don't be a wiseass."

He handed me the knife.

"Now hold the flashlight right here."

"Your wish is my command, princess, but put these on before you go monkeying with anything else. You've already had your hands all over this cart, so your fingerprints will be on it in any case, but now that we know what we're looking for, it's better to take precautions." He handed me a pair of latex gloves. I've never known him to be without several pairs. Must be an occupational thing, like carrying a gun.

I gripped the knife in my teeth pirate fashion while I put on the latex gloves. Then I waggled the knifepoint carefully into the seam to widen it just enough to get two fingers inside. "I feel something," I said. "It's lumpy."

"Hurry up."

"I'm hurrying." By the time I had worried the object far enough out of the upholstery to get a grip on it and pull, I was sweating. "Gotcha," I said. "Give me a hand here."

Geoff grabbed me around the waist and

pulled me up and into his arms. I think he was considering kissing me, but it would have been difficult while I held a lethal weapon in each hand — his knife in one and a six-inch hatpin without a guard in the other.

I tore my eyes from his as he dropped his hands and aimed his flashlight at the pin. It looked rusty.

Not rust. Dried blood. I recognized it at once. I know whose hatpin it was, although I prayed I was wrong. I looked closer.

I was right.

"Oh, dear God," I said. "Oh, my."

"Whose is it?"

I hesitated.

"You know who owns it." He laid his flashlight on the seat, pulled a clean hand-kerchief from his pocket, and laid the pin gently in it. I couldn't take my eyes off it.

"Doesn't mean the owner is the one who used it. Maybe the killer stole it from her."

"Dammit, Merry. Who owns the pin?"

I didn't want to say the name even now. "Look at the end of it. That's not a bead. It's an antique topaz. I've seen it dozens of times."

"Who, blast it?"

I sighed. "Catherine Harris." I cut my eyes at him. "But she has an alibi, doesn't she?

403

Both she and Troy? And why on earth would she kill Raleigh? I know they didn't like one another, but . . ."

"Go get Peggy's hatpin out of your truck. Don't let anyone see you do it." He wrapped Catherine's pin in the handkerchief, then slipped it carefully into his jacket pocket.

I went. He took Peggy's hatpin from me, bent down and carefully inserted it in the upholstery where Catherine's had been.

"You're setting up a sting, aren't you?" I said.

He nodded. "Worked for Stan and the cocaine."

"Would you please wait until after the clinic to arrest her?"

His jaw dropped halfway to his belt buckle. "I beg your pardon."

I drove my hands through my hair. "I'm crazy and selfish, but she's no danger to anyone here, is she? Think about the money for Casey's carriage. Think about the bad publicity to the farm. Oh, God, I sound like the mayor in *Jaws.* Don't warn people about the twenty-foot shark. It might disturb their afternoon at the beach."

"Even if it is hers, *she* may not have used it. I need to check a few things before I arrest her or anyone else."

"Don't you need a warrant?" I asked in a

small voice.

He shook his head. "I can arrest without a warrant. You'll have to act as though nothing unusual has happened."

Just great. How could I treat Catherine as though I hadn't a clue she might be a killer? Heck, if Troy really was my half-brother, then she was my kinfolk. Sort of. I dropped my head in my hands. "I wish all these people would go home. I should never have had this show."

He pulled me against him and propped his chin on the top of my bent head. "Hang in there. You say you're good in a crisis. Prove it."

"How?"

"Keep this door locked until I tell you to open it. Stay the hell away from Catherine, Troy, and anyone else who had a reason to kill Raleigh."

"What are you going to do?" I sounded whiny. I hate that.

"Some elementary police work. I'm headed to Mossy Creek to borrow Amos's office."

"What are you looking for?"

"I'm going to try to break an alibi and isolate a motive." He shoved his flashlight into his back pocket, took my face in both hands and kissed me. He took his time. So did I. The man could *kiss,* I'll say that for him. I dropped his knife — never a good thing to do with a knife. Since I didn't spear either of us in the instep, we ignored it for some time. I suspect by the time he let me go, I was cross-eyed. I certainly couldn't breathe.

"Does that mean I'm no longer a murder suspect?" I gasped.

"In my book you never were, but I still had to avoid the appearance of impropriety. I explained all that last year."

"Screw propriety." I took hold of his polo shirt and kissed him again. He responded quite nicely, then held me against his chest. "I'm scared, Agent Wheeler."

"I know, Merry. I won't take long. Just act natural." He bent down, pulled his knife out of the dirt floor, closed it and dropped it into his pocket. He turned away before I did. I didn't think my feet would work right anyway. He unlocked the door and slipped it open a crack. "Lock this after you leave and don't open it again until I tell you to."

And don't get killed in the meantime. I would definitely try not to, despite what Peggy calls my *speaking countenance.* I'm a terrible liar, which is why I try to tell the truth whenever possible. By the time I locked the deadbolt, Geoff's Crown Vic was out of sight.

How was I supposed to make nice with Catherine?

How was I supposed to keep my mind on the show and not on that kiss?

How was I not going to tell Peggy?

I forgot to tell Geoff I knew why Catherine wanted Raleigh dead.

CHAPTER 35

Geoff

Geoff hoped Troy was too scared to refuse to drive to Mossy Creek when Geoff called his cell phone.

"What'll I tell Catherine?" he asked. "She doesn't want me to leave the show."

"Don't tell her anything. You won't be gone long. Just come."

"Can't we do this by phone?"

"Troy, drive down to Mossy Creek and talk to me." Geoff was annoyed. The kid was within his rights, but Geoff wanted to ask his questions face to face, see his reactions, watch his body language.

"Okay, I guess."

Geoff spent the twenty minutes it took Troy to drive from Merry's show to Amos's office going over the ME's reports on Raleigh and Gwen that had been faxed to Amos's office. He also wrote out a time line that was more conjecture than fact.

When Troy knocked on Amos's door, his first words were, "Catherine said I should have her lawyer with me when I talked to that sheriff."

"That's your right, but I'm not Sheriff Nordstrom. If you call your lawyer, I'll have to hold you until he shows up. At the moment, I'm not accusing you of anything. I just need clarification."

Troy looked at the small police station. He obviously thought that Mossy Creek's cells would be smaller and more uncomfortable than Sheriff Nordstrom's. After a few seconds, he said, "If I want a lawyer later I can ask for one, right?"

Geoff nodded. "At any point you can refuse to answer questions and ask for a lawyer. I doubt you'll have to." He checked that the voice-activated tape recorder on the table between them was working.

Troy nodded. "Okay."

Geoff opened his yellow legal pad and picked up his pen. The page was blank, but he hoped it wouldn't stay that way long. "I'm checking out cell phone calls last weekend," Geoff said. "You said Catherine called you at the motel early Sunday morning to tell you to meet her downstairs for breakfast. Correct?"

Troy nodded.

"You'll have to say the words." Geoff pointed at the tape recorder.

"Yessir," Troy said.

"You're certain *she* called *you,* not the other way around?"

Troy dropped his head into his hands. "I told you and that Nordstrom guy. Catherine called me just as I was coming down to breakfast Sunday morning to tell me to get my butt in gear."

"You took the call? You didn't let it go to voice mail?"

"Catherine hates voice mail. I picked it up."

"How long after that did she come downstairs and join you?"

Troy hesitated, narrowed his eyes as though trying to visualize the scene.

"Five minutes? Ten?" Geoff pressed.

"Thing is, she didn't actually come downstairs."

"She was already in the breakfast room?" Geoff felt his heart speed up.

"Not exactly. She'd been out in the parking lot checking out the fog. It was so thick she was afraid people might not be able to drive their trailers to the Tollivers' safely."

Geoff steadied his breathing and nodded as though this new information meant nothing. "Okay. She came in from the parking lot. How long after she called you?"

"I don't know, man. Does it matter?"

"It's my OCD. I like to get things exactly right."

Troy sighed, closed his eyes. He was visualizing the scene. Good. Another little bombshell would be helpful.

"Okay. She called as I came down the stairs. I told her I was already walking into the breakfast area. She asked if Morgan was driving out with us. I said she was still asleep. She was driving back to school after she woke up.

"I picked up some o.j. and a blueberry muffin, then after I put them on one of the tables, I went back and poured me some coffee. I was sitting down with the coffee when Catherine came in from the back door."

"Not the lobby door?"

"No. I guess she'd walked around the building. I saw her come in and waved to her. She came on over and said she was dying for coffee."

"Did she seem upset or worried about the fog?"

"Nope. She said it wasn't too bad to drive through, but she said she had to go change her shirt because she'd gotten damp."

"How about her hair?"

411

"Man, I don't remember." He sounded sulky. "Anyway, she was wearing that khaki jungle hat — the canvas one with the wide brim. Water just beads up on it."

"What did you and Raleigh say to one another when he called you Saturday night?"

"What?" Troy sat up straight. "He *didn't* call me."

"Texted you, then."

"No, man. I told you. After what happened in the morning, I was staying way clear of him. I didn't want him to make the connection between me and that banner. Man, I can't believe we did that."

"Neither can I," Geoff said. But he understood it. The kid was not the brightest bulb in the chandelier, and Morgan had all the electricity required to flip his switch. "So, he sent you a voice message?"

"No, man! How many times I have to tell you? The only people who would have called were Morgan and Catherine and they didn't."

"No calls to your room?"

"No!"

Geoff spread his hands. "Okay, settle down. Thing is, we pulled your cell phone records — yours and Catherine's. They say you got a text message from Raleigh's cell phone at eight-thirty Saturday night. It was deleted, so I'm asking you what he said."

Troy came up out of his chair. "That's not true! Ask Morgan. We cut out early. By eight-thirty we were already headed to the motel. Last thing I wanted was to run into Raleigh . . ." He cocked his head. "Why would Raleigh text me? I barely knew the man."

Unfortunately, Geoff had no idea. But he'd bet Catherine knew why. "Calm down. I believe you. Your records say *you* called *Catherine* Sunday morning."

"No way. She called me."

"Your cell records a call from you to *her* on Sunday morning."

Either Troy was a better actor than Geoff gave him credit for, or the confusion in his eyes was genuine. If it were genuine . . . "Can I see your cell phone?"

"Sure." Troy handed it over. Geoff checked its history. One text from Raleigh Saturday night. One call six-thirty on Sunday morning from Catherine. "Your phone says you're lying," Geoff said. He held onto it.

"Huh? This is crazy."

Geoff nodded. "Mind if I keep this for a little while?"

"Yeah, man, I *do* mind. I need my phone.

If Catherine tries to get me, I have to answer or she'll freak. I mean, she bought and paid for it."

"Even on Saturday I can get a court order. I promise I won't keep it long." Geoff peered at the phone. "It's not an iPhone or a Droid, just a simple phone."

"Yeah. Same as hers. She bought them at the same time — some two for one deal. I'd like an iPhone, but she says she can't afford it and I sure can't."

"Go get one of those cheap pay-as-you-go phones at Wal-Mart."

"Who's gonna pay for it?"

Geoff pulled a twenty from his wallet. "Here. Get a cheap one. Then go back to the show."

Big sigh of relief. Troy was only too glad to leave. As he started out the door, Geoff said, "One more thing."

"What?" Not happy.

"Catherine ever use your phone?"

"Why would she? She keeps hers practically Superglued to her side."

After Troy left, Geoff leaned back in his chair. He now knew how the alibi worked and why Troy had not met Raleigh at the dressage arena, but he was afraid he'd never be able to prove it.

Catherine must either have known or

suspected that Raleigh was going to try to get in touch with Troy Saturday night, but Geoff had no idea how or why Catherine didn't want Raleigh communicating with the kid.

She must have swapped phones with Troy — they were identical after all — sometime Saturday, then swapped them back after she called Troy on Sunday morning. She was taking a big chance that Troy would notice the phones had been swapped before she could change them back. Not so big a chance, however, as if Troy had been using a Droid or an iPhone with a bunch of apps.

She'd gotten away with it.

It was the only thing that made sense. Maybe Raleigh boasted he was going to hire Troy away from her. Did the kid matter that much to her? Apparently they weren't sleeping together.

Say she'd swapped phones with Troy on Saturday night without his knowledge and intercepted a text message from Raleigh setting up a meeting before the show in the dressage arena. Why Raleigh would set such a time and place made no sense to Geoff, but it must have made sense to Raleigh.

Catherine used Troy's cell to agree to meet Raleigh in Troy's name. Then she used Troy's phone to call him from the parking lot of the motel Sunday morning. Sometime, possibly during breakfast, she swapped the phones back. The kid had been too preoccupied with Morgan to use his cell phone Saturday night or Sunday anyway, so he wouldn't have paid enough attention to his phone to know it wasn't actually his.

Next he called the motel where the horse people had stayed Saturday night and spoke to the owner. "What's your policy about late night incoming phone calls?" Geoff asked.

"No policy," said Mr. Patel. "You call room directly, you get through."

"How about if I don't know the room number?"

"No calls."

"Anyone ever ask not to have late night calls put through?"

"Oh, sure. No problem. We flip a switch at desk."

"How about last Saturday night? Anybody request not to receive calls?"

"Man, how would I know?"

"Don't you write it down somewhere? For the next person on shift, maybe?"

He finally got the name and number of the woman who had been the desk on the previous Saturday night. She was off duty this weekend, but Geoff was lucky enough to reach her at home. When he asked her if anyone had specifically requested not to receive calls, the phone went silent. Geoff hoped she was thinking and not painting her fingernails.

Finally, she said, "Yeah. There was a woman paid for adjoining rooms Friday and Saturday. She asked us not to route calls to either room Saturday night." She snickered. "Guess the guy in the next room was sleeping in her room, and they didn't want to be disturbed."

"You remember if there were any calls?"

"Lord, I have no idea. We don't keep records. Everybody uses cell phones anyway so they don't have to pay extra."

He thanked her and hung up.

He needed one more piece of hard evidence, but he was unlikely to get it until Monday at the earliest, unless he called Sarah Beth Raleigh. Dawn was at Merry's show and he didn't have her cell phone number. She probably wouldn't return his messages anyway.

Sarah Beth hung up on him. He had busted the father of her unborn child for transportation of drugs with intent to distribute. He didn't think Sarah Beth was involved, but that was Stan Nordstrom's problem. He wondered whether Sarah Beth would post bail for Brock. If she did, he suspected Brock would jump bail and head for parts unknown.

He called back until she stayed on the line. Grudgingly, she gave him the name and cell phone number of Raleigh's personal attorney in Atlanta.

Geoff expected to reach him at the eighth tee on his country club golf course.

"I'm not golfing," Wilson Waters said. "And it's your fault, Agent Wheeler. Raleigh's estate is so screwed up, I'll have auditors and IRS agents and the SEC and I don't know who all in my hair for a year."

"For which you are billing the estate by the hour," Geoff said. "You actually owe me." Geoff had encountered Wilson Waters several times in the course of his investigations. Atlanta might be big, but the legal community wasn't. Not for a GBI agent who spent a good deal of time in court.

The man had an excellent reputation. He suspected Raleigh kept as many of his business transactions in other hands as he could manage, leaving his personal finances relatively clean. He hoped Waters was not only honest but cooperative. "I need the answer to one question."

"Will it help arrest his killer?"

"And convict."

"Ask away."

CHAPTER 36

Peggy

Merry acted very odd at lunch. On one hand, her face had that glow Peggy's got after an evening with Dick. On the other, she couldn't sit down and didn't pay attention to the people asking her questions. Very un-Merry.

The garden club ladies had pushed what furniture there was in the clients' lounge against the walls and set up long tables and folding chairs for lunch. Since the alternative to their sandwiches was a drive into Mossy Creek, almost everyone participated.

Catherine couldn't share tables with participants. Everyone was cordial to the judge at a show, of course, but there was a fine line that wasn't crossed. The garden club ladies set up lunch for Catherine and Juanita Tolliver, who was scribing for her, under the judge's tent by C.

"So far, so good," Peggy whispered as they

419

finished their chocolate cake.

"What?" Merry reacted as though Peggy had lashed her with a whip.

"I said, so far, so good. No accidents, no runaways, there's still toilet paper in the restrooms, and people are picking up their trash. The clinic tomorrow is full and bound to be a success, and Sandi says we've cleared over two thousand dollars so far. Add the money from the food, and after we pay the expenses and Catherine's fee, we should have enough for a down payment on Casey's carriage and a nice chunk of change for the farm."

"Don't tell anyone," Dick whispered, "but I've already got a deal working on the carriage. I'll make up the difference."

"Dick, you can't," Peggy said.

"Shut up, Pretty Peggy. It's my money. It won't be much. I've got my eye on a Norwegian Fjord pony for her as well. Broke to death and kind as they come."

No wonder Peggy was crazy about the man.

"Merry! Isn't that wonderful?"

"What? Oh, yeah, Dick, wonderful."

Peggy didn't think Merry even knew what they'd been talking about.

"Anybody see Geoff?" she asked, scanning the room.

She didn't wait for an answer, but dumped her leavings in the trashcan and left without a word.

"Before you ask," Peggy told Dick, "I have no idea what that's about."

"We can talk tonight. You gonna give me a hand getting the cart ready for Casey?"

They had scheduled Casey's dressage test first after the lunch break to give them time to set up her carriage and warm up for an extra-long time before she drove her test.

Peggy was glad Dick was driving with Casey. The way Merry was acting, she'd drive off course. Unfortunately, Merry's Halflinger, Golden, the old campaigner, was trying to develop an abscess in his right front hoof and was therefore slightly lame. That meant only Ned, Peggy's Halflinger, was available for Casey to drive. Merry had suggested she scratch, but Casey would have none of it. "Is he safe?" she asked.

"Mostly," Merry said.

"Then I'm driving," she said. "Dick won't let anything happen to us." Ned had been a perfect saint since his dunking at the Tollivers'. Peggy figured he was afraid that if he misbehaved, they'd try to drown him again.

There was no shortage of helpers to get Casey's wheelchair strapped into the cart. Her husband, Hank, the veterinarian, was a big man, and Louise's grandson Pete had played high school football.

As Casey and Dick settled themselves and walked Ned around outside the arena to enter at A, Geoff found Peggy in the stable.

"Where's Merry?" He looked grim.

"Looking for you. Why?"

"I have to talk to her *now*." He peered around the arena and spotted Juanita Tolliver alone under the judge's tent checking the afternoon dressage tests. The boxes containing the remains of their lunches sat on the table beside her. He headed for the table.

Peggy followed him. She wanted to hear what he said.

"Mrs. Tolliver, have you seen Merry or Catherine?"

"I think Catherine went to the restroom, Agent Wheeler. The last time I saw Merry she was back by the hazards course in the back pasture."

Geoff started toward the lane between the pastures, then turned back and pointed to the open plastic lunch box on the judge's table. "Is this yours or Mrs. Harris's?"

"Hers. The other one's mine. Why?"

Catherine's paper napkin was balled up, but there were several streaks on it that looked like blood. The garden club hadn't

422

brought catsup for the turkey sandwiches, and there was none on the judge's table.

"Has Mrs. Harris hurt herself?" Geoff asked.

"Bless her heart," Juanita said. "She's got a couple of nasty cuts across the underside of her little fingers. She said she found a piece of rusty barbed wire in her pasture and cut herself yanking it loose from the dirt. Swear to God, that stuff ought to be outlawed around horses."

Whoever had pulled that wire tight around Gwen's throat must have exerted a great deal of force. Pulling hard on alfalfa wire even wearing gloves could slice your fingers so badly they bled.

Using a fresh napkin, Geoff closed the box holding the remains of Catherine's lunch with her used napkin inside, borrowed Juanita's ballpoint and wrote his name, date and time across the top and side of the box. He picked up the brown paper sack the two lunch boxes had come in, put Catherine's box inside and folded it closed. "Mrs. Tolliver, you wouldn't happen to have any tape, would you?"

Her eyes were wide and scared, but she realized something about that lunch box was important, and not in a good way. She shook her head and said, "But I've got a staple gun." She handed it to him.

"Great." He wrote his name and both Peggy's and Juanita Tolliver's on the sack, then stapled the top together. "Ladies, mind writing your name across the flap?"

Peggy and Juanita locked eyes. Peggy's hand shook, but she signed, then Juanita signed.

"Thanks," Geoff said. "Hang onto this for me, please." An enormous leather satchel sat at Juanita's feet. "Put it in your satchel, but don't let anyone know you have it."

Juanita took a deep breath. "My God." She slid it into her bag.

Catherine had been wearing thin driving gloves all morning. Peggy thought at the time that was weird considering the warm weather, but then she'd dismissed it.

But Catherine wouldn't have been able to explain eating her lunch with her gloves on. And her fingers were still raw enough to bleed.

Geoff was nearly running down the lane toward the hazards set at the far end of the mare's pasture. Peggy wanted to see Merry, talk to her, warn her, although there was no reason Catherine, even if she were guilty, should attack Merry. Was there? She said to Juanita, "Don't mention this to a soul."

"But what am I supposed . . ."

Peggy couldn't see Merry, but then, this was nonsense. Catherine wouldn't kill anyone. There had to be a mistake. Geoff would find Merry and look after her.

Surely, Merry would come to the arena to watch Casey warm up. This was their first judged dressage test, and both she and Ned were nervous. Peggy knew Dick's coaching would relax both of them. What she didn't know was where Merry had gone. She looked for Merry with her fingers crossed and a prayer on her lips.

"She's not down by the hazards," Geoff said from behind her. "I don't see her anywhere."

"She's probably in the loo." She looked carefully into Geoff's eyes. "Are you worried?"

"Where's Catherine?"

"She's due back in ten minutes. Probably still in the bathroom."

"Yeah, putting fresh bandages on her fingers."

Ned passed them at a strong trot. From time to time he took a couple of canter strides, which would be penalized in the actual test. Casey brought him back under control expertly. Peggy began to relax.

Merry

I know Geoff said not to unlock the barn for any reason until he got back, but he wasn't running a horse show. I was. I should have known Marvin Cudlow and Becca would continue to cause problems. Marvin decided to drive the hazards course flat out. Unfortunately, he couldn't steer his pair at a gallop worth a darn.

He'd been the last on course before the lunch break, which was fortunate, since he demolished one of the plywood gates we'd constructed. The plywood, painted to look like gray stone, was relatively intact. One of the two-by-fours that kept it upright, however, was in pieces. The horses were lucky they hadn't picked up shards in their legs.

No barn is ever without two-by-four studs and plywood. Our supply was kept in the front corner of Hiram's barn, where they were presently under lock and key along with my carriages. Louise's grandson Pete could nail up a new upright and set the hazard back in place after he finished eating, but he needed wood, a hammer and nails.

Pete followed me into Hiram's barn, balanced a couple of two-by-fours on his shoulder in case another one got broken, stuck the hammer and nails in his back pocket, and trotted off across the parking lot as the remaining two-by-fours shifted and began to slide to the floor.

I ran over to catch them, rearranged them and turned to leave.

Catherine shut the barn door behind her quietly, and said, "I've never been in here before. It's huge."

"Plenty of space for the carriages Hiram was repairing." My mouth felt dry, but I think I sounded normal.

She ran her hand over Dick's marathon carriage. "I've never seen a cover drape all the way to the floor like this. Custom made, of course, nothing but the best for Dick."

"He can afford it."

She tittered. She was nervous and making me nervous too.

"Hadn't you better get back to the judge's stand?" I asked.

"Oh, I've got ten minutes or so. No hurry."

I couldn't walk out and leave her. She'd pull that hatpin out of the Meadowbrook. The minute she saw Peggy's substitute, she'd know somebody had found hers and probably recognized it. She'd be certain it was *me*. I knew she'd killed Raleigh. That meant she'd probably killed Gwen as well.

We were almost the same age, and I was two inches taller, but she was tough too. I didn't want to go up against her, hatpin or no hatpin. I had to keep her calm and get her out of the barn without it.

She trailed her hand over the miniature Meadowbrook. "You brought this back on Sunday from the Tollivers', didn't you? Where was it? Under that cover?"

I nodded. "It folds up."

"Why on earth would you lock your trailer in your own parking lot?"

"Why would you tell me Hiram was Troy's father?" I knew the minute the words left my mouth I'd made a big blunder. "Didn't you think I'd check our DNA? As his daughter, my DNA would be close enough to his for comparison."

"You couldn't possibly have the results back yet." She was suddenly tense. She must have realized she'd admitted knowing that my trailer had been locked. And now, this.

I had no intention of telling her I was bluffing about the DNA. "Geoff pulled strings. He already had Troy's DNA."

She sighed and her shoulders slumped. "I'm sorry, Merry. I know it was a despicable thing to do. If you thought Troy was your half-brother, I felt certain you'd try to help him."

"But he's not. Hiram didn't seduce you. Who did?"

She waved a hand. "Good ole roofies at a frat party my sophomore year. I have no idea who Troy's father is. I didn't want to admit that."

"You know, all right. You've always known. But I'll bet Giles Raleigh didn't know until recently."

"Giles?" All confusion. *Right.* "Giles Raleigh? Why would you think . . ."

"Cut the crap, Catherine. Was it consensual or did he rape you? Don't bother denying it. Geoff has already had Raleigh's DNA tested against Troy's." Another lie, of course, but I hoped she wouldn't think too hard about it. Since all those CSI shows seem to take ten minutes to do ten DNA tests, I hoped she wasn't certain how long it took to get the results back.

She leaned back against the marathon cart. "The roofie part was true. Giles must have doped my drink at an exhibitors' party. The drinking part was true too. Only it was Giles who did the deflowering. Hiram never knew I was pregnant. That part was true. All of it was true, really."

"Except for the part about my father deflowering an eighteen-year-old virgin. Catherine, all you had to do was ask for my help. You didn't need this big charade."

"I was so frightened, I couldn't be sure

unless I had some hold over you." Her hand strayed to the seat of the Meadowbrook again.

It hit me then. Catherine didn't know about the medical examiner's findings that there were two wounds. She must have thought if she could get the hatpin back with Raleigh's blood on it, no one would ever know she'd used it.

"It's not the same hat pin," I said.

"What?" She jerked her hand away from the Meadowbrook as though it was on fire. That's when I noticed her little fingers were bandaged.

"That pin's Peggy's. Geoff has yours."

Her face went slack. "I don't know . . ."

"He's testing it for blood. Think he'll find Raleigh's?"

"That's crazy. How would I know how to kill anyone with a hatpin?"

"You worked in your husband Paul's office for years. He was a neurosurgeon. You knew," I said.

"Why on earth would *I* wait all these years to take revenge on Giles? Don't be ridiculous."

"Because he was going to tell Troy who his father was. And you couldn't have that."

She must have heard the sympathy in my voice. It did what my confrontation hadn't.

Geoff always said that the worst problem killers have is that they're lonely. They can't share what they've done with anyone. When they finally get the chance, they are almost relieved. For a minute or two, until they realize what they've said.

"It's over, Catherine. You wanted me to help Troy, let me help *you*. I'll go with you to Geoff . . ."

"No!" All of a sudden I was looking at an angry woman pointing a very small but deadly handgun at my stomach. "I can't go to jail. Mother and Sandra and Paul would be mortified."

"Do they know who Troy is?"

She waved me away. "He's willing to wait to tell them. We were thinking maybe at our big family Fourth of July picnic."

I nearly giggled. I could hear Catherine speaking to Sandra and Paul, "Illegitimate half-brother with your barbecued ribs, kids?"

"If you didn't want to mortify your family, how stupid was it to use your grandmother's antique topaz hat pin to puncture Raleigh?" I was scared pea green, but that last statement made me furious. Poor Troy. No wonder he fell for Morgan's antics. First his mother abandons him at birth, then she finds him, but hides him from the only real relatives he's got.

"It was an accident. I never meant to kill Giles."

"Come on. You don't stick a six inch hatpin in somebody's brain by accident."

"It was the only hatpin I had with me. I stuck it in my rain hat because the wind was blowing."

I didn't believe that either. Who uses a topaz hatpin in a khaki rain hat? "Tell Geoff it was an accident. I'm sure he'll understand."

She snorted. "Will he understand about Gwen too?"

Uh-oh. I kept hoping the drug people had killed her, but those bandaged fingers said otherwise. I knew exactly how she'd hurt herself.

"Little bitch saw me stick the hat pin in the Tollivers' Meadowbrook and tried to blackmail me." She narrowed her eyes. "Are *you* trying to blackmail me?"

I was coming to see that Catherine was more than a little nuts, but then all killers must be a tad nuts to see the death of another human being as the solution to a personal problem. "I am not trying to blackmail you. I'm trying to help you. Does Troy know who his father is?"

"Certainly not. Giles saw Troy and me

together at a show six weeks ago and knew at once he was Troy's father. Troy has his eyes, his nose, his build. Most people wouldn't see the resemblance, but that egomaniac Giles guessed. Then he found out when Troy was born. Once he discovered Troy was adopted at birth in a private adoption, he stole Troy's coffee cup and had Troy's DNA tested. Would you believe Giles already had a copy of his *own* DNA chart? He told me, 'In case of a paternity suit.' "

"What's that got to do with last Sunday?" I asked. "How did we get from Troy's paternity to a four-in-hand team at six-thirty in the morning?"

Catherine sank her rump onto the marathon carriage's front wheel. "I begged him not to tell Troy. I held him off until last weekend, but Saturday he announced to me he didn't intend to wait any longer to reveal himself." She gave a sad little laugh. "He said he could use a *son* to keep the rest of his family in line."

"Those words?"

"You bet."

What a rat!

"I managed to keep Troy so busy and far enough away from Raleigh on Saturday that I knew he hadn't spoken to Troy, but I just knew he'd pull some grandstand play before the weekend was out. If he couldn't speak to Troy, the next best thing was to text him. That's what they all do. I wanted to head him off there as well.

"So I swapped phones with Troy at the motel before the party. I was right. Troy got a message asking him to come to the dressage arena at six-thirty on Sunday morning to hear some good news." She snorted. "Good news. I assumed Giles would simply walk over from the arena, tell Troy he had a new sugar daddy, then take Troy to breakfast. I texted him in Troy's name that he'd be there."

"You didn't plan on the four-in-hand?" I asked.

Catherine laughed. A perfectly normal laugh. We might as well be chatting over tea. I wasn't fool enough to think she'd let her guard down completely, however. When the story was over, she was going to make her move. I just didn't know what it was.

"That team scared me half to death."

Just the way it scared me.

"He planned to loom up out of the mist in that damned four-in-hand. It would have been Cinderella's coach — the opening salvo. 'All this can be yours, my son.' Giles was surprised to see me, but he wasn't afraid of me. He held all the cards, after all.

I said Troy had sent me in his place, that I'd told him Giles was his father — which of course I hadn't. Said Troy was too stunned to meet him yet. All that mattered was Troy's well-being, that we could work out our differences. I climbed up on the box beside him to talk."

"You never planned just to talk, did you?"

"Maybe if he hadn't been so — the only word I can think of is gleeful — I'd have let him live. He'd won again, you see? But I came prepared, just in case. I laid my hand along the back of the seat, then . . ." Catherine shrugged.

"It was much easier than I thought it would be. He made a funny sound and fell off the box onto the ground." She smiled. "The horses stopped the instant I said whoa. I was proud of them. Giles always did have well-trained horses."

Merry closed her eyes.

"I wrapped the reins around the whip holder before I climbed down so they wouldn't get tangled."

Always thinking, even in the middle of a murder. A true horsewoman. Just not a real sane human being.

"He was lying up against the edge of the arena. Dead, of course. I decided I could use the stake to cover up the original wound, so I pulled my hatpin out from under his skull, and stuck the stake in to cover the first wound."

She looked at me quizzically. "I was certain that would work. Why didn't it?"

"According to Geoff, the first wound would have been nearly impossible to conceal." I was working my way around so that I was between her and the door.

She didn't seem to notice.

"The medical examiner realized that there were two tracks the minute he opened the wounds," I said. "Why on earth did you stick the pin under the seat of the Tollivers' Meadowbrook?"

"You showed up too early. I grabbed the pin and hid in the trees, then while you were trying to catch Giles's horses I slipped around the end the stable. That's when Gwen saw me.

"That little Meadowbrook was the first cart I came to. I know you can't ever remove all the traces of blood, and everyone knew that was my hatpin, so I stuck it between the seat and the cushion and assumed I could sneak back and remove it later that day and take it home to boil it clean. When I went back to get it, the Meadowbrook wasn't there. Harry Tolliver said you'd borrowed it. I had to get the pin back, so I took one of his SUVs and tried to run you off the road. I got back to pick up my own truck before anyone noticed I'd left."

"You could have killed the horses."

"I *had* to take that chance. I prayed they'd be all right."

I noticed she hadn't prayed over me and Peggy.

"So you came to Hiram's farm to try to remove the pin."

"Only I couldn't find the cart," Catherine sounded put upon, as though I had hidden the cart to spite her. "I was very annoyed."

"That's why you nearly killed me?"

"When you followed me across the pasture, I hid behind the road grader just to get away from you."

"You hit me with a two-by-four and tossed me into a cellar to get snakebit!"

"I simply wanted to get away. You'd have been fine if you hadn't chased after me."

So it was my fault for chasing her? If I'd been a fire-breathing dragon, she'd be a small pile of ash right now.

"And then you put all those deadbolts everywhere and the keypads and all that security. I couldn't get in to hunt for the cart."

"So you tried to shoot us."

"I most certainly did *not!* If I'd been aiming for you, I'd have hit you. I shot out the light. I am an excellent shot. I merely wanted time to get away. Again."

"Through the governor's land? I nearly broke my neck in the daytime. How'd you manage at night?"

She waved the hand not holding the gun. "Paul and I hunted that land for years with the governor. Even so, finding my way down to the parking area where I left my truck hidden under the brush wasn't easy. I twisted my ankle and got a nasty case of poison ivy. After that I decided to leave the hatpin where it was until the show, when I'd be free to wander around as much as I wanted. I knew I could get it back then."

"Only we got it first. Face it, Catherine, it's over. You can't get out of here. One of Amos Royden's deputies is down by the road waiting for your car." Actually, Mutt wasn't waiting for any special car, but I didn't tell her that. "You're trapped."

"Not if you come with me. He'll let us through. I'll put you out on the road somewhere."

Of *course* she would. "No."

"Either that or I'll shoot you now and say you killed yourself. You're right. I have nothing to lose."

"You're too far away from me for it to look

like suicide. Suicides by pistol are hard to fake. Don't you watch all those forensics shows? They can check the stippling pattern to see precisely how far the gun was from the subject when it was fired. You're what? Six or seven feet away?"

She frowned, took a deep breath and pulled herself erect. She looked exhausted. "Come closer."

"Not on your life. Or mine."

"I can just shoot you where you stand and say you attacked me."

"As if."

"Then I suppose I'll have to come to you."

She was expecting me to recoil. Instead, *I* raised both arms under her gun arm and threw myself full force against her.

In that enclosed space, the gunshot through the metal roof sounded like a canon. Kicking a woman in the groin doesn't do a whale of a lot of good, but whacking her across the wrist with both fists sure can. The pistol went flying.

Catherine screamed. I hoped I'd broken her wrist, but I didn't stick around to find out. I also didn't stop to lock the barn. I ran around the stable toward the dressage arena where any moment now they'd start to wonder where she was.

She'd find the gun quickly, but I didn't

think she'd shoot into a crowd. She wouldn't want to hit a horse by accident. I expected her to try to run away.

I jumped the two foot high dressage arena rail.

"Strong trot!" came Dick's voice from Casey's carriage as they warmed up.

I heard Ned's hooves coming fast and raced to the center of the arena.

"Merry, get out of there!" Geoff yelled.

"Catherine's behind me! She's got a gun!" I'm not sure he heard me over the hoof beats. I raced for his side of the arena and did a grande jete across the dressage fence into Geoff's arm. Only one. The other was already pulling his gun.

He threw me past him. "Get down!" he yelled.

"Geoff, no!" I shouted.

I saw the khaki hat before I saw Catherine. I'd expected her to make a run for her truck in the parking area. Maybe I'd pissed her off so badly she wanted to kill me at all costs. Maybe she'd simply lost it. I threw myself face down into the dirt and heard the whine above me. It's like a rattlesnake. Nobody had to tell me what it was.

"Stay down," Geoff dropped to his knees beside me. "I can't risk a shot. Put it down, Catherine!" he shouted. "It's over."

"Jesus!" Dick's voice.

Catherine ran across the arena toward me and dead in front of Ned. He hit her chest high. The impact tossed her six feet away to land in the dirt on her back. Her gun flew out of her hand, landed butt first in the dirt and fired a single shot straight up.

Maybe if Casey's carriage hadn't been so heavy and tough to stop because of her wheelchair, maybe if Dick had grabbed the reins from her and stomped the brake that she couldn't, maybe if Ned hadn't spent his first years as a child's jumping pony, none of it would have happened.

The shot must have sounded like a mortar shell to Ned. He stood on his hind legs, then galloped for the edge of the arena.

Ned jumped the short rail of the dressage area, while Casey hauled on the reins and Dick clung to the fender. Straight ahead the four foot pasture fence loomed.

Ned tried valiantly to haul the carriage across the pasture fence, too. Instead, he stuck on the far side with his front feet on the ground and his rear end in the air scrabbling for purchase. The front wheels hung on the top rail of the arena, leaving the carriage canted up at a forty-five degree angle, while Dick held on to keep from being tossed out. Casey, thank God, was strapped into the carriage in her wheelchair.

Her chair was hanging at a scary angle, but it wasn't going anywhere. I could hear her husband Hank yelling at her.

She called back, "We're all right. What happened?"

Peggy shouted at me, "Go!" and ran toward Dick and Casey.

Geoff and I ran to Catherine.

She'd had all the breath knocked out of her, even if the horse hadn't crushed her sternum and punctured her heart. I knew that feeling . . . terror that you'll never breathe again, suffocating in awful pain. I dropped to my knees beside her and grasped her hand. "It's gonna be okay, Catherine." What a dumbass thing to say! Of course it wouldn't be okay.

She gripped my hand and turned frightened eyes to me. Her mouth gaped, but she couldn't speak.

Our EMT on call shoved me out of the way and put an oxygen mask over her face. I saw her chest heave. The hand I held gripped harder, but her chest lifted once, twice . . .

The EMT slid a cervical collar under her neck and fastened it. Her legs were thrashing, so she hadn't severed her spinal cord, but the EMT fought to strap her to a body board to keep her still.

"Mamma?" came a male voice, and a moment later Troy knelt beside me. "Mamma, how bad are you hurt?"

She dropped my hand and reached for his.

He wheeled on me. "What the hell did you do?" His face was a mask of fury.

"Move away, son," the EMT said. "Goes for all of you."

"Which hospital?" Geoff asked.

"Bigelow General, and we're moving now. Y'all get out of the way." He signaled to the ambulance, and no more than a minute later Catherine slid into the ambulance on a body board.

Geoff climbed in behind her and I heard him Mirandize her. That's all I could hear with the noise around us. I assumed she'd lawyer up. She'd admitted what she'd done to *me,* but I doubted any of it was admissible in a court of law.

I held Troy back. "You can't go with her. Come with me."

Peggy materialized on his other side. "Casey's all right," she said. "Dick's handling it." She took Troy's other arm and dragged him to his feet. I thought for a moment he'd fight us, but he seemed to collapse instead. We led him to the in-gate and out. The ambulance blew by us with its siren blaring. He raised his head and followed it with his eyes — eyes that were spilling tears.

"Why'd she shoot at you?" he asked me. "She could have killed that horse."

So her indoctrination had worked that far, at least. He didn't mention killing me.

"I'm afraid she killed Giles Raleigh and Gwen Standish."

"No way."

"Your mother . . ."

He blinked and caught his breath. "You know she's my mother?"

I nodded. But she wouldn't have told Troy that Giles was his father, even though a dead Giles no longer posed a threat to her relationship with her son.

"But why'd she kill him? The banner thing was barely a misdemeanor. He couldn't hurt me."

I looked across at Peggy. Should I tell him?

One look at the confusion on his face, and I decided he ought to know before he saw Catherine.

"Raleigh'd found out he was your father," I said. "Catherine thought he was trying to take you away from her. Afraid his money would ruin your life."

"No way. She's the one went looking for me."

"She was also the one who put you up for adoption," Peggy said quietly. "Raleigh didn't know you existed until recently."

I decided not to mention Gwen unless Troy did. He had enough on his plate already. He looked poleaxed. I didn't blame him.

We led him into the stable and sat him down on a bale of hay. Peggy sat beside him and held his hand. He clutched it, seemingly grateful for the human contact.

"Did she think I'd prefer Raleigh because he's rich?" Troy shook his head. "Never happen."

He sounded sure, but would he have felt the same when Raleigh dangled a Ferrari under his nose, gave him a penthouse condo in one of the Raleigh properties, a corner office in Atlanta? Paid for an engineering degree at MIT and made certain he was accepted in society? Catherine, obviously, hadn't thought Troy would hold out long.

Juanita came up and asked, "We don't have a judge or an EMT. What should I do?"

"Tell everybody I'll speak to them in ten minutes."

She disappeared. She could handle an infantry division. A bunch of rowdy carriage drivers would be a piece of cake.

"She was going to tell everybody I was

445

her son," Troy said.

"When?" Geoff asked. I glanced around. I hadn't heard him come in, but then he could move like a cat.

"You didn't ride to the hospital with them?" I asked.

He shook his head. "I wanted to be here." He grabbed my hand right out in public. "Amos and the Bigelow cops will meet her at the hospital, and Amos is calling Stan to tell him about the arrest. It's really Stan's jurisdiction."

Troy was obviously trying hard to believe Catherine's motives, but even I could see the doubt behind his eyes. "She had to tell her family about me first. Explain to them. Tell Sandra and Paul, Junior, and her mother."

Like I could hear *that* conversation. "Sandra, Paul, may I introduce your half-brother Troy? Mother, meet your grandson. And the best part? His father is that great southern gentleman, Giles Raleigh. How about that gene pool, huh?"

I didn't doubt Catherine loved Troy, but she loved her reputation and her other family too. No wonder she'd tried to convince me that Troy was Hiram's son and my half-brother. Everybody knew Hiram had mistresses. Plus he was dead and couldn't deny it. And everybody loved him. Nobody loved Giles.

How Giles would have gloated. I could hear him now. "Shape up, Dawn, send your polo player back to Argentina and do what I tell you or you'll be out on your ass while your brother takes over the company.

"Get your adulterous little tail out of my house and my life, Sarah Beth, honey. I don't need you to produce a male heir. I've already got one. And I *know* he's mine."

"Get lost, Brock. You and my wife can ride off into penury together on your mortgaged Harley."

The list went on and on. Having Troy in his camp, and acknowledged as his son, would checkmate many of Raleigh's enemies.

But, give Catherine credit, she'd known the risks when she didn't get an abortion, and even more when she went hunting for Troy as soon as Paul died. What she couldn't endure was sharing and possibly losing him to a self-serving monster like Giles Raleigh.

She didn't trust Troy to remain loyal, so she didn't give him the opportunity to choose. She made the choice for him.

And lost when she might have won.

Geoff jerked his head at me and cut his eyes. "Peggy, can you keep Troy company?"

447

he asked.

She nodded. I followed Geoff out of the tent and leaned back against the front of the stall.

"You okay?" he asked.

"Is it against protocol to ask for a hug?"

He wrapped his arms around me and pulled me tight against him. He rested his chin on top of my head and whispered, "You know how lucky you are not to be in that ambulance on your way to the hospital?"

"Or the morgue."

"I warned you not to open the barn until I got back."

"It wasn't my fault. I had to get some two-by-fours. She was supposed to be in her tent."

"She tried to shoot you."

"Will she survive?" I asked.

"One of the shaft ends caught her. Probably at least one punctured lung and some broken ribs, but I'd guess yes."

"Will she confess? She told me everything, but I didn't record it or anything. It probably isn't admissible."

"I think she'll confess, but what the actual charges will be, I have no idea. At least two counts of first degree murder. They may ignore the assault on you. My guess is she'd rather go to jail than face the scandal of a trial."

"I never dreamed she'd fire across the arena that way." I sniffled. "She might have shot Ned."

I could feel his chest shake.

"What?" I pulled away from him. "You're *laughing?*"

"I ought to know by now — horses first, people second."

"God, the horses!" I pulled away from him and ran to the judge's tent. Drivers, grooms and spectators were hanging around gossiping and grousing, not having a clue what had happened. I wasn't about to enlighten them. Not about Catherine, at any rate.

First I apologized for the uproar and offered to refund their money for their cancelled classes this afternoon and the clinic scheduled for Sunday.

"Why can't *you* teach the clinic?" Harry Tolliver asked from the crowd. "You have the skill and the credentials. I'd value a lesson with you." He looked around. Several heads nodded. "How about it, people? Same schedule, different clinician?"

Amazingly, everyone agreed, even Marvin Cudlow.

That left the remains of Saturday afternoon's show. We had no dressage judge, until Peggy stepped up and whispered, "Casey still wants to drive her dressage test. If you'll drive with her, Dick can judge her *hors de concours*. He can judge the rest of the afternoon."

"She wants to drive?" I looked over Peggy's shoulder at Hank heading Ned. Casey's carriage only had a couple of scratches in the paint. Carriages have to be tough. All we had to do was to put back the PVC rails Ned had knocked down. I nodded. "We don't have an EMT."

"Sandi's had some training. She can help out in a pinch. Please God we won't have any other accidents," Peggy said.

"Then if Dick's agreeable, have at it."

I made the announcement, and again everyone agreed.

Geoff walked across the arena with me. "I can see killing Raleigh," I said. "Heck I could have killed him myself half a dozen times. But trying to run us off the road with Golden and Ned in the trailer?" I shook my head. "There must have been a better way to handle the situation with Troy."

"Killers can't see any other way out."

"In the end, she only made things worse for everybody."

"Murder frequently does."

The rest of the show went well. Casey

drove Ned brilliantly, and all the clients and spectators seemed happy. I am a good teacher. A number of people asked me to have another fun show and clinic in another couple of months.

We'd see.

Peggy finished feeding the horses in pasture, while I settled the boarding horses down. Geoff leaned against the wall opposite and watched me. We'd agreed to pick up burgers and eat at my little apartment. What would happen during the meal and afterwards — mostly afterwards — I couldn't guess, but I had hopes.

I was coiling the water hose when I heard his cell phone behind me. He answered, listened, and let forth with a string of cusswords. The ones in English I knew. The Spanish ones, not so much.

"All right, dammit," he said, flipped his phone off and came to me.

"Problem?" I asked. Stupid question. His face told me he was furious.

He took my arm, guided me into the feed room and shut the door.

My heart sank. "What's happened?"

"Some boaters just found a cigarette boat beached on Jekyll Island, full of holes and covered in blood." He looked grim. "I'm headed down there." He shook his head.

"What is it with us?"

"Bad karma?"

"Nuts." He kissed me, and this time there was no tenderness. It was more like a ten round title bout. When we finally separated, he said, "Stay out of trouble until I get back."

What trouble could I possibly get into?